√ 75

CHR   Christian, John
        Five gates to Armageddon.

Date Due			
DEC 28 75			
JAN 9 '75			
JAN 24 '75			

FIVE GATES
TO ARMAGEDDON

John Christian

FIVE GATES TO ARMAGEDDON

a novel

ST. MARTIN'S PRESS
NEW YORK

C h+

Library of Congress Cataloging in Publication Data

Christian, John.
    Five gates to Armageddon.

    I. Title.
PZ4.C5553Fi [PS3553.H73] 813'.5'4 752

Prologue: Jerusalem 1985

In a private house on the outskirts of the new city of Jerusalem a group of men and two women were gathered round an ordinary dining-room table. It was late at night.

None of the faces of those present, except that at the head of the table, would have been recognised by the general public locally—let alone in the rest of the world. But all were united in their total devotion to a common cause, the preservation of the State of Israel, and they listened intently to the one already identified, whom all recognised as their natural leader, as he spoke to them:

"Gentlemen ... and ladies. Time is no longer on our side. The successors of those who entered into a freely negotiated agreement with us grow impatient for more, and the continuing pressure upon our friends in America from both without and within means that the moment is fast approaching when the crude might of the Soviet Union looming behind our immediate enemies will no longer be balanced by the unequivocal support of the United States; and it is clear to all who do not bury their heads in the sand that, when that moment arrives, we may count the months left to us on the fingers of one hand."

The speaker's eyes swept round the table to meet with a few nods of agreement; but none said anything, and, after a pause, he continued:

"The time to act, therefore, is now: to strike our enemies such a blow that, no matter what help may arrive later, they will be crippled for at least a generation, at the end of which time the United States, with all her resources, will undoubtedly have found an answer to the blackmail being wielded against her."

He lowered his voice, but his expression reflected the depth of his feelings.

"But ... when we turn to those who form the majority in the Knesset and in the Government—even ..." he almost choked, "even to the Prime Minister herself—what do we find? Alarm? Determination? A plan of action? On the contrary. We find wishful thinking; an inability to appreciate how the underlying realities of our national security have changed—which is almost totally; and, in some quarters, I am ashamed to confess, a shrinking away on the grounds of so-called humanitarianism that is little short of cowardice."

He took a deep breath, and then continued more calmly. "I do not know to what extent the current penetration of our institutions by the Left is responsible for these attitudes; but, whatever the explanation, it is clear that the time for argument and persuasion is over. The fate of Israel rests in our hands, and we must not flinch from whatever action is necessary—no matter what the effect may be on the rest of the world. And this is only just, for one thing is certain: if we fail, and as a result the long cherished ambition of our enemies to drive us into the sea is realised, the rest of the world will stand to one side—pitying, perhaps, but inactive if to be otherwise would put their own people in danger —as they have so often in the past."

At this a murmur of agreement rose from those listening. A grey-haired woman at the far end began to speak, but the one at the head of the table raised his hand after a moment, and she fell silent.

His face took on an expression that those who had served under him knew well. They smiled inwardly, for it was not for nothing that his soldiers had nicknamed him "The Fox".

"Nevertheless," he went on quietly, "our one real friend remains the United States. And if it is possible to reconcile the action we must take—no matter how desperate—with that friendship, even if it is strained for a while, so much the better. And I think it *is* possible, provided that a sufficiently convincing provocation is forthcoming—against us, of course. One that will not convince *all* our American friends perhaps, but a sufficient number for the issue to be confused long enough for those who fight our propaganda battles for us in Washington and elsewhere to move into action."

The speaker paused for a few seconds, and when he spoke again it was slowly, and looking at each of them in turn.

"In order to achieve this, it will be necessary to take certain steps that would be unthinkable in any other circumstances. But, in considering the plan I am about to put before you, I ask you to remember the consequences of failure. Even if we succeed, how many more of our people will die unless the United States is content to remain at least quiescent?"

He reached into a briefcase on the floor beside his chair, and produced a map, which he then stood up to unfold on the table in front of them. He allowed himself a brief smile.

"I don't know how many of you are familiar with the ancient prophecy beloved of our Christian friends concerning the final battle between good and evil? A predecessor of mine and the then Prime Minister, who were not without a certain sense of humour, borrowed the name for a procedure known only to a small circle, to be used if the State of Israel was in dire peril. As this is the position I believe us to be in today, I intend to use that name for our own plan which, amongst other things, involves the procedure from which it takes its name . . ."

Chapter 1

As the taxi neared Ben Gurion Airport, an Englishman in his early fifties punctuated glances out of the rear window with urging his driver on to even greater excesses than were commonplace amongst a race who spent most of their weekends practising with tanks out in the desert. When at last they drew up outside the main terminal building, he got out quickly with a small overnight bag, and after adding the promised tip for covering the forty odd miles from Jerusalem in as many minutes—much of it through heavy traffic—he nodded briefly to the grinning driver and hurried inside.

He made at once for the British Airways reservation desk, glancing at his watch as he did so and checking it against the clock over the stairs leading to the departure lounge. He managed to overtake an elderly couple obviously making for the same place by breaking into a run, and turned his back on them, thus blocking any protest they might otherwise have made.

"When's the next plane for London?"

The girl, who had noticed his action, was looking at him disapprovingly. She then kept him waiting while she smiled sympathetically at the two who were now muttering behind him before turning back and saying primly: "Not until eight o'clock ... sir."

"Damn!"

"I beg your pardon?"

"I'm in a hurry."

"So I saw."

"Has anyone anything sooner?"

"Not direct."

"Well, indirect then."

The girl glanced down at her list.

"El-Al has a flight to Rome."

"El-Al?"

"Yes. It arrives just after six. You could easily get a connection from there."

"Isn't there anyone else?"

"Besides El-Al?"

"Yes—besides El-Al." He swallowed trying to keep his temper in check while the girl once again deliberately consulted her list. Surely there couldn't be all that many flights from an airport like this? You'd think she'd know them off by heart! It suddenly, and quite irrationally, reminded him of his father-in-law who had been a devoted churchgoer, but had never learned the responses as long as he had lived.

"There's a TWA flight to Rome an hour and a half later."

"You're sure there's nothing sooner?"

The girl smiled thinly.

"Positive. But please don't take my word for it. Do check with someone else."

"Where's the El-Al desk?"

"Right behind you."

"Thank you."

The girl, an Israeli who happened to work for British Airways, watched him go. He was like a lot of Europeans, she thought contemptuously—afraid in case he got hijacked!

In fact, she couldn't have been more wrong.

By the time the ticket had been issued and he had paid for it with an American Express Credit card bearing the name Paul Close, the flight had been called twice, and he passed through the exhaustive searches that preceded any flight out of Tel Aviv without delay, straight on to the aircraft itself.

The doors banged shut, and after an interval the aircraft started to lumber towards the end of the runway.

Instinctively, Close glanced in the direction of the observation lounge. The darkened glass prevented him from seeing anything; but he knew someone would be there by now watching, and he felt for reassurance inside the flap of his right-hand jacket pocket.

It was strange; even the most diligent security officer invariably failed to check the flaps. Perhaps it was because not many people had jackets with such things nowadays, or maybe they were subconsciously dismissed as too old-fashioned to present any kind of threat. But they all did the same thing: bang the pockets from the outside, then lift the flaps as their hands slid past and inside. And often a small piece of paper was all that was necessary.

Anyway, it was there. And they would be there, wondering what to do now. But it was too late.

He knew what they would try to do. But with luck, it wouldn't be any use.

One of the men who had been at the meeting in Jerusalem watched the plane for a few seconds as it taxied. Then he nodded to his companion, and they went down into the main lounge where the public telephones were.

They were all occupied for the moment, but there was no hurry. The plane was not due to touch down in Rome before six o'clock, local time—all the time in the world to make the necessary arrangements. In a way, it couldn't be better; a British businessman killed in Rome would attract less attention than if it had happened on the road from Jerusalem.

Chapter 2

El-Al Flight 453 for Rome—estimated time of arrival 18.00 hours
—left on time. As the big jet climbed into the afternoon sunshine,
those passengers who were already relaxed looked down at Tel-
Aviv spread out beneath them, and a few noticed the Shalom
Tower—the tallest building, and a popular tourist attraction—just
before the plane crossed the coast and headed out to sea.

In front, the Captain, the young Co-pilot (who also doubled as
navigator) and the Flight Engineer went about their routine tasks
with a practised efficiency that had acquired, perhaps, just a little
extra edge from knowing that, from the moment they left until
their return, they were as good as in the front line, and a prime
target for more than a thousand enemy agents throughout the
world waiting for the slightest relaxation of security that would
give them the chance to strike.

The Captain wondered how long it was fair to go on asking
his wife to accept the strain of seeing him off from the front door
of their villa just outside Herzliya without knowing if she was
ever going to see him again. It was true that she had known all
about his job when they had married; she had worked for the
Airline before, and on the administrative staff for several years
afterwards—in fact, until their son was born. But those were in
earlier—harder, undoubtedly—but perhaps less vicious days, when
shootings and bombs were confined to the armed forces of both
sides or those who guarded the borders in one form or another,
and civil aircraft were sacrosanct.

Now their son was flying Goldas, a squadron leader in the
finest air force in the world. But he knew his wife worried about
him far more. Although he never admitted it to her, it was probably true he was in greater danger—at least, as long as these
uncertain times continued—and the signs were that the young

Arabs were turning more and more against the treaty their fathers had signed.

In theory, he could go on flying for another seven years, provided that he could pass the medical; but Mike Shwerdt, the General Manager, had promised him there would be an interesting and worthwhile desk job any time he wanted it. So what was stopping him from taking one, so Ari could stop worrying herself sick—she wasn't strong anyway—and he could be at home and look after her for a change?

The plane was flying on the automatic pilot, and he looked up at the blue vault of the sky overhead before glancing down to see the shadows of a few clouds masking the glint of the sun on the sea far beneath them, even though the clouds themselves were almost invisible. Over to their right a dark line on the horizon marked the southern coast of Cyprus.

"Nicosia reports slight clear air turbulence at thirty thousand feet over the northern Aegean." The Co-pilot turned to look at him, holding the earphone firmly against his left ear. "They ask if we'll let them know what it's like to the south as we pass through."

His superior nodded without replying, and the other responded over the radio in English before checking the route map in front of him. "We pass a good eighty miles south of the Athens track," he remarked after a few seconds, reverting to Hebrew. "I doubt if it'll affect us at all."

This time the Captain grunted without even looking in his direction, and the younger man looked at him curiously. Unlike most airlines, for security reasons the flight crews of El-Al planes tended to stay together for months at a time, and consequently got to know one another pretty well; this was the idea. But he had rarely seen the Old Man so preoccupied as he seemed to be this afternoon. He glanced round at the Flight Engineer, who was himself in his early forties, to see if he had noticed anything; but he was busy checking some readings and noting them down in his log.

The young man turned to face forwards again: Oh well, if it was reminiscing time, he had a few memories of his own he didn't mind indulging for a while!

Frankly, he was in love; and the object of his devotion not only reciprocated his feelings—as they had discovered to their mutual delight only the previous evening—but, as one of the stewardesses, was travelling in the main cabin only a few feet away. And tonight he and Sharon would be in Rome with another evening together in front of them!

Close felt his stomach contract and expand. It was not that he minded flying, except in really bad weather—he did it all the time—but he knew, as certainly as anything he had ever known before in all his life, that if the aircraft he was in touched down in Rome representatives of those he had just managed to elude would be waiting for him, and he would never get the chance to tell London what he knew. And that was more important even than his own life.

Not that he was unafraid of death—he had seen too much of its ugliness and had lost too many friends to be otherwise. But if some means were not found of stopping the madmen he had left behind, the chances were that not only he would perish, but countless millions besides.

He knew it was useless trying to persuade the Captain to change course. No one would believe him without proof—except those who would be waiting for him. Unless, of course, he was one of *them*. That was always possible, and it was one of two reasons why his heart had sunk when he realised it was El-Al, the Israeli national airline, or nothing. The other was that, somehow or other, he was going to have to take over the aircraft, and he knew that he could not have picked a harder nut to crack, for El-Al, alone among Western airlines, had a policy of shooting first and asking questions afterwards, which was why aerial hijackings were so rarely attempted against them.

Bluff wouldn't work—that was certain. Among the passengers were at least two armed guards; at the first sign of trouble they would go into action, and he had no weapon of his own—the searches had seen to that—not that he would have been stupid enough to try and conceal one, knowing how thorough they always were.

Even so, the guards were his best chance. Each would be carrying a loaded revolver, and he had to get one of them, first to defend himself against the other guard, and then to take command.

He was sorry for the other passengers. He knew it would be a frightening experience; but if all went well, no harm would come to them, and their long-term interest was every bit as much at stake as his own.

He was banking on there not being more than two guards. If there were, he would probably be shot and killed.

If only he knew which they were!

More than an hour passed; drinks were served and the flight proceeded uneventfully. Close glanced at his watch and felt the hairs on the back of his neck beginning to tingle.

From where he was sitting he had a pretty good view of most of the plane, and he had even risen to his feet suddenly before walking to the toilets at the back of the aircraft, in the hope that someone would reach instinctively for their hidden weapon before smothering it on realising his purpose. But despite all this, and a welcome wait half-way to the back while one of the stewardesses dispensed drinks from a trolley, which had given him an opportunity to study closely those sitting at the rear, he was none the wiser when he returned to his seat. One of them could even be a woman.

Then suddenly the door at the front of the aircraft opened, and the Captain stepped into view. It was unusual for any of the flight crew to leave the cabin these days, but sometimes this was unavoidable. On this particular occasion a query had arisen over the number of packages in the hold. The lists had been agreed before they took off, as security required, but an eagle-eyed chief steward had noticed that they had on board one more item than they could account for. In normal circumstances no-one would have bothered the Captain with what appeared, on the face of it, to be a trivial matter; but in these days the extra item could be a bomb, and only the Captain, who was ultimately responsible for all security, could override the standing order either to turn back or to land at the nearest airfield while the matter was investigated.

The Captain paused before starting his walk to the back of the plane until he heard the door safely locked behind him, and swore under his breath. Ground staff were becoming progressively more incompetent, and the chances were this was the third false alarm he had had to deal with this year; but the unions had become so strong, that nothing the flight crews ever had to say on the subject seemed to make any difference.

Close's attention was held as the other began to walk down the aisle towards him. Then he saw what he was waiting for. Just for a second, the Captain's eyes strayed to a man sitting in an aisle seat on the opposite side two rows in front of him—a short, bald man whom he had noticed at the beginning of the flight sweating a lot and mopping his brow repeatedly, which he had put down to nervousness.

The Captain did not smile. No word was spoken, but his eyes widened involuntarily in recognition, and the other gave an almost imperceptible, but quite definite, nod.

That was it. It was as if one had said: "Ah, there you are! Everything all right?" And the other had replied: "Yes. No problems." It was all over in a moment, and the Captain passed on. But it was enough. He'd stake his life on it—literally!

He waited for the Captain to go on past, then he rose to his feet, quite nonchalantly this time—he even smiled at the woman sitting on his right as he stepped past her.

Then suddenly he sprang ... Before his victim had even glanced up, he was felled by a blow to the back of the neck.

The Captain spun round at the resultant commotion and Close dropped to a crouching position—partly so he could reach for the shoulder holster he was now totally committed to finding, and partly to offer as small a target as possible.

His hand closed with relief on the handle of a revolver. As he wrenched it free, another man who had been sitting at the back of the aircraft was on his feet as if by magic with a gun in his hand, and began to fire.

Close fired back. His opponent was evidently unsighted by the

18

Captain, and hesitated as if trying to avoid hitting him; but the Englishman continued and within a few seconds the exchange was over. The second guard falling back, clasping his right shoulder and dropping his gun.

Close paused watching for the slightest sign of movement, but no one tried to pick it up—in fact everyone else seemed stunned. After a few more seconds, he stepped over the body of the Captain to retrieve it himself.

Only when the second gun was clasped firmly in his right hand did he flick open the chamber of the first with the thumb of his left to confirm something his instinct had told him as certainly as the identity of the first guard: His last shot had been the last. He had walked the entire length of the plane with an empty gun in his hand.

He was equally sure there were still two shots left in the second gun, but this he did not check. If they had rushed him, he wouldn't have stood a chance. But a man with two guns in his hands looks twice as frightening as it he only had one, even if one was empty.

He glanced towards the front of the aircraft. Undoubtedly they would have some sort of weapon on the flight deck, but the door of the cabin had remained tightly closed in strict accordance with instructions. He might have taken command of the passengers, but he still had to take over the plane itself.

The fact that the Captain was incapacitated for the moment gave him a better chance. It would be a test of wills between him and the Co-pilot. If the Captain had been sitting in there he wouldn't have been so sure; but the second-in-command were usually comparatively young.

As he looked towards the locked door, he saw a young air hostess cowering in the first class compartment. It gave him an idea, but first he turned to the chief steward who was already bending over the injured guard and said: "Tell everyone not to worry. No one will come to any harm. We're only going to London."

The other glanced up momentarily then went on with what he was doing without replying.

"When you've attended to him, see what you can do for the other two," Close went on. "Then I suggest you serve everyone a drink on the house."

The steward looked up again, and this time he said: "Don't tell me what to do, you bastard. You'll never get out of this alive, I promise you."

Close said: "Try and control your temper. If not for your own sake, then for the sake of the passengers. It may be as you say . . . but they, at least, will be unharmed if you behave yourself."

So saying, he backed away. Then he turned and strode up to the front, collecting the frightened girl just before he reached the locked door. He just had time to register the fact that she was exceptionally pretty before turning his attention to those on the other side and raising his voice.

"If you have a gun, don't try and use it. I have one of your stewardesses here. I'm about to make her stand with her back to the door."

He pushed the girl into position then whispered: "What's your name?"

"Sharon," the girl stammered back.

Good. An identified hostage was always more effective.

"It's Sharon," he repeated, raising his voice again, little realising the impact of his words on one of those on the other side. "Now listen carefully: I'm not going to play games. I'm in too much of a hurry. Either open this door and throw out your gun by the time I count ten or I'm going to start by shooting her in the leg. Is that understood?"

"We haven't got a gun" came the answer after a few seconds.

"I don't believe you. One . . . two . . ."

He had no idea what was happening on the other side of the door and continued to count, glancing over his shoulder all the time to make sure no one was sneaking up behind.

The girl's eyes widened as he reached eight, and she bit her lip as she saw the barrel point downwards; but to her credit she remained silent.

The fact that he reached "ten" without anything happening— apart from some woman passenger having hysterics behind him

20

—came as no surprise. Knowing the people he was dealing with, he would have been amazed at anything else. But he was aware the Chief Steward had now left the prone body of the Captain, and was moving slowly towards him. His next move had better work.

He turned and fired at the steward, who was obviously determined to be a hero, hitting him in the shoulder. The sound of the report in the confined space was deafening, and simultaneously, as well as rather ungallantly, he kicked the girl in the shin—hard enough to make her shriek with pain but not hard enough to break anything. And after all, it could have been a lot worse.

The reaction was almost instantaneous. The cabin door was torn open, and a young man stood there with gun in hand. But he didn't stand a chance; his attention wavered between the girl, who half fell into the cabin—as he thought, possibly crippled for life—and the would-be hijacker, and in the instant it took him to make up his mind, the gun was knocked from his grasp and it was all over.

For a while the flight resumed at least the outward appearances of normality. The door leading to the flight-deck was relocked with the girl on the outside, and the injured steward was removed to the rear of the aircraft with the others, as well as the body of the Captain who never regained consciousness—having been hit in the chest and in the back, he died shortly afterwards.

The knowledge that he was now entirely responsible for the safety of the big jet went some way to steadying the young Copilot. His relief on learning that Sharon was comparatively uninjured was almost counterbalanced by the knowledge that, by his precipitate action in opening the door, he had broken one of the standing orders laid down for dealing with such situations, and he had delivered the aircraft into the hands of an enemy.

He glanced at the Flight Engineer, but the man's face was expressionless. He knew, if they ever lived to face an inquiry, his future would depend on the evidence his colleague might give—no one else had been close enough to see what had really

21

happened, except the one who now stood pointing the revolver he had dropped at his head—and he was hardly likely to appear.

He drew a deep breath, and dismissed the thought. He would face it, if and when it arose. For the moment, his responsibility was to the passengers and the rest of the crew.

He had landed the aircraft dozens of times in the course of training, and one of the things he had liked about the dead Skipper was that, unlike some, he often gave him the chance to do so; but he had never gone "solo" before. It was one thing to put down nearly two hundred tons of aircraft at a hundred and sixty miles an hour under usually good conditions knowing that an experienced hand was never more than a few inches from the other set of controls; but no one ever worked completely alone, and certainly not with passengers on board: there was the co-ordination of the four throttles with the control column, for one thing.

He glanced again at the Flight Engineer; he would be able to help to some extent, but it wouldn't be the same as having two hands one upon the other as if controlled by one brain.

The injured were made comfortable, and, after a while, the chief steward grudgingly acknowledged the wisdom of the hijacker's earlier advice, and ordered the drinks trolley out again for "one on the house."

Shortly afterwards, the Flight Engineer's voice came over the speaker system to inform them that there was nothing more to worry about: they were diverting to London, where the gentleman who had taken charge had promised to give himself up, and no doubt a plane would be put at their disposal to fly them back to Rome within hours.

The first reaction was of intense relief. Some even began to laugh, until they were reminded of the injured and fell silent again. Then another, deeper anxiety began to be felt. If they weren't being taken to Libya or some place like that and weren't going to be held hostage, it wasn't a political act. Besides, who diverted planes to London? He must be mad! And knowing he was up front pointing a gun at the remaining pilot didn't make them feel any safer.

The young Co-pilot's first reaction on being told to change course was to argue that they didn't have enough fuel to reach London; but Close knew that any long distance aircraft always carried enough capacity for at least two hours extra flying in case of traffic congestion or bad weather, and when the pilot still argued he pointed the gun sufficiently convincingly at the Flight Engineer's left knee-cap to shut him up. The memory of what he thought had happened to Sharon when he heard her scream was too fresh in his mind. Perhaps he was also hoping that his colleague would remember how he had felt when his face was already tense with anticipated agony when he came to give evidence.

Traffic control informed them that air lanes into Gatwick were being cleared. It was true that under normal circumstances they had enough fuel to reach London, but it was reported that the weather over northern France and south-east England was deteriorating rapidly and, although Gatwick was only thirty miles south of Heathrow, anything that widened the margin of safety was considered by those responsible to be worth introducing into a situation that now had half Europe sitting on the edge of its seats. As if to prove the truth of this, first Yugoslavian, then Italian, then French fighters provided an escort for a while. This quite irrationally cheered those travelling in the main cabin.

As they passed the Paris beacon it began to get dark, and, as their last escorts turned away, a bank of thunderous cloud extending across the horizon reared up in front of them as if a blanket were being drawn over their heads to hide the end of the story. Turbulence became extreme as they crossed the French coast, invisible now except on the radar screen, and started to descend. Visibility became nil as rain began to sheet across the windscreen; despite the closed door and the noise of the engines, the crew could hear sounds of distress coming from the main cabin behind them.

"Slightly less than half an hour left," the Flight Engineer reported solemnly after checking the fuel gauges.

23

The Co-pilot glanced at Close, who was holding on to a bank of instruments to prevent himself being thrown around by the plane, which was bucking up and down now as if on a switchback.

"We've no business going down in these conditions," he protested. "I've never landed like this. It takes two people."

The Englishman looked pale in the reflected light of the instruments, but the gun never wavered for more than a second at a time.

"You said you could use him," he said, and moved the barrel to point at the engineer for a moment.

"Under normal circumstances, yes. But not like this. We should return to Paris."

Close's eyes were tired but cold.

"I said London."

"I'm not sure I can do it."

The other examined him carefully to see if he was telling the truth, and decided he probably was. But it was London or nothing.

"Try," he said quietly.

"Don't you care anything for those people back there?"

The engineer had spoken so infrequently, and then only to repeat some technical data, that Close looked at him with surprise.

"Haven't you scared the shit out of them enough already?"

Close's eyebrows rose a fraction. Bad language was something with which he had never compromised, in business or, even earlier, in the Army.

"It has not been my intention to frighten anyone more than was absolutely necessary," he said coldly.

"Then why can't you do as he suggests? Paris is near enough to London, damn it. You can take a train which gets you there in three hours!"

The suggestion made the Englishman smile in spite of himself; but, before he could reply, he saw the other stiffen and hold the radio earpiece which he had taken over earlier more firmly in position. He also saw the Co-pilot listening intently.

"Thank you, London. We are turning two degrees to the

right." He leant forward and adjusted the automatic pilot, causing the Boeing to bank slightly before righting itself. Then he continued: "But if you don't mind we would prefer not to climb. Reserves are already critical."

There was a brief pause, and he made another adjustment which immediately gave the impression of going up in a lift. But Close had flown enough to realise they had simply levelled out. The plane steadied slightly, but the sound of the rain pounding on the windows became even more intense.

The pilot glanced at him.

"We're being diverted to Luton. It's not too good there either, but both Gatwick and Heathrow are closed in by thunderstorms. I'm afraid it's going to get worse before it gets better. We haven't enough fuel to climb, so we're going to have to go through."

Close gazed back at him. The boy of only a few hours ago had somehow been replaced by a man, and he knew that if the other failed it would not be for lack of nerve. He then glanced at the engineer. But the other, being a man of few words, remained silent.

Not so the pilot, who turned and said: "Ask Georgina to make sure everyone's sitting down and stays strapped in until after we land. Give them the usual ... then make sure *they* all stay in their seats as well—unless anyone's really ill, of course."

"Right."

The Flight Engineer picked up the 'phone, and after pressing a button began to repeat the orders. But Close's attention was drawn by a flash of lightning immediately in front of them that penetrated the encompassing gloom and left him half blind for a second.

"Do you mind putting that thing down now?"

Again it was the young pilot who was looking directly at him.

"We've no choice but to go where you want now, and it might help if I hadn't got the feeling you might shoot me by accident!"

Close stared back at him, then grinned for the first time since the long ordeal had begun.

"All right, I won't point it at you." He glanced at the Flight Engineer. "But I'll hang on to it, just in case."

25

"Suit yourself."

From then on all three were taken up with the fight to get the plane through the storm and find the end of the runway.

The Englishman had experienced bad weather; but none even approached the beating they took now, and he marvelled that the plane stayed in one piece. Even through the hydraulic controls, he could see the battle the young pilot was having to keep level, and when they finally turned for the approach the engineer reported they had only ten minutes' fuel left.

Nobody said anything, but Close realised he was saying in effect they'd better make it first time, because there wasn't going to be a second.

The engineer climbed into the vacant seat beside the Co-pilot and strapped himself in to stop getting thrown out again. Close picked up the spare earphone, and from then on was able to hear the calm voice of the traffic controller who was talking them in—so much in contrast to the raw savagery of the situation as they rode a potential fire-bomb, bucking and kicking through the night towards a piece of rain-drenched concrete barely half as wide again as the wing span of the plane itself.

Without that calm English voice it would have been like trying to find a button on the wall of a darkened cellar first time with the tip of one finger.

"Your direction's good ... you're right on the glide path."

The pilot concentrated on his instruments oblivious of the monster outside that was trying to tear them to pieces or smash them into the ground short of the runway; but the engineer peered into the darkness, although he knew it was too early to be able to see anything.

"... You're a little too high.... That's right.... Now half a degree.... Well done."

The pilot's face was bathed in sweat. But it wasn't fear; there was no time for that now. Only Close was afraid. And the engineer—he was afraid too; he could see that.

There were people in houses only a thousand feet below them now, sitting in their front rooms watching TV. They probably

26

didn't give a thought to the plane passing overhead—except to curse it for interfering with their favourite programmes.

". . . you've just passed the three-mile marker. You're still a bit too high."

The pilot edged the stick away from him a fraction, and the plane lurched forward sickeningly.

"That's enough. As you were."

Again a bump, and the feeling of going up in a lift. He must have extended the flaps ages ago.

"Undercarriage."

The engineer leaned forward and threw a switch. A whine, heard even above all the other noises, followed by a thump as the wheels locked into position. The nose of the aircraft began to dip, and simultaneously the pilot edged the stick back and knocked the throttles forward a fraction to compensate for the drag.

At once the plane became even more difficult to handle, and Close realised why he had left it so late.

"A fraction too much to the left . . . that's better."

"Air speed?"

"Two hundred knots."

"You're one mile from the end of the runway. Your direction is good. You're right on the glide path. You should be able to see the lights at any moment."

Close stared outside, and suddenly he saw them.

For a second his heart was in his mouth. They seemed to be crossing the runway at an angle. Then he realised it was the M1 motorway.

"There it is!"

They all saw it, almost simultaneously, right in front of them.

"OK. I see them."

The pilot knocked the throttles back a fraction.

"Speed?"

"One-sixty."

"Good."

He watched fascinated as they rode towards the double column of lights bobbing up and down quite gently now, as if on a ship which had just passed into the lee of a harbour wall.

"You're over the runway." It was the last message they received before touch-down.

They flared out, and after what seemed an agonising delay, felt the jolt of the wheels against the tarmac. It was so quiet now, comparatively; they even heard the tyres squeal. Then the nose settled gently. It was all so easy.

Close looked at the young pilot in admiration, and saw he was actually enjoying it.

"Reverse thrust."

While the pilot held on to the stick with both hands, the engineer, using both his, pushed the throttles right back; and as the engines rose to a shriek the speed cut to the point where the wheel brakes could take over.

"Hello, Charlie Apple Baker. This is the control tower. There is a Land-rover waiting for you at the end of the runway. Follow it, please."

Close peered outside again, and saw the lights of the seemingly diminutive vehicle a few hundred yards in front of them. He also noticed several fire engines which had been parked beside the runway pulling away, but as the plane proceeded, three ambulances fell in behind.

"Charlie Apple Baker here. Wilco!"

The Land-rover led them away from the main buildings to where a mobile ramp was waiting together with several other vehicles.

"Charlie Apple Baker. This is the Airport Police, Inspector Funnell speaking. May I talk to Mr. Close, please."

The pilot glanced at him. The plane had come to a halt now and the sound of the engines died away.

"Just speak normally. It acts both ways."

Close cleared his throat.

"Paul Close here."

"Ah ... Mr. Close. Are you a British subject?"

"Yes, I am."

"And do I understand you are prepared to give yourself up without any trouble."

"That is correct."

28

"Very well. Two officers will come on board first. Captain?"

"Yes?"

"Please see everyone else remains in their seats. I understand the wounded who are still alive are not in imminent danger?"

"That is correct." The pilot swallowed, then opened his mouth as if to say something else; but, before he could do so, the Inspector continued:

"Then we'll see to them afterwards. I think it's best we remove Mr. Close first."

"I understand."

"Mr. Close?"

"Yes."

"Please stay where you are until my men arrive. We're bringing the ramp up to the forward door, so you won't have to go through the main cabin."

Close suppressed a smile.

"That's very considerate."

"Not at all. We don't want any trouble."

In a short space of time there was a knock on the cabin door, and Close nodded to the Flight Engineer who unlocked it. A young policeman stood in the doorway with another just behind him.

"Mr. Close?"

"That's me."

"Would you come with us please, Sir."

"Certainly."

He moved to comply.

"Perhaps we'd better take that?"

He glanced down and saw he was still holding the revolver.

"Oh . . . yes, of course." He handed it over, handle first.

"Thank you, Sir. Please follow us."

Close moved to comply, the first policeman standing to one side, the other leading the way, but he paused at the door and glanced back. He was about to say something and the other two looked at him expectantly; then training took control, and he turned away without a word. It had even stopped raining.

Half-way down the ramp he paused and looked back.

"Is something the matter, Sir?"

"Yes, I almost forgot. My briefcase. I was sitting in Sixteen B."

One of the stewardesses was sent to fetch it, while Close waited at the bottom of the ramp with the two policemen.

Perhaps that was the mistake. There was nothing very important in it. Just his pyjamas, toothbrush and shaving kit, as they discovered afterwards. There was no reason to wait, but habits die hard, and a man and his briefcase are seldom parted.

Just after it was put into his hand, and they started to walk across the tarmac, a shot rang out and Close suddenly found himself lying face downwards on the ground. Then—suddenly—incredibly—he realised his life was coming to an end.

He opened his mouth to protest even as one of the police dropped beside him and the other crouched down with drawn revolver looking round for his attacker.

Their first reaction was to look back at the plane. Then they realised he had been shot in the chest and they peered into the darkness while waving frantically at one of the ambulances.

But they saw nothing. Whoever it was, had gone.

He was dead before they lifted him inside.

Chapter 3

The Director sat at his desk long after the meeting had broken up, sucking an unlit pipe and staring at infinity. He did not even look up when his secretary came in and quietly drew the curtains and turned on the desk light, which she knew would not disturb him, before going out and closing the door behind her. It never occurred to her to say anything. She knew that look.

Paul Close had been one of his ablest and most experienced agents. His cover had been excellent, and information had already been leaked to the press concerning the British businessman who had gone berserk on the flight to Rome hinting at a previous history of psychiatric treatment. The Foreign Office had expressed its deep regret to the Israelis that a British subject should have been responsible for such an incident, and arrangements were being made to make an *ex gratia* payment from the Prime Minister's discretionary fund to the wife of the dead Captain, although it had emerged at the post mortem that the latter was in fact slain by one of the bullets from his own side; a detail that, with a little prompting in the right quarters, had been seized upon by BALPA—the British Airline Pilots' Association—as a perfect example of the necessity of dealing with potential hijackers on the ground and not in the air, and thus succeeded, without any official comment, in making it appear as if it was really the Israelis' fault. But all this was a gloss, as his counterpart in Jerusalem would undoubtedly have realised by now.

In earlier, happier days—or, as some preferred to think of them, the "Middle" period—there had been close links between Israeli and British Intelligence; but, as the "Energy" crisis had developed, a divergence of interests had arisen, and now that relationship had reverted to one of watchful neutrality. Each country was aware of the operations of the other's agents within its borders. The identity of many were known, but rarely were they requested to leave. They would only have been replaced, and then the business of discovering the newcomers would have begun all over again. So it was easier to leave things as they were —unless there were strong reasons to the contrary.

Of course, each had a few whose identity was unknown to the other. Close had been one, but by now the Israelis would have put two and two together, and would have realised moreover, as he had himself, that whatever information he had been about to impart must have been quite out of the ordinary for him to have ignored the usual methods of communication and to have driven him to such desperate measures to reach London.

Or perhaps they already knew. Perhaps it was because Close had realised he was blown that he had left so precipitously; or had he intended to go to Rome in the first place? Naturally, they were checking every possibility. But so far all they had to go on was a piece of paper sewn into the flap of one of his jacket pockets on which was written a phrase which had meant nothing to anyone so far. It was certainly not in one of the usual codes. But they were working on that too.

The Director got up slowly and sighed, automatically banging the empty pipe against the heavy glass ashtray.

He had given orders that none of those on the spot were to do anything. Most had not even known of the existence of Close, and he dared not contact for the moment the only one who had worked with him, and whose identity, he hoped, was still unknown to the other side.

He turned slowly and walked towards the windows.

Whether they had known what the agent had been about to reveal or not, they had got to him in a great hurry.

He pulled the curtains aside and looked outside. He hadn't really cared for that side of it. Still, it might come in useful as an excuse one day. Meanwhile, eyes would be upon them, waiting for some response.

What was needed was a completely new element. One that no one but himself and, perhaps, his immediate superior would know about. And he had better not take too long introducing it either. He had known Close for years, and nothing would have induced a man of his experience to have blown cover so spectacularly—unless the matter was of a gravity almost unheard of in peace-time.

Rain was lashing down now, forcing the few pedestrians to seek the temporary shelter of doorways. As he watched, someone managed to dislodge an empty milk bottle so that it rolled off the stone step and smashed on the pavement, to the consternation of the guilty party, who decided to risk another soaking by running on, rather than face possible retribution.

Why would anyone live in a God-forsaken climate like this unless they had to?

Richard Deutsch—"Dutch" to his friends—heard the rain pattering against the window panes of his studio apartment in a comparatively new development of what used to be dockland at Wapping. But that only seemed to make the room that much more cosy and, glancing at the figure of the sleeping girl beside him, which he could see in outline by the lights from across the river, he turned his head back to look at the ceiling and, after a few moments, closed his eyes contentedly once more.

At forty-three he found he did not need as much sleep as before, although the life he led was every bit as strenuous; but he had taught himself to lie quietly and rest, without worrying over it.

It was often at such times that he had some of the best ideas for the thrillers which now provided most of his income, but more often his mind just free-wheeled gently until he drifted to sleep without realising it.

The flaw in his character of which he was most aware, when he thought about it, was his temper. Over the years he had learned to master it reasonably well—the US Air Force had been a help in that respect—but his mother and father had been so worried about it when he was at school, and the other parents had complained that he was always going round attacking their children, that keeping his temper had become almost an obsession, which had only got him into even more fights when some of the other kids mistook it for turning yellow.

Probably, on balance, he hadn't got into any more fights than any other kid of his age, but his reactions were so fast—a fact which had helped qualify him later for pilots' school, and had certainly saved his life thereafter on more than one occasion —that although his style wasn't much to write home about, the others always seemed to be moving in slow motion, which gave him all the time in the world to step in and hit them on the nose.

It was true he still got angry. More often, nowadays, it was when he saw some injustice or indignity heaped on someone who, for one reason or another, was unable to defend himself. But most of the time he was easy going, and this, allied to looks that were almost indecently boyish—with the exception of his eyes, which were penetratingly blue, and a smile that came at un-expected moments, especially when someone mistook his usual good nature for softness—left him rarely without friends, and made him almost irresistible to women. Except one.

He had come to Europe with the USAF as a fighter pilot, mainly stationed in Germany. But his leaves were spent mostly in England, which he had come to love, in the company of the daughter of an English Squadron-Leader whom he had met during a routine change of posting.

He had met Helen several times socially before he eventually asked her to go out with him. He had thought her beautiful but snooty—the main reason for the latter being that she was shyer than most of the girls he had known, and as she had been to one of the better English girls' private schools, she had an upper class drawl which at first he mistook for boredom with things in general and with him in particular. But when they got to know one another better he forgot he had ever thought there was anything unusual about the way she spoke and, given a little encouragement, the Squadron-Leader's daughter showed herself to be anything but bored. In fact, once awakened, she developed an enthusiasm for making love that was great while they were together, but contained within itself the seeds of destruction.

They were married after a few months, and spent their honeymoon at the Westbury Hotel, just off New Bond Street. Jane was born exactly nine months later; her mother had not wanted anything to spoil the short time they were to spend together before Dutch had to rejoin his unit. The child was nick-named "Billie" because, while Dutch was away, Helen often took her down to the tennis club and Billie Jean King's name was on everyone's lips at that time.

They had been happy enough as long as he had remained in the Air Force; but when he decided against renewing his contract of service and they went back to live in the States for a while, things had started to go wrong. He had tried a number of jobs connected with aviation that had taken them from Virginia, out to California, and back; but things got no better between them, for the root cause was nothing to do with either his work or where they were living.

Helen loved a full social life and to have friends in all the time, while Dutch needed a period of tranquillity in which to find himself again in his new circumstances. Furthermore, completely unbeknown to him, she had become accustomed to taking a variety of lovers while he was away—with the greatest discretion of course—and whereas it had been comparatively easy to bury her guilt when she had been able to forget his existence for long stretches of time, to practise infidelity on a day-to-day basis, with all the ingenity and deceit it required, was only slightly less of a strain than having to accept the limitations his constant presence imposed.

After all, she told herself, she only wanted to be happy. Was it her fault if she required a higher level of sexual activity than any one man was able to give? She still loved him at times, and she loved their daughter deeply. In spite of everything, she was a remarkably good mother.

And so, after hurting each other deeply in their different ways, they separated when Billie was eleven. She was now twenty-two, and working as a secretary in Jerusalem, having emigrated there two years previously.

After the divorce, for which Helen returned to London, Dutch had gone back to America. He had written detective stories and thrillers as a hobby since boyhood, and, having salvaged most of his gratuity from the settlement—Helen's father had died leaving her extremely well off—he eventually decided to try his hand at it full-time. But New York had been too unsettling; besides, practically all his friends were in London, which was still a cheaper place to live. And so, after little more than a year, he had returned, had rented an apartment and had begun to write; augmenting his earnings until he was established as a writer—which he hoped would not be too long delayed—as a part-time instructor at a flying club just north of London.

In fact, success did come fairly quickly—thanks partly to help from a friend—but, until a film company bought the rights of his third novel, he learned what many had before: that it was perfectly possible to practise the art of novel-writing with good reviews and evident success, and at the same time starve to death; and the flying lessons, occasionally supported by winning a variety of races and staging aerobatic displays, became a vital factor in making ends meet. And when these activities were no longer strictly necessary, he found he had become so accustomed to running the two careers together that, when he attempted to give one up, the other faltered badly, and he hurriedly resumed his former way of life. Besides, in his heart of hearts, he loved flying and knew he was probably better at it, despite his by now considerable earnings as a writer, than anything else—well, practically anything!

After a few early experiences, Dutch had made it a rule never to have an affair with any of his female pupils. But in the case of Angela, the girl who now lay beside him, breathing softly, he had made an exception.

He had known from the beginning that she was extremely well off. She had turned up at the Club for her first lesson in a Bentley; he had seen her get out of the car and, as he watched her walk across the park towards the women's dressing-rooms, he thought he had never seen anything so coolly, elegantly beautiful in all his life, and had scarcely dared to hope that this was the Angela Romay to whom he was due to give a first lesson.

Lying in the dark now, he could remember exactly how she

had looked. It had been a hot day, and she had been wearing a pale lemon linen suit with light gloves of the same colour. Despite the glare, she had left her dark glasses in the car, and he had been able to see her face properly. Just about everything he had seen had been perfection, from the shape of her face to the wide-set eyes and dark hair, cut short, unlike most of her contemporaries at the time, but in a style that accentuated her features and the slenderness of her neck. It had been in the days when skirts were worn shorter than was fashionable then, and the last he had seen of her as she mounted the steps leading into the clubhouse was a pair of legs which shouted provocation.

The next time they met she was wearing a flying-suit which disguised a figure that he was to discover later had the ability to swivel heads at five hundred paces. On closer examination, her looks more than confirmed the impression they had given from a distance. Despite the colour of her hair and eyebrows, her complexion was fair, as well as being flawless; but her eyes were as dark as the sea at sunset, and seemed to reflect doubt as to what the next day might bring.

She had been bored. She confessed that when they knew one another better. This was why she had decided to learn to fly. But there was nothing in the least aloof in the smile she threw him as she came into the instructors' office to introduce herself; in fact, although he realised later it was unconscious, it was the kind of smile guaranteed to make any man feel he had to prove something, even if he had to take an unfair advantage to do it; and when they went up, he did several things with the plane that he knew he had no business to do with a beginner—and as a result she had been violently sick. But she forgave him, and that was how they had gone out together for the first time. She hadn't wanted to hang around the clubhouse, having made an exhibition of herself, and since the least he could do was to buy her a brandy to settle her stomach, he drove her to one of the better pubs close by where they sat outside under the trees.

They talked of all kinds of things. He even discovered her age (twenty-six); but he never discovered she was married until he took her out to dinner after the next lesson—and then it was too

37

late. He learnt that she was the wife of an extremely wealthy exporter of engineering products who spent at least three-quarters of his time abroad, and much of the remainder either recovering from his last trip or preparing for the next.

Angela never said a word against him. Henry was kind and generous, and she had great respect for him. But after sweeping her out of the West End show in which she had a minor part into a whirlwind honeymoon round half the countries of South America, he had deposited her in a mansion not far from Epsom, with a stupendous allowance. He had refused to let her take up a career of any kind and, as they had such an efficient staff, there was nothing for her to do at home either. She had begged to be allowed to go on some of his trips, and eventually he had consented. But he was scarcely ever available to take her out, and more often than not the places they ended up in were those where it was simply not done for a lady to wander around by herself. It was not long, therefore, before she had had to agree that, on balance, she was probably better off at home.

She had proved to be an apt pupil and went solo after only eighteen hours; but she continued to see Dutch afterwards. He never asked if he was the latest in a long line of diversions—at least to begin with, he didn't want to know the answer. To his surprise, Angela revealed herself to be a competent typist—her mother having insisted on her learning before allowing her to go on the stage—and as he had never learned to type himself, she helped him a great deal by typing his first drafts, which made editing them so much easier.

The day came when she had confessed to being in love with him and asked to be allowed to leave Henry, or rather Henry's house—that very day, if he would only give the word. She wouldn't ask for a penny; just her freedom. But she had not pressed the point, and had seemed to accept the fact that Dutch was not willing, at least for the moment, to remove the limitations he had placed on their relationship from the beginning—or to devote himself exclusively to her.

If she was jealous, she hid it well; and as a result, although he had reserved his freedom of action in theory, he saw other women less and less, apart from a few old friends with whom he did not have that kind of relationship.

He supposed he would have to agree to marry her one day, or say goodbye. And although he had been settled in his former way of life the latter alternative was something he could not really imagine. Still, there was no desperate hurry; things could drift along as they were for quite a while yet . . .

He was almost asleep again.

He wondered if Angela would alter after they were married. Or perhaps his attitude would change. At the moment they were having a ball. But it made it difficult to think it out properly. He didn't want to make another mistake. But, that was a long time ago . . .

It would all work out. There was plenty of time.

The bedside 'phone shocked him awake, heart thumping, the very instant he dropped into unconsciousness.

He kept meaning to have the damned thing moved. It was a stupid place to have put it in the first place. Enough to give anyone heart failure.

The 'phone continued to ring.

Had he really been asleep?

He turned on the light and looked at the watch, which had been a twenty-first birthday present from his mother. Someone had once told her that if you wore one with a luminous dial over a long period it made your hand fall off, so for years he had put up with not being able to see the time in the dark.

It was two-thirty!

Angela stirred and groaned, then turned away from the light. He picked up the 'phone.

"Hello?"

"Richard?"

"Helen!" No-one else ever called him by his first name.

"Darling, who is it?" Angela raised her tousled head from the pillow and was looking at him frowning. Dutch covered the mouthpiece.

"Just your husband. Go back to sleep."

39

"Oh. I thought it might be important!" She made as if to settle down again.

"Richard, are you there?" He uncovered the mouthpiece.

"Yes, Helen."

"Is somebody there with you?"

"That's a hell of a question!"

There was a brief pause. Then she said: "I'm sorry."

His contact with Helen—who had remarried some years previously—had been confined to matters concerning Billie. After the initial bitterness—in fact, after his return to London—they had found they were able to meet and discuss their daughter's welfare without acrimony. Dutch had never contested the fact that Billie had needed her mother more, no matter how much he had needed her at the time and, in return, Helen had put no restriction on the amount of time they could spend together. They had even had a couple of holidays, the three of them together—just like the old days—and he was beginning to wonder if they shouldn't try again, when Helen suddenly told him that she was engaged to be married to one of the officers in her father's old squadron, and that was that.

They had gradually seen less of each other as Billie had grown up. Not that Helen's new husband, whom Dutch had met a couple of times and quite liked, made any difficulties; but in the natural course of events Billie grew away from both her parents without becoming any less fond of either of them, and by nineteen she had quite taken control of her own destiny.

He became aware of Helen's voice once more.

"Richard, it's Billie."

"Why? What's wrong?"

"Well ... nothing, as far as I know. But I'm worried about her."

"Why?"

"I'd rather not discuss it over the phone. Can you come round?"

"Helen, it's nearly three o'clock in the morning!"

"I don't mean now."

"Are you sure there's nothing wrong?"

"I just don't know. That's what's worrying me."

"Is John there?"

"No. He's away. Can you come round straight after breakfast —or make it *for* breakfast, if you like." He caught a flash of the humour which had been the side of her he had most missed when they were no longer together. She knew by now, of course, he had a girl with him.

He was about to say he would come round straight afterwards, when suddenly he remembered he had a lesson to give at ten o'clock.

"Helen ... I can't do either. Honestly, I have a lesson lined up. But I'll drive straight to your place as soon as it's finished."

He glanced at Angela, who was now also wide awake and listening intently. They had arranged to work on the latest draft of the new book after lunch, but that could wait.

"... That is, if you're sure it will keep till then. If something's really not right, I'll cancel it, of course, and come straightaway."

There was a moment's pause, then he heard Helen sigh.

"No. I suppose it's just me being mummish. A few more hours won't make any difference—except to me, of course. But I expect you'll say the whole thing's just my imagination, anyway."

He hesitated.

"You're sure you don't want to tell me about it now?"

"No. It'll keep." He thought he heard her yawn. "The pills I took are starting to work, at last."

"All right then, if you're sure. I'll see you tomorrow."

"Come as soon as you can."

"I promise."

"Goodnight, Richard."

"Goodnight, Helen."

There was a pause, then the hint of a chuckle.

"Think of me!"

He put the 'phone down and looked at Angela. He knew exactly what she had meant. He was never going to sleep now.

"What was all that about?" Angela asked. He told her.

"She probably wants to keep you in suspense to make sure you go round," she said afterwards, and Dutch grinned.

41

"Yes. That idea had occurred to me."

"If she told you what it was now, you'd realise it was nothing and wouldn't go."

"Why should she do such a thing?"

"To see you, of course."

"She's never done anything like it before."

"There's always a first time. She's probably remembering what she's missed."

"After eleven years?"

"Some people are naturally slow."

"If she felt like that, there are plenty of other people."

Angela looked at him for a moment, then changed what she had been about to say.

"Well ... either way, try and not worry about it," she said soothingly. "Billie's a grown woman, and from what you've told me, she's lot of friends. If she's in any kind of difficulty, I expect there are dozens of people she can turn to."

Dutch looked at her gratefully, and Angela went on with a smile: "I expect she wants to get married, or something like that."

"Yes." Dutch paused thoughtfully, then he smiled too. "Could be that."

"And the way Helen feels about marriage, I expect she wants you to go out there and talk her out of it."

Dutch lay back and looked at the ceiling.

"I'd never try to do that. Not that it would be any use; Billie has a mind of her own. And I certainly wouldn't want to celebrate seeing her for the first time in two years by having a row!"

Angela didn't say anything. She didn't really want to talk about Billie. Not that she had anything against her—except that she was the one person in the whole world she was afraid of. That was ridiculous, because they'd never even met and, as she was nearly three thousand miles away, they weren't likely to. But she knew Billie was the one person for whom Dutch would give her up without a second's hesitation, if he thought her welfare needed it; and so, whenever the subject came up, she was terrified of saying the wrong thing. She didn't want to seem uninterested on the one hand; on the other, she felt, while such conversations lasted, like a skater on melting ice, unable to reach safety quick enough.

She watched him for a while. Then, when she judged the moment right, slipped out of the covers, and put out her hand to touch him.

"Let me make love to you," she whispered.

He turned his head to look at her, and thought how beautiful she was, leaning on her right elbow, searching his face for some sign of approval. He guessed what she had been thinking and knew that, in spite of it all, she loved him very much.

Not for the first time, he marvelled that such a creature should be his for the asking, and wondered if he wasn't being very stupid not making sure of her by allowing her to leave her husband and his money at once to marry him.

What was holding him back? Was it really a reluctance to part with his freedom of action? He had parted with that already, quite voluntarily. Or was it something deeper?

He put out his hand to stroke the rounded smoothness of her hip which, due to the position in which she was lying, was accentuated into a rounded hill which ran away into the plain of her upper leg whose skin, as he bent down to brush his lips against it, had the flawless texture of the very young. He heard her draw in her breath quickly and looked up. Then he drew her into his arms.

Chapter 4

As soon as the lesson was over, Dutch walked towards the club-house intending to change as quickly as possible; but before he was more than half-way he saw Helen coming out to meet him. Even from a distance he could see something was badly wrong, and as soon as they were close enough she blurted out: "Richard—Billie's missing!"

"Missing! What d'you mean?"

The two of them stopped a few feet away, facing each other.

"Just what I say. Nobody knows where she is. Everyone's looking for her—even the police."

"For crying out loud! Why didn't you tell me this last night?"

"I didn't know till ten o'clock this morning, and by then you were up there." She glanced momentarily at the clouds above his head.

"Then why did you 'phone?"

"I told you. I was worried about her."

"Although you didn't know then you had anything to worry about?"

"Of course I had. But now I've got proof."

They looked at each other for a few moments; then Dutch said: "Look. You'd better tell me everything." He glanced over his shoulder at the clubhouse. "We can't talk in there."

Helen smiled thinly.

"Not unless you want everyone standing you a drink. That was quite a display you were putting on. What were you trying to do—show your young friend how much he had to learn?"

Dutch looked at her sharply. During their last years together she had consistently attributed the worst motives to anything he had tried to do, but it had been a long time since he had heard her speak like this.

He opened his mouth to retort; but he managed to control

44

himself, and instead he said evenly: "We'll go and sit in your car. It's bigger than mine."

Helen stared at him, but after a few seconds she lowered her eyes and nodded.

When he thought they were settled, Helen asked for a cigarette, which meant he had had to dash back to his own car and fetch some. He smoked so little these days he rarely had any on him; but he remembered Angela had left half a pack in the glove compartment. Then she began by telling him that she had not had a letter from Billie for more than three months.

Dutch remembered he had not had one himself in that time. True, he and his daughter did not exchange letters on a regular basis; sometimes they wrote two or three times a week, then perhaps not again for quite a while. But now he came to think about it, he realised, with a stab of guilt, that it had never been so long before. What with Angela and his new book, he had simply not noticed. Helen, for her part, reminded him that she and Billie had always written to each other regularly once a month, so she had noticed at once when their daughter had failed to reply to her most recent letter. She had not begun to worry, however, until a second month passed without hearing from her; but after almost three months she had become very concerned indeed.

Dutch listened with respect. He had never had reason to doubt her love for Billie, or criticise her as a mother.

"So I decided to 'phone her," Helen continued.

"At work?"

"No, at her flat."

"I didn't know she had a 'phone."

"Well, she got one eventually. She must have forgotten to tell you."

"After waiting two years?"

"Well, I don't know. Perhaps she didn't want you to 'phone."

Seeing his expression, she went on quickly: "No—I didn't mean that. I don't know. She must've forgotten she hadn't told you."

Helen paused for a moment.

45

"Anyway, it didn't make any difference. I tried and tried, but it was no use; no matter what time of day or night I called, there was never any reply."

"Perhaps she's away on vacation."

"For two whole months?"

"On business then."

"No. I thought about that. But Israel's not that big. There's nowhere they could have sent her from where she couldn't have got back, at least at weekends. And I know she'd have wanted to. She loves her flat and all her friends there."

"Yes, I know."

"So that's why I 'phoned you. I'd just tried again, and still no reply."

"You're sure her 'phone's in order?"

"I've had them check it so many times they groan whenever they hear my name."

"Then how do you know she's missing?"

"I had a letter from her this morning."

"To say she's missing?"

"No, of course not!"

"Let's see it, then."

"I left it behind."

"Helen, you're not making sense."

"Neither did the letter. Of course, she didn't know I'd been trying to 'phone, but she made no mention of having been away. It was written as from Jerusalem. The whole thing was obviously an attempt to put my mind at rest."

"How do you know?"

Helen looked at him in exasperation.

"It wasn't a normal letter at all; it was obviously written in a hurry. She must have suddenly remembered she hadn't written, and that I'd be worrying."

"Did she say why she hadn't written for so long?"

"Yes. She apologised, and made some excuse about having to work late and getting back so tired she didn't feel like anything, except flopping into bed." Helen hesitated, then went on in a rush: "Of course, I knew she wasn't telling the truth, and that

46

something must be badly wrong. So I put through another call straight away, and this time I got through. A man answered."

Dutch swallowed. No man really likes to think of the little girl for whom he had once been the only man in the world having any sort of intimate relationship with another, and he had to push the mental image conjured up by his wife's words firmly to one side before he could look back at her with some semblance of a smile and say:

"Well—there's your answer."

But Helen shook her head vehemently.

"No! I asked to speak to Billie, but after a few seconds he said she wasn't there."

"He spoke English then?"

"Just."

"Where did he say she was?"

"He didn't. He just started asking *me* a lot of questions. And when I said I was Billie's mother and unless he told me where she was and what he was doing in her flat my next call would be to the police, he put down the 'phone."

"Burglars?"

"That was my first reaction. Then I thought, no burglar would deliberately prolong a conversation just to ask a lot of questions. So I rang again."

"What happened?"

"The same man answered the 'phone. And when he realised it was me he asked me to wait. Then another man came on— quite a different sort of voice—who spoke English almost perfectly—and he said they were the police, and that they were making enquiries into Billie's disappearance."

"Oh, God!"

"According to him—he said he was Inspector Ezra, by the way—Billie didn't report for work after her two-week summer holiday. Her employers thought at first she had simply been delayed coming back from wherever she had been; she might have been visiting us, for all they knew—when she left, she apparently told them she hadn't made up her mind what to do. But, after a few more days, they became worried and sent someone round to see if she was ill."

"But she wasn't there."

"No. And when they still hadn't heard after a couple of weeks, and someone had gone up a second time without finding her, they became really worried and contacted the police. That was yesterday."

"And that's why they were there today?"

"Right. The Inspector told me to try not to worry. He sounded very nice. He said young girls were always going off by themselves these days for months on end. His own daughter disappeared for five whole weeks without letting them know where she was, or anything; then she suddenly walked in through the door one day as bold as brass, wearing the same clothes she had gone away in, and more or less told them to mind their own business when they asked where she'd been."

"But Billie's not like that."

"I know. He was only trying to be kind."

"It probably wasn't true anyway. About his own daughter, I mean."

"Why should he lie?"

"What happened then?"

Helen paused for a moment looking at him with a frown. Then she went on: "He said Israel was a small country. No-one could disappear for long. Then he asked me if I'd heard from her recently."

"Why?"

"Presumably, in case I could give them a lead."

"And you told them about the letter you had this morning?"

"No."

"No?"

Now it was Dutch's turn to frown. "Why not?"

Helen shrugged uncomfortably, and shook her head.

"I don't know. There was nothing in it really." She paused for a moment, then went on: "I don't know why I didn't tell him. He was being so nice, and only trying to help. Several times after I put down the 'phone I nearly called back. But I didn't."

Dutch looked at her. He had learned a long time ago to respect

48

Helen's intuitions, and he knew that, whatever the reason for not telling Ezra about the letter, it had to do with their daughter's safety. He wasn't going to argue.

"So how did it finish?" he said eventually.

"He told me not to worry—again—and promised to let me know the minute he knew anything definite. And I promised to let them know if I heard anything."

"I see."

"Richard—I'm frightened! If Billie had gone off with a man somewhere, she'd have *told* me. We've never had that kind of secret from each other."

She saw his look, and went on hurriedly: "Oh, you needn't worry, she's nothing like me. As a matter of fact, I don't think she approves of me really. You're the one she looks up to."

She paused again, then continued with a touch of defiance: "But she loves me more. She probably thinks I need it."

Helen's eyes filled with tears, but she regained control of herself.

"Anyway, if it was anything like that, she'd know I'd understand. But she didn't even mention a boy's name. So I *know* it's something else."

"What?"

"I don't know, damn it. That's why I've come to you."

Dutch took a deep breath.

"Do you think she's in trouble with the police, but they're not letting on?"

"I don't think so. Billie said a long time ago their police force is modelled pretty much on ours. Can you imagine an English police inspector not telling the mother of an American girl if she was wanted for some crime or other?"

"No. The usual drill is to ask the parents to advise their children to give themselves up for their own sake."

"Exactly."

"On the other hand, I can't imagine an English police inspector getting a warrant to enter someone's apartment just because their employers said they hadn't turned up for work."

"They might, in some circumstances."

They looked at each other while the significance of this sank in. Then Dutch said quietly: "What do you want me to do?"

Helen put her hand out to touch him, and her eyes became misty once more.

"Go and find her," she said huskily. "I don't know what she's got herself mixed up in, but I know she's in trouble and needs help. I'd come with you—or go myself—but John's so difficult these days. He'd be furious if he came back and found I wasn't at home!"

In spite of the seriousness of the situation, Dutch found himself suppressing a smile. He could well imagine the conclusions his successor might jump to over her absence, and there was such a thing as the "last straw", as he knew only too well. Besides, he didn't really want her tagging along; it would only cause difficulties with Angela, and he had little doubt he would manage much better by himself.

As he drove back into town, his anxiety began to lessen slightly. In spite of Helen's assurance that Billie would confide in her, he had a suspicion that a man was probably at the bottom of it. The bit about Billie not approving of her mother's infidelities was probably true; but she was no prig, and there was a chance that precisely because she *didn't* want her mother to associate a new found love with her own adventures—particularly if she was really in love for the first time—she was keeping it from her, at least, until she saw how things developed. And the more he thought about it, the more he began to look forward to the forthcoming trip.

As soon as he got home, he made a call to book a seat on the regular Saturday flight to Tel Aviv. After all, Billie must be alive and well, or Helen wouldn't have received a letter at all. He just couldn't imagine her in any kind of trouble with the police.

After he had put down the 'phone, he frowned. The next problem was Angela; he knew she'd hate him going away. But before he had made up his mind what to say to her, the 'phone rang. It was Helen once more.

50

"Richard?"

"Yes."

"I've just been looking at Billie's letter."

"I've just booked the flight."

"I told you it was written as if she was still in the flat?"

"The apartment—yes."

"Well, I can't think why it never occurred to me to look before—at the postmark, I mean."

"What about it?"

"It was posted three days ago—in Haifa."

There was a long silence.

"Are you still there?"

"Yes."

"Well?"

"Helen, listen carefully. Tear that letter up. No—better still, burn it. And make sure you burn the envelope as well."

Suddenly there was a chill running down his spine, and he couldn't say why.

"And whatever you do, don't mention it to anyone. Do you understand? No one. Police . . . anyone."

There was a moments silence, and when Helen spoke again her voice was fearful.

"You feel it too, don't you?"

"Yes."

Helen paused, then she said: "I'm glad. I know she's in danger. But now I know you'll do whatever's needed."

"I'll try. I promise."

"I know. I'll pray for you."

He put the 'phone down almost with a sense of shock. The thought of Helen praying for anything, let alone his safety, did nothing to still the alarm bells that were jangling at the back of his head. Although this last piece of information added little to what he already knew, and in some ways even confirmed his suspicions, Helen's call had succeeded in communicating somehow her own instinctive fear, and it was a long time before logic and reason managed to thrust it sufficiently to the back of his mind to remember to call Angela.

51

Chapter 5

"Dutch—darling!"

The flight had already been called, and he had just reached the top of the escalator which led to the departure lounge when he heard his name. He looked down to see Angela waving to him from the bottom before getting on herself.

He suppressed a twinge of irritation. She had been sweet reason itself when he had told her of his need to go to Israel, even when he confessed that it was just the excuse he had been waiting for to make the trip so he could see Billie. But when she came into sight smiling at him, she looked so radiant he could not bring himself to be so churlish as to remind her that they had said their goodbyes the previous evening.

Angela walked up and kissed him. And it was only when she stood back that he noticed she was carrying a small flight bag.

"What's that for?" he said, pointing accusingly.

"What? This? Oh—just for carrying one or two things." Seeing his expression, she linked her arm in his and, after glancing round to see where they were supposed to go, said hurriedly: "Now, you know we agreed not to say goodbye at the airport?"

Dutch found himself being borne along in the direction of passport control.

"Well, after last night, I *had* to see you again. And the only way I could think of doing it, *and* keeping our promise was to come with you."

"What?"

"Don't make a scene, darling. People are looking."

It was true, a lot of people were looking—mainly men—but only for the reason they always looked whenever he appeared with her in public: sheer envy.

He stopped and faced her, hissing between his teeth, while the

52

passport officer watched with interest: "What about Henry?"

Angela's brow cleared at once.

"Oh, you don't have to worry about him—honestly. He's not due back from Caracas for at least a week, and it'll be days afterwards before he even realises I'm not at home."

"What about then?"

"I've left him a note he's bound to find eventually, saying I've gone to stay with Peggy in Cornwall. We were at school together, and I 'phoned her this morning so she'll cover for me if necessary."

They both heard the flight being called a second time.

Angela said more seriously: "Look, darling, if you really don't want me to come, I'll go back. But I thought it would be so lovely. I won't interfere, I promise. I'll go shopping or sunbathe and so on while you're doing whatever you have to. And then, when you've got it all straightened out, we can have a lovely holiday together instead of you rushing straight back." She paused for a moment, then looked wistful. "We've never had a holiday, or any time before, when we didn't have to worry about who was going to see us." She paused again, then added softly: "I really won't interfere. I'll be as good as gold. And I would like to meet Billie."

Looking at her, Dutch realised any other man in the world, standing where he was, would think him mad for even hesitating, but he did so for more than one reason. In the first place, he wasn't sure how Billie would take to her father arriving with a girl friend who was someone else's wife. And he knew he would have to tell her the truth. On the other hand, they might marry, sooner or later, and he hoped his daughter would be sufficiently loving, if not sophisticated, to give them the benefit of the doubt.

The other objection concerned Angela's safety. Ever since his wife's last call, he had sensed there would be more to this trip than simply "helping the police with their enquiries", as they said, even if a man *was* at the bottom of it. Perhaps it was the boy friend the police were after?

He turned back to see Angela studying his face intently, but before he could say anything, she said quietly: "Look, I love

53

you very much, and I know you love me. But I don't want you to feel responsible for me. I know how to look after myself. I can drive—fast if need be—and you taught me to fly. I'll stand on the side lines as long as you want—but I can pitch in and help, too. Who knows?—You might be glad of a friend before we've finished."

Damn all women! Why did they have to keep reading your mind?

Suddenly she gave him a brilliant smile, and tucked her arm into his as they walked the remaining few yards.

One of those who looked in their direction after they had boarded the aircraft was a man who joined the flight at the last minute and took a seat at the back. He had experienced the same pang of envy as every other man as he walked up the aisle between the rows of seats and saw the occupant of 11C sitting next to the gorgeous looking girl who was obviously madly in love with him. But he had a professional interest and, after glancing over one more time just after he heard the doors close to make sure they were still there, he studiously ignored them for the rest of the flight.

His passport bore the name Isaac Codron.

The flight to Tel Aviv took longer than it might have done, because the plane touched down at both Paris and Geneva to take on freight and additional passengers.

In both places, the plane halted a good way from the terminal buildings for security reasons. The passengers were not allowed to remain on board, and they had to wait for a bus to take them to and from the transit lounges, after which all hand-luggage was taken off, and had to be reidentified before being allowed on again.

In the normal course of events Dutch would have found the whole process incredibly irksome, but with Angela it was something of an adventure, and they were both mercifully unaware that, in addition to the official checks, someone else made quite sure they reboarded the plane before he did likewise.

54

The result of all these diversions was that, although the plane left London at eleven-thirty in the morning, it was almost eight o'clock local time and quite dark before it touched down at Ben Gurion. But the lateness of the hour was partially compensated for by the sight of Tel Aviv as they passed over the coast, a welcoming blaze of light after the darkness of the past hour, with only the light of an occasional ship to break the monotony.

After they had passed through Customs and Immigration, Dutch managed to secure two places in one of the communal cabs which plied between the airport and Jerusalem and, apart from a garrulous rabbi who had arrived to visit his son and who insisted on pointing out items of no great interest for the benefit of the American couple with whom he shared the front row of seats, they travelled in silence. Their companions seemingly were affected by the same mixture of fatigue at the end of a long day and relief at their safe arrival.

After a while, Dutch began to realise that the phrase "going up to Jerusalem" was literally, as well as metaphorically, true. The air became appreciably cooler, and, even as they were climbing, the distant lights of the city in front of them showed it to be at least a thousand feet higher still. Every inch of this road would have been trodden at some time or another by Moses, Samuel, David or Jesus Christ—not to mention the Greeks, Romans, Arabs, Turks and British who had followed. They were moving towards the cross-roads of the world.

The cab eventually dropped them off at the King David Hotel, which Billie had recommended when he had once suggested he might pay her a visit. It had been the headquarters of the British security forces at the time of the Mandate and, when they had had a considerable difference of opinion with the Jews concerning the ending of their responsibility, a section of the Stern Gang, the extremist wing of the Jewish underground, had managed to smuggle enough high explosive into the cellars to do the kind of job Guy Fawkes had in mind for the Houses of Parliament.

The resultant explosion had killed more than fifty British officers —some while they were asleep in bed, a detail which many at home found more difficult to forgive than the deed itself. But there was no trace of those less comfortable days now, either in the building itself, which had been even more sumptuously rebuilt as well as modernised, or in the warmth of the welcome from a charming Jordanian who introduced himself as Doctor Nasheeb and informed them that there would be no difficulty in accommodating them. The best double room in the hotel would be put at their disposal instantly.

By the time they had unpacked, it was ten-thirty. They had opted for some chicken sandwiches and a couple of bottles of beer to be sent up instead of going down for dinner, but by the time they arrived, even these seemed too much effort; and after they had undressed, they both flopped on the big double bed and drank from the bottles like a couple of legionnaires at the end of a route march.

When she had finished hers, Angela rolled over to put the bottle on the bedside table, and while she was doing this Dutch picked up the 'phone and asked Reception to put a call through to Billie's apartment. If she was there, he wasn't going to say anything about their fears for her safety. It would just be a surprise visit, and if, when they got used to each other again, she wanted to tell him anything, all well and good.

But as it turned out, this contingency plan remained unused. The 'phone rang for half a minute, and then a man answered. The police must still be there. He put the 'phone down without saying anything, and frowned.

What the hell *was* going on? Surely they wouldn't still be there if all that had happened was that she had disappeared. Whatever it was, he intended to go round first thing in the morning and find out.

Angela, who had been watching, moved closer and rested her head on his shoulder. She knew he would have resented anything else at that moment. But, despite her concern, she was so exhausted she fell asleep within minutes.

When he heard her breathing regularly, Dutch shifted his position so that her head was resting on the pillow. Then he turned out the light. But it was a long time before he managed to go to sleep himself.

56

Chapter 6

Despite the fact that he had not slept for more than four hours, Dutch woke up feeling completely refreshed. After showering and eating one of the chicken sandwiches to save time, he left Angela to take a more leisurely breakfast before she spent the morning going round the shops and, without waiting for the elevator—their room was on the second floor—ran swiftly down the stairs, and then across the crowded lobby towards the main entrance.

As he did so, he did not notice the man from the plane talking to one of the bellhops; but as soon as he appeared the other cut short his conversation and, after glancing briefly at the now empty elevator, he seemed to change his mind, and followed Dutch outside just in time to see him getting into a cab.

He immediately hailed the next one in the rank.

Billie had never described her apartment to him in any of her letters, apart from its size, nor mentioned where it was; but somehow Dutch had expected it to be in one of the modern blocks which always seemed to appear in any photographs he had seen of Jerusalem recently—particularly those taken in the context of features deploring the effect of speculative development in the Holy City. In the event, it turned out to be in an old house in a quiet, tree-lined avenue—probably one of those laid out by the British who, like the Romans before them, had tended to leave their mark on those places they had occupied more by their institutions and architecture than in the affections of those they eventually left to their own devices.

He asked the cab to wait, and the driver promised to do so a few yards further down the street where he could park in the shade.

Closer inspection revealed the lower part of the house, which was built of stone, to be covered with some kind of vine. He could never remember the names of such things, but this was covered with purple flowers, which not only added to the attractiveness of an already quaint design, but filled the morning air with perfume.

The front door had in front of it a stone-flagged patio, from which the vines had been encouraged to grow up to the balcony on the floor above, thus creating an oasis of shade protecting it from the direct rays of the sun which had already climbed well into the sky and was threatening to scorch everything within reach.

It appeared from the bell-push beside the front door that the house was divided into three apartments. The names alongside were in Hebrew, so Dutch pressed the one at the top and waited, hoping for the best. There had been no sign of a police car in the road outside, but that didn't mean anything—necessarily.

The door opened after a while, and an attractive young woman stood in front of him holding a baby in her arms.

She said something to him in Hebrew, which he couldn't understand, so he gave her one of his best smiles and said: "I wonder if you can help me. I'm looking for my daughter. My name's Deutsch—Richard Deutsch. I've just arrived."

She looked at him frowning for a few seconds, and he was just beginning to wonder if she understood, when she suddenly smiled. She really was very pretty.

"Oh yes, Mr. Deutsch. I recognise you from one of Miss Smyth's photographs."

"Who?"

"Miss Smyth. Your daughter." Suddenly she looked unsure again. "You *did* say you were her father?"

"Yes, of course!" Of all things he had forgotten that Billie had taken her mother's new name when she had remarried. He had found it hurtful at the time, in spite of Helen's assurance that it was simply for convenience's sake, and was obviously only a temporary expedient as their daughter would eventually take her own husband's name. He had seen the sense of it, but had

58

been almost more upset about it at the time than anything else. Now he had forgotten all about it. It might be a truism, but time did change a lot of things!

He looked back at the girl and smiled again.

"Are you a friend of hers?"

"Yes. My husband and I occupy the apartment on the second floor. We've known Billie since she came to Israel. My husband works in the same firm."

"I guess that's how she came to move in here?"

"Yes, my husband told her about the apartment when the couple who had it before moved out. It's on the ground floor, but it's smaller than the others because of the hall."

"Is Billie in?" Dutch asked as lightly as he could. The girl looked at him again for a few seconds before answering.

"I think you'd better come inside."

When the door closed behind them they stood in a cool, tile-flagged hall from which a concrete staircase led to the floors above. The baby smiled, evidently having decided that he must be a friend; but his mother's face was serious.

"Mr. . . ?"

"Deutsch."

"Mr. Deutsch. Don't you know your daughter has disappeared?"

"Yes. But I didn't know how much *you* knew."

"We don't know anything. Except what's been going on round here. Is that why you've come?"

"Billie's mother spoke to the police over the 'phone from London. They told her what had happened."

"They were here every day for two weeks. Then suddenly, last night, they disappeared, and haven't been back since." She paused for a moment, and then went on: "We're terribly worried about her. She must be in trouble of some kind. If only we knew where to get in touch with her we'd help. We'd do anything. I can't tell you how wonderful she was to us just before and after Rudi was born. And even when I was better, she sat for us, more or less whenever we wanted."

"She didn't go out much, then?"

"No. That's the stupid thing. She can't possibly have done anything wrong. Uri says it must be all a misunderstanding, but if we don't know where she is, what can we do?"

Dutch saw her eyes suddenly fill with tears. He said: "Perhaps I can help. At least, I hope so."

"If she knew you were here, I'm sure she'd contact you."

"Well, that's the first thing I wanted to say. I'm staying at the King David Hotel—um, with a friend—and I don't intend to leave until this is cleared up. So if you do see her ..."

"Of course. We don't care what she's done. We'd do anything for her."

"I thought you said she couldn't have done anything?"

"No, of course not. Well—you know what I mean. No one knows anyone that well—no matter how much they love them. I only know, if Billie's in trouble, it's not her fault."

"Did she have any boy friends?"

"Yes ... several. But, like I said, she didn't go out much in the evenings, except at weekends. Sometimes they used to come here." She looked at him hurriedly. "But they never stayed."

"Do you know if any of *them* has disappeared?"

The girl shook her head.

"No. All the ones we know have been here looking for her."

"Did she have any other friends?"

"A few. Mostly people at work. She used to exchange visits occasionally. But I think we were her closest friends."

" And you've no idea at all why the police are so interested in finding her?"

"No. They asked questions for hours when they first came here! Miss Dieter, who lives in the middle apartment—she got very annoyed. She's retired now, but she used to work in the Civil Service, and she told them if they didn't accept our word, that we'd told them all we know, she was going to call a friend of hers in the State Attorney's office."

"And after that they left you alone?"

"Yes. But they still disturbed us with their continual coming and going—until last night."

"When they left for good?"

"Yes. And good riddance!"

"Could you tell me when that was?"

The girl frowned for a moment. Then she said: "I should say . . . about half-past eleven."

It had been about then he had called. But he hadn't said anything. They couldn't possibly have known who was on the other end. It must be a coincidence.

The baby was starting to get restless and, after struggling with him for a while, his mother looked at Dutch and smiled apologetically.

"Would you like to come upstairs and have some coffee? I'm afraid Rudi is getting bored."

"Thank you. But I rather think I should go and see this Inspector Ezra."

"Who?"

"The man in charge of the case."

"Oh. Is that his name?"

"Didn't he tell you?"

"No. They didn't tell us anything. They really were quite objectionable. You hear stories about the police, but I never believed them, until now. I always thought ours were different."

Dutch wasn't really listening.

"There is *one* thing you can do for me."

"What's that?"

"I'd like to look round Billie's apartment. Do you have a key?"

"Yes. As a matter of fact I have it here."

She produced it from the pocket of her smock.

"I thought it was the police back again when you rang. I wanted to save myself another journey."

"They gave you the key?"

"No. Billie gave it to me just before she went away—just in case."

"In case what?"

The girl shrugged.

"I don't know really. A burst pipe—fire—anything. We only thought she was going away for a few days."

"It didn't strike you as strange at the time?"

"That she should give us her key?"

"Yes."

"No." The girl looked at him more closely: "You aren't a policeman yourself, are you? Back in England, I mean."

"No." Dutch grinned. "Why do you ask?"

"You talk like one. In a nice way, of course. Not like the others."

"I write crime stories sometimes. That's the nearest I ever come."

"Yes, I remember now. Billie showed me some of your books. She was very proud of you really."

"Why do you say 'really'?"

The girl blushed slightly, and shook her head. Then she said gently: "I suppose the child of any divorce is bound to get hurt."

Dutch looked at her. There were many things he would like to have asked this friend of his daughter, but this was neither the time nor the place. After a few more seconds she turned away and took a few steps towards the inner door, where she fitted the key into the lock.

Dutch said: "The police always asked you for the key?"

The door swung open, and the girl stood back.

"No. They kept it for two weeks. But this morning we found it in our letter box. That's why we thought they must have gone for good—until you rang."

The apartment consisted of a bedroom, living-room, minuscule kitchen and bathroom. There was nothing that would have told him it was his daughter's home. No photographs—nothing to remind her of home. She had evidently decided on a complete break. It was understandable, but sad.

In the living-room there was the smell of stale cigarette smoke. His companion snorted with disgust and went over to open the windows before turning back.

"I'm sorry. They left everything in such a mess. The first thing I did this morning when I knew they had gone was to give it a good clean, but I can't have left the windows open long enough.

Suddenly the 'phone in the bedroom rang, and for a moment Dutch and the girl looked at each other without making a move. It almost seemed she was frightened, and when he made as if to go and answer it, she nodded quickly.

He went into the room where the 'phone was still clamouring for attention, and picked up the receiver.

"Hello?"

He waited for a few seconds.

"Hello?"

Again, there was no reply.

"Put your money in, or whatever you have to do."

A moment later he became convinced the line was alive.

"Billie! Is that you? Don't ring off. It's Dad. Where are you?"

He could have sworn he heard an intake of breath; but a second later the 'phone went dead, and the contrast was so marked he was certain someone had been listening.

He looked up at the girl who had been watching him from the doorway.

"It *was* her. I'm sure of it."

Dutch put the 'phone down slowly, and then got up off the edge of the bed. The girl moved to let him pass, but he stopped, facing her.

"Leave the door open, so you can hear the 'phone if it rings again. If it's Billie, tell her I'm at the King David."

"Is that where you're going now?"

"No. I'm going down to Police Headquarters. But she can leave a message. If she doesn't want to use her own name, tell her to say anything, just so long as I know where to contact her."

"Yes. All right."

He rested his hand lightly on the arm which supported Rudi, and smiled; but his eyes were serious.

"Tell her ... I don't care what's happened—but I must see her. I only want to help. And I'm not going until things are straightened out, one way or another."

"You think she *has* done something?"

He paused for a moment, then dropped his hand.

"Why wouldn't she talk to me?"

63

"Perhaps she didn't believe you—or couldn't be sure. It might have been a trap. After all, as far as she knows you're still in London."

"In which case, when she's had time to think, or perhaps put a call through to England, she'll ring back."

"I hope so."

"So do I. Goodbye."

"Goodbye, Mr. Deutsch."

"I hope we'll meet again soon."

"So do I."

"By the way, you never told me your name?"

"It's Helen Borsch."

"Well, goodbye, Helen. And thank you for being a friend to my daughter."

He gave her another smile, then ruffled the baby's hair before stepping out of the front door onto the patio.

He walked down the stone-flagged path to the front gate, paused for a moment to close it behind him, then with a final wave to Helen, who was walking slowly towards the gate to see him off, started back down the avenue to where he could see the cab waiting.

He did not notice at first the sound of a car accelerating up the road behind him—his mind was so full of thoughts concerning Billie and what might have happened to her—and only a screamed warning from the girl, followed by a squeal of tyres alerted him when, for most people, it would already have been too late.

Without wasting time trying to see what was happening, Dutch flung himself away from the sound, and even as he did so, heard the repeated crack of an automatic and felt the bullets thudding into the ground where he had just been standing.

A moment later he picked himself up, again without looking round, and dived into the front garden of the house next door, just as his would-be assassin must have taken second aim. He heard the fence splintering behind him, and hit the turf with a thud that knocked most of the wind out of him; but he was unharmed.

While he lay there, his brain trying to catch up with what had happened, he heard a man shouting and the car, which must have stopped close by, starting to pull away.

Two more shots rang out, but these sounded different. A few seconds later Dutch raised his head above the fence in time to see a Citreon Safari rounding the corner at the end of the avenue at breakneck speed, and his own driver, who had produced a Colt revolver from somewhere, loosing off two more rounds after it.

He got up, brushing bits of dried grass from his trousers and jacket, and after a reassuring wave to the girl, who was now joined by an older woman as well as several others who came running out of their houses to see what was going on, he left the garden—this time by the gate.

The cab driver came to meet him, and when he was assured that his fare was unharmed, grinned broadly and would scarcely let Dutch thank him for the prompt action which had undoubtedly saved his life. But a sizeable crowd was beginning to gather, and the two men got into the cab. Dutch asked to be driven to Police Headquarters.

When they had gone, Codron moved from behind one of the lime trees about a hundred yards away unnoticed by anyone, and walked off in the opposite direction.

Chapter 7

Dutch had no idea why anyone should want to kill him. He had only been in the country twelve hours, and not even Americans became disliked that quickly. Someone had obviously mistaken him for someone else.

The driver, to whom he undoubtedly owed his life, introduced himself as Eli Kassim, a Christian living in Bethlehem, and, without slackening the speed with which they were proceeding towards Police Headquarters, turned round in his seat, eyes shining, and insisted on shaking him by the hand while emotionally dismissing his own part in the affair as of quite minor significance. It had been the gentleman's own reactions which had saved him. Never had he seen anyone move so fast. The gentleman was undoubtedly used to living with danger.

He continued to look back admiringly at Dutch with nerve-racking frequency and duration, considering their speed and the fact that they were now approaching the centre of Jerusalem, chatting excitedly the whole time and re-living every micro-second of their shared experience; and it was only when they actually pulled into the small courtyard of the building, beyond which it was impossible to go without intensive screening, that Eli asked him not to mention his own part in the affair while making his report. Much as it grieved him to be such a nuisance, but the law frowned on taxi drivers carrying guns—particularly Jordanian ones.

After being cleared by Security, Dutch had to wait while someone went off to find the Inspector.

They brought him a cup of coffee, but more than an hour was to elapse before a girl with the best pair of legs he had ever seen beneath a police uniform finally appeared, and asked him to follow her.

In the event, the long wait had done him no harm. During a short period of his life—in Vietnam, immediately before coming to Europe in fact—he had lived with sudden death, and the whole time he was in the Air Force he knew he was taking risks which, but for the good offices of the American Government, would have made him uninsurable. But being shot at—repeatedly —in a quiet sunlit street was something new again, and it had taken quite a while for his heart to stop thumping.

As he walked along the corridor and up some stairs, the girl's legs twinkling in front of him, he knew he was now completely calm and would be able to give a more objective account of what had happened. There was no sense in jumping to conclusions, and he had to gain Ezra's trust if he was to persuade him to reveal the real reason why they were so concerned at Billie's disappearance. Only by doing so, could he hope to be of some help to her.

He was shown into a small, well-lit office where a dark-haired man in civilian clothes rose to meet him with a smile.

"Please sit down, Mr. Deutsch. I'm sorry to have kept you waiting, but there were one or two points I wanted to check arising from the story you told downstairs. Several people 'phoned the police after the shooting, but I wanted to wait until one of my own men had returned from the scene before seeing you. Also we took the precaution of 'phoning your publisher, who was able to confirm who you were." The Inspector allowed himself a brief smile. "I gather we should feel honoured!"

Dutch returned his smile, but sat in the chair indicated, immediately in front of the desk, without replying.

The other continued: "There is, however, the other aspect of your story which is causing us some bewilderment. The reason, if I understand correctly, for your being in Jerusalem in the first place."

Dutch nodded.

"You mean the disappearance of my daughter. I don't want you to think I'm trying to interfere, but naturally, her mother and I are very worried."

The Inspector frowned.

"You say your daughter has disappeared. When was that?"

Dutch looked at him in complete astonishment. Then he said: "I'm sorry, I don't follow you."

The Inspector sat in his own chair, and leant forward with his arms folded across the desk.

"I said, 'When *did* your daughter disappear?'"

"About five or six weeks ago. But surely you know?"

The other shook his head.

"On the contrary, that's why I'm asking you. If the citizen of a foreign country—or anyone, come to that—disappears, naturally we do what we can to find them." He shrugged. "Of course, regrettably, in the case of young girls, they often don't want to be found, and that makes it difficult."

Dutch stared at him.

"Are you serious?" he said eventually.

"That's what we're here for."

Dutch shook his head impatiently.

"No. I mean ... that this is the first time you've heard of my daughter's disappearance?"

The other looked at him steadily.

"I give you my word," he said. "But, first of all, let me introduce myself properly. My name is Morgan."

"Morgan!"

"That's right. Chief Inspector. I was born in Wales. I thought you might have realised. It was a long time ago, but I'm told the accent persists—even in Hebrew!"

"What happened to Ezra?"

"Oh, yes. We've gone into that. There is no one of that name holding the rank of Inspector in the Force. In fact, according to the computer, there's no one of that name in the Police anywhere in the country."

Dutch's eyes widened still further.

"Clearly you have been dealing with an impostor, Mr. Deutsch. And apart from whatever else may have happened, impersonating a police officer is a serious offence. I think you had better tell me the whole story from the beginning, a step at a time." He

68

touched a key on a small machine on the top of the desk.

"And now, it is my duty to warn you that our conversation is being recorded and, although you are not on oath, failure or refusal to confirm anything you are about to say in court later, if called as a witness, may be considered evidence of having attempted to mislead a police officer in the course of his duty and might be the basis of police prosecution. Do you understand?"

Dutch nodded.

"Please say so out loud, Mr. Deutsch."

"I do."

"Thank you." Morgan smiled. "I'm sorry if that sounds a bit awesome, but it's for our mutual protection. Now ... your story please, from the beginning. How long has your daughter been here, and when did you first know she had disappeared?"

Dutch went back to the first call from Helen. He digressed slightly to explain their relationship. How Billie had changed her name by deed poll, and then, how she had emigrated to Israel.

"You are Jewish, then?" Morgan asked.

Deutsch shook his head. "I'm not," he said, "but my wife is; and I gather that's good enough?"

The Chief Inspector nodded.

"That is correct. Under rabbinical law, a child takes the nationality of his or her mother."

Dutch was tempted to ask if that was how a man with the name of Morgan happened to be a Chief Inspector of Police in Jerusalem. But he thought better of it, and went on instead to tell about the series of calls Helen had put through, culminating in the conversation with Ezra. In the circumstances he saw no further reason for withholding knowledge of Billie's last letter, his ex-wife's feelings concerning its contents, and finally her discovery that it had been posted in Haifa.

He then paused for a moment, and Morgan, who had not interrupted for some time, said quietly: "And so you came here to find out what you could do to help?"

"Yes."

"And so you have, Mr. Deutsch. You have discovered the

69

reason for your daughter's disappearance."

"I have?"

"Not in detail, of course. But clearly she has run away and is afraid to return home because she knows the men who were passing themselves off as police officers were lying in wait."

"But why. Billie wouldn't hurt a fly."

"Possibly not." Morgan rose to his feet and went to look out of the window which faced inwards into the courtyard. (Dutch had noticed earlier that all those facing the street were of frosted glass, and probably bullet-proof.)

"But obviously she's done something to hurt *them*," the Chief Inspector went on without turning round. "So much so that she is obviously in fear of her life; and not without cause, judging by what happened to you!"

"You think there's a connection?"

The other turned, and his expression was grave.

"My dear chap, can you doubt it now?"

"You mean they've already found out I'm here, and tried to kill me because I'm Billie's father?"

"It's possible." Morgan paused for a moment, then perched on the edge of his desk. "Or possibly they mistook you for someone else she's associated with."

Dutch's mind was in a whirl. It seemed all Helen's worst fears were coming true.

"Naturally, we'll start at once to track these people down, whoever they are. But I must say the fact that your daughter didn't come to us at once and ask for protection doesn't look very promising. If she would rather face such people alone, she must have a reason; and I'm afraid that the usual explanation in such cases is that whoever is being threatened is more afraid of the police finding out what they're mixed up in."

Dutch shook his head helplessly. He had to have time to think. What could Billie have got herself into that she would rather risk her own life than ask for help? Dope smuggling? Diamonds? Espionage? He couldn't bring himself to believe it. But the Chief Inspector was right. The facts spoke for themselves.

Morgan went on: "We'll get on to it straightaway. But my

70

advice to you is to go back to London on the first plane. There's already been one attempt on your life, and there could be another."

"Is that an order?"

Morgan looked at him.

"No, of course not. As long as you stay within the law, I've no authority to ship you out. I'm just giving you a bit of friendly advice."

Dutch thought about Angela. He had no right to expose her to known danger; but the more he thought, the more his heart went out to Billie, hiding somewhere, afraid for her life. He wasn't going until he could take her with him. It wasn't that he loved her more, but she was his in a way Angela could never be.

He became aware Morgan was looking at him sympathetically.

"Well?"

Dutch shook his head.

"I couldn't," he said simply, and Morgan nodded.

"That's what I thought you'd say."

Dutch noticed the machine was no longer working. The Inspector must have turned it off when he had finished his statement.

"But it wouldn't look good on the record if you got yourself killed and I hadn't advised you to leave, see?"

The other got up off the edge of the desk and grinned. Then he went round and sat in the chair.

"As long as you're here, there's a fair chance your daughter will make contact with you somehow. Don't ask me how—or how she'll know you're here . . ."

"I think she knows already."

"How?"

Dutch told him about the 'phone call while he and the girl were in Billie's apartment. Morgan looked serious.

"You say there's another girl living there?"

"Not in the same apartment. The house is divided into three."

"Then we shall have to put them all under police protection. Until we get to the bottom of this, they are the only ones—apart from your daughter, of course—who can positively identify the

71

people concerned."

"Oh, my God!" Things seemed to be going from bad to worse. Now the young family were threatened!

"Don't worry. We'll see they come to no harm. And by the way, hasn't it occurred to you that the call might not have been from your daughter. How else did your would-be murderers know you were there?"

"But that was only a few minutes later."

"They might have given up direct occupation in favour of watching from a distance, to try and tempt your daughter home. They might have seen you go in there, and put a call through to try and find out who you were."

Dutch looked crestfallen.

"And I went and told them!"

"Precisely." The Chief Inspector looked cheerful again. "But don't worry. It's just that sometimes there's a difference between writing about this kind of thing and actually being in it."

"I'm beginning to realise that."

"And above all, remember—*if* your daughter contacts you, do everything in your power to persuade her to come to us. Not only for her own sake—possibly she doesn't know yet just how far her enemies are prepared to go—but for yours, and for the sake of her friends, all of whom are in danger as long as this continues."

"I'll do my best."

Dutch rose to his feet. Morgan pushed a bell, and a few seconds later the door opened and the girl who had brought him up appeared in the doorway.

"Yes, Sir?"

"Mr. Deutsch is just leaving."

The girl stood to one side, and Morgan held out his hand.

"You're staying at the King David, I understand?"

"That's right."

"Well, I shouldn't think anyone would try anything there. But I'll have my people keep an eye on things, just in case."

"Thank you."

"Don't go out more than you have to. And stay away from

your daughter's apartment for the time being."

"Am I to be followed?"

The Chief Inspector shook his head, and grinned: "No, we have our own way of doing things here. Good day to you Mr. Deutsch, and let me know the minute you hear anything."

At the very moment that Dutch was leaving Police Headquarters, a bell-hop knocked on the door of their room in the King David Hotel. He had seen the woman return, then leave again soon afterwards, and he was paid to be curious—well paid, as it happened.

He knocked again, to be sure—but not too hard. He didn't want to attract the attention of the floor maid. Still getting no reply, he took a pass-key out of his pocket and, after sticking his head in first to look round, slipped inside.

He was about to check the bathroom, when a note scribbled on one of the hotel's cards and propped against the dressing-table mirror, where it could not fail to be seen, caught his attention, and he picked it up to study it more closely.

He spoke English perfectly as well as Arabic, Hebrew and a little German; but Angela's writing caused him some difficulty, and it was a good half-minute before he drew in his breath, replaced the note where he had found it, and left, closing the door behind him.

He left the hotel by a side entrance, and made his way to a public telephone box standing at the corner of the street outside the YMCA—there to dial a number which had been burned into his memory by a mixture of fear and greed—greed, for what he would get paid for such information acquired at such little risk compared to some previous occasions; and fear in the knowledge of what would happen to him if he ever imparted the number to anyone else, for whatever reason.

Chapter 8

Dutch returned to the hotel, where he paid off the cab-driver, adding a generous tip to his thanks. But before allowing him inside, Eli insisted on handing Dutch his card, and made him promise to call him day or night if ever he was in the need of a driver who was utterly fearless in the face of danger. Bethlehem was only a short drive from Jerusalem, and his wife always knew how to contact him during the day; he pulled a face as if this last had not always been to his advantage, but brightened instantly when Dutch assured him that he wouldn't dream of relying on anyone else in such circumstances. They shook hands for the last time. Then Dutch strode inside.

He was surprised to find the key still at the desk. It was almost two o'clock, and, although they had made no special arrangement to meet so early, he would have thought the heat would have made Angela give up shopping and retreat to the air-conditioned sanctuary of the hotel long ago. Either her stamina was better than he had given her credit for, or she had found somewhere to have lunch—or possibly someone had found it for her.

He knew that as long as their present understanding lasted, Angela's pride made her insist on the same freedom he reserved for himself, but he had always assumed this was more a matter of theory than practice. Of course, one could never be sure—and that was the idea. He had to admit that she was a walking provocation for any man, and Billie's letters had not led him to believe that the young—or even not so young—Israelis were less adventurous than anyone else.

These thoughts occurred to him as he went up in the elevator —he would have walked up, but the little Arab boy who operated it gave him such a brilliant smile as he walked across from the desk he hadn't the heart to refuse. As he let himself into the room, a sense of unease added to the disappointment of not being able to enthrall her at once with his morning's adventures.

He knew Angela was good at concealing her true feelings— particularly when uncertain of his own reaction to them—and, in spite of the fact that she had known from the beginning his purpose in making this trip, no woman could really enjoy being left to her own devices while the man she loved devoted his time and energy to another woman, no matter who; and the certain knowledge that the love which bound him to his daughter had a known and tested strength, while theirs still remained in doubt, could not make it any easier.

He took the key out of the lock and closed the door behind him. Like anyone else, his next move would have been across to the bathroom to take a shower before changing his clothes and sending his suit out to be cleaned; but then he too saw the note and walked over to pick it up.

"Darling," he read. "Guess what? Billie 'phoned!! (How's that for one-up-manship? There's you chasing all over Jerusalem and I find her just sitting here!)"

"Anyway, she sounded fine. I'd just got back from shopping, as a matter of fact (the shops here are dreary, but a girl I met said that in Tel Aviv they're fabulous) and she asked me to meet her at the Damascus Gate leading into the Old City. Don't ask me where it is—I'll have to take a cab.

"Sorry not to wait, but she made it sound important I came right away. Back soon. Love you! A."

Dutch had torn open the door and was running down the corridor with the note still in his hand before his conscious mind had begun to work out why he was suddenly so afraid. But by the time he was half-way down the stairs he knew.

Angela had never heard Billie's voice in her life, so how could she have known it was really she? And of course, she had no reason to suspect her own life might be in danger.

He managed to run across the lobby without hitting anyone— although several people were forced to execute swerves which would have done credit to any rugby wing-half—and dashed out of the main entrance just in time to elbow someone dressed like the Pope to one side as he was about to get into the only cab in sight, and jumped in ahead of him.

"The Damascus Gate," he barked—having no idea where it was either.

The driver spun round to protest just as the Archbishop, or whoever he was, recovered sufficiently to utter some unsaintly words of admonition; but his eyes lit up as soon as he saw who it was.

"Mr. Deutsch!"

"Eli!"

"Where did you say?"

"The Damascus Gate—and hurry!"

As it was, his two previous trips with the same driver had been made only just below the speed of sound, but now the other, eyes bright with excitement, trod on the accelerator with such ferocity that the car leaped forward, rear tyres fighting for a grip on the loose gravel—almost machine-gunning the still protesting Cleric to death—and hurtled towards the narrow entrance where the hotel drive joined the main road.

"Is it a matter of life and death?" Eli shouted over his shoulder.

Dutch's eyes fixed on the twin pillars rushing towards them; but before he could say anything they had flashed past. Because it was early afternoon and the heat was such that anyone in their right mind was resting indoors, the traffic was light, and they managed to join the stream going south down Tachana Street without killing anyone.

Dutch waited until he was absolutely sure all four wheels of the car were on the ground. Then he said: "Yes. But try not to attract too much attention. We don't want to be followed."

He was rather proud of this remark. It should have encouraged a more relaxed state of mind, but the effect it produced on Eli was to make him fling the wheel round so that, without losing any speed at all, they plunged down a dark, seemingly impossible narrow alley. From then on, until they emerged on to the main road which encircled the Old City, they sprang from the darkness into the light like a pouncing leopard, inducing appropriate reactions from passing traffic. Almost the whole of the rest of the journey was made down side roads, only touching the streets where the sun shone for a few seconds at a time, or just so long as it took to cross from one side to the other at right angles to hurtle once more into the labyrinth of alleys from which, for a while, Dutch wondered if they would ever emerge in one piece.

That it would have been difficult to follow them could not be denied. The trail of dustbins upset by the speed of their passage would have ensured that for a start, but Dutch realised he was going to have to be very careful in future about his choice of words when dealing with Eli—particularly now, when he obviously saw himself well into chapter two of a new adventure, and was desperately trying to establish his position as a central character. But one thing was certain: Eli was technically a superb driver, and if he seemed to handle his Mercedes with apparent disregard for his own safety as well as that of others, Dutch knew after a while that he had much more control than at first seemed possible—nerve-racking though it was to anyone not brought up in the "Interceptor" style of motoring—and that, one day, he might be glad of it.

They left the car in the park outside Herod's gate. Eli explained that no cars were allowed inside most of the Old City—the fastest conveyance permitted being a donkey cart—but he insisted on coming too. Most of those who lived within the walls spoke only Arabic, and his new friend would undoubtedly need an interpreter.

Dutch realised that by permitting this he might find it difficult to get rid of him later. Besides, the longer they spent together, the more the other was finding out about him—things that, if known by his hidden enemies, would make his already precarious situation even less tenable. But although Eli had been a complete stranger until a few hours ago, the affection and loyalty he had already shown with such an open heart was hard to resist, and Dutch felt that, if he could not be trusted, his belief in his own judgement would be destroyed for ever. How and on what basis he was going to pay him later he had no idea; but no doubt they'd work something out when it was all over, and for the time being nothing seemed further from Eli's thoughts.

The Gate itself was an archway leading through the thickness of the Ottoman-built walls into the overcrowded mass of shops, houses, churches, mosques, shrines and relics which comprised the Old City.

It was the busiest gate leading in and out of the City, the one most used by tourists and by those who lived there. The group of shops just inside were selling mainly souvenirs. Although it was the rest period, they were open, for the coaches were still discharging tourists in a seemingly unending stream outside the walls in the charge of guides before being escorted on walking tours of the City.

There was no sign of either of the two girls, but Eli asked Dutch to give him descriptions of them. Then he went up to a blind beggar sitting in the shade of the archway, rattling his tin at the tourists who swarmed around him—without much success—and spoke to him in Arabic.

The beggar seemed to glance in Dutch's direction, then held out his tin.

"What are you doing?" Dutch walked over to join them.

Eli said: "Sir, this man may remember the two ladies we are looking for, but he is very poor and has to ask the favour of money in return."

"But how can he possibly ..." Dutch began, then stopped and shrugged before reaching into his pocket.

Seeing his expression, Eli shook his head.

"No, Sir. If you will forgive me, but you are mistaken. See ... look at his eyes. His parents were so poor they did not have enough money to feed him. So they put the maggot of a fly under his eyelids when he was a baby, and thus gave him the chance to live by begging. It is a terrible thing, is it not? But at least, he is alive; and, having been blind as long as he can remember, he hears things that are impossible for you and me."

Dutch pulled out some money, and put a five-pound note into

the tin. Eli looked at him with a smile while the beggar's agile fingers examined it before tucking it inside his ragged jacket.

"One would have been sufficient. But that will buy enough food for his wife and children for two days."

Dutch looked at him in amazement.

"He has a wife and children?"

The beggar grinned as Eli nodded.

"Oh yes, they live better than many. You see, his parents knew what they were about."

"He's not going to do the same to his own children?"

"No, no fear of that. Those days are gone, thank God. Now they pay him a pension. It's not very much, but they live on what he can earn here, and by the time the eldest son is old enough, he will have saved enough to send him to the University in Amman."

"What will happen to him then?"

Eli shrugged.

"Who can tell? Perhaps he'll become a doctor. Then his father will be looked after in his old age."

"I hope so."

"I hope so too, Sir. Excuse me."

He bent down and the beggar began to talk in rapid, short phrases. Then Eli stood up again.

"He understands English, but hopes you will excuse him not addressing you in such. It would be bad for business!"

"I understand."

"He remembers two girls who spoke in English accents."

"What did they say?"

Again Eli bent down to consult the beggar before straightening up again.

"He couldn't hear much owing to the noise from the tourists."

"Then how is he so sure it was them?"

Eli shrugged again.

"Even to me, two English voices would stand out here. But he heard enough to be able to say with certainty that one of them was trying to persuade the other to go with them into the walled City where she said they would be safer. He thought at the time

79

it was a strange thing to say, for the Old City is not really the place for two young girls to be walking around by themselves, but eventually the one prevailed, and they went off in the direction of the Pool of Bethesda."

"How long ago was that?"

"About half an hour."

"Do you think we have any chance of finding them?" Already Dutch's heart had sunk. If it *was* a trap, Angela had walked straight into it.

Eli looked at him puzzled.

"If they are walking around, it is possible. But if they have gone indoors somewhere . . ." he let the sentence hang in the air. "If you could tell me why you are so afraid for them," he began again.

"Which way's the Pool of Bethesda?"

The beggar pointed over his right shoulder without the charade of translation. Dutch nodded.

"Thanks." He turned to Eli. "Come on . . . I'll tell you on the way. Only let's hurry."

Just after they had disappeared into the throng, another figure ceased to pretend to be interested in buying some mementoes, and pushed his way through to the beggar who had begun to rattle his tin once more. He also put a five-pound note into the tin, then bent down and whispered in his ear. But the beggar shook his head as he answered, and Codron straightened up with every sign of annoyance before reaching into his pocket and adding another similar note.

Betrayal came more expensive than straight information. Even after two thousand years.

An hour later they found themselves standing in the large open space which had once been occupied by Herod's Antonia fortress, long since destroyed. The result of the search had been negative, and now the hundreds of small shops in the various arcades were beginning to open again, adding the odour of sweetmeats, vegetables and delicacies of all kinds to the background stench of donkey dung and too many human beings closely confined. The main thoroughfares, not one of which was more than ten feet across and most only just wide enough to let two laden donkeys squeeze past one another, had become so crowded that further search was impossible, and they had come out to where they stood now for a breath of air and to review the situation.

Dutch glanced at his watch. It was a few minutes to four. He then turned to Eli, who was wiping his forehead with a handkerchief.

"I don't think it's much use continuing," he said.

Eli shook his head.

"I'm very sorry, Sir. Perhaps we should try all the main gates. Someone may have seen them leave."

"With all these tourists?"

Eli allowed himself a brief smile.

"I believe you said both young ladies were very attractive?" He glanced round at the various groups who were standing around listening to the guides and lowered his voice. "Such would still stand out, I believe!"

Dutch returned his smile. Despite their failure to catch up with them, the fact that the beggar had referred to both girls speaking with an English accent had raised his hopes that the second was indeed Billie, now he had come to think about it. An imposter who knew nothing of his background would have assumed that his daughter also spoke with an American accent.

"OK. But unless someone can give us a definite lead, I think we should go back to the hotel. My . . . fianceé is bound to try and contact me there, even if she does not intend to return immediately."

During this conversation, the barrel of a rifle had poked through the balcony round the top of the minaret which stood in the south-west corner of the square, and a cross-wire had settled on a spot just behind Dutch's right ear. But, even as the trigger-finger was tightening, it struck four o'clock, and from the loud-speakers behind the marksman, as from every other minaret across the City, the recorded voice of a *mullah* burst forth calling the faithful to prayer.

Eli glanced up, as did everyone else nearby, except those to whom the call was addressed, who laid out their prayer mats and dutifully turned towards Mecca. He was about to remark ruefully that even in such matters, automation had taken over. But the words stuck in his throat as he saw a man holding a rifle start to his feet in alarm before realising that it was only a recording, bring the weapon to his shoulder and aim once more in their direction.

"Sir! Look out!"

Dutch sprang to one side a split second before an explosive bullet smacked into the ground beside him and went off with an ear-splitting crack. In doing so, he inadvertently collided with an elderly gentleman and his wife who had also been looking upwards but who had not been able to see clearly what was happening; he tried to save himself, and them, but somehow their feet got mixed up and the three of them went down. He instantly rolled to one side, conscious that in lying at full length on the ground he was presenting the best possible target to one almost immediately overhead, but the din of the *mullah* was such that he was not able to hear the report which followed.

Someone began to scream and, as he leapt to his feet, he saw that everyone was looking up at the top of the tower as if hypnotised. Even Eli was standing stock still.

Dutch repressed his instinct to run just long enough to follow their gaze, and he saw that the man in the tower had dropped his rifle, and was bending almost double over the low parapet as if intent on seeing what lay immediately beneath. Then he slipped forward and took to the air, for all the world as if doing a stunt in a circus. The body described a complete somersault, turning over slowly in the afternoon sunshine. Then it hit the stone flags with a thud that was heard even above the noise coming from above, and everyone began to rush forward.

The first to reach the side of the man who had just fallen, a youth wearing shorts and a skull cap, was felled a split second later by the rifle which must have come to rest momentarily in the gutter. Those close on his heels fell back in horror, looking heavenwards as if expecting further missiles to be dispensed from a cloudless blue sky—perhaps as a rebuke to the over-curious.

Dutch glanced round at rooftop level, but no further danger seemed imminent, and he moved forward to gaze on the face of the one who, but for a miracle, would have slain him half a minute earlier. Encouraged, everyone else surged forward, and consequently no-one saw Codron step from the cover of the cypress trees which ran the length of the western side of the open space and walk away.

He knew it was no conceit to acknowledge that he was by far the best shot he knew. He had, after all, worked hard enough, but even for one of his experience it had been a very long shot indeed. He had glanced up at the tower a few seconds earlier and had thus seen the protruding rifle quite by chance. He sincerely hoped that the success or failure of his mission would not rest on such odds again.

Dutch saw that the man whose sightless eyes stared back into his had been shot near the heart. He glanced quickly at Eli beside him, and the other, reading his thoughts, shook his head.

Whether the dead man would have survived the wound without the fall, or the fall without the wound, was of only academic interest; but the youth who lay face downwards almost beside him groaned and started to try and sit up. Judging from the way he was holding himself, the rifle had hit him on the shoulder breaking his collar bone, and it was only the fall to the ground which had knocked him out briefly.

Willing hands reached forward to help him; and simply by allowing those who wanted to take a closer look push him to one side—after all, it wasn't everyone whose walking tour of the Holy City included attempted murder—Dutch soon found himself at the back of the crowd which was still gathering. He saw Eli emerge a few seconds later.

"I've never seen him before," Dutch muttered in answer to the other's unspoken question. But Eli said:

"I think he was one of those in the car this morning. I only had a quick look . . . but I would swear."

"Well never mind about that now. Let's get out of here. We'll exchange notes later."

Already he could see out of the corner of his eye two policemen running towards the centre of the disturbance. In another few minutes someone would remember that it had all started with him getting shot at and point him out, and he didn't want to spend the rest of the day back at Police Headquarters.

On regaining the car, Dutch insisted on being driven back to the hotel. The relief at knowing that Billie was alive had passed; he felt sure that someone else had seen Angela's note before he did, and that there was a connection between this and the second attempt on his life within hours he felt reasonably certain. How else would anyone have known where to lie in wait?

The incident had also had its effect on Eli, and by his standards they returned to the hotel quite slowly. If he hadn't been so concerned about Billie and Angela (perhaps they had walked into a trap too, but hadn't been so lucky), Dutch might have wondered if perhaps the driver was beginning to have doubts about being associated with someone who was getting shot at quite so regularly; but suddenly Eli pulled into the side of the road.

"Look, Sir. I really am very worried."

"I can't say I blame you." Dutch looked at him; but the other continued:

"I don't think you should go back to the hotel. Your enemies, whoever they are, know you're there, and it will only be a matter of time before they try again."

"What do you suggest?"

Eli's expression brightened.

"Come home with me, Sir, to Bethlehem. We will look after you—my family will consider it a great honour—and from there you can telephone the hotel to find out if the two ladies have returned. And you could leave a message asking them to ..." his voice trailed away as the obvious objection hit him.

"Let them know how to contact me?" Dutch prompted gently. Eli shook his head.

"No. They must have someone in the hotel. If you do that, *they'll* know where to find you."

"Quite."

84

Dutch smiled. In spite of everything, he couldn't help being moved by his new friend's concern. "But, apart from that," he went on briskly, "I wouldn't dream of involving your wife and children. I've no idea who wants to kill me, or why. But I've no reason to suppose they would hesitate just because some innocent people might get hurt."

"But there is more to my family than women and children, I assure you. My father was a sergeant-major under Glubb Pasha, and my three brothers, who live close by, all fought in the wars."

Dutch put his hand on Eli's shoulder.

"I don't doubt their valour," he said, forcing himself to remain calm. "And I thank you from the bottom of my heart for your kindness. But this is not their battle. If you choose to throw yourself on my side, that is one thing; but I cannot allow you to involve anyone else. You must accept that, if you are my friend."

Eli hesitated for a second, then nodded. Dutch saw tears of emotion shining in his eyes.

"Very well," he said, after a few more seconds; then he reached into his pocket, and pulled out his gun.

For just two seconds Dutch's blood ran cold. Eli had led him into the trap at the Antonia fortress; now he was going to kill him! Then he saw the other was extending the gun towards him, handle first.

"At least take this, please, for your protection. It is fully loaded, and I will bring you a box of shells this evening."

Relief mingled with shame swept over Dutch as he looked down at the weapon. His only hope was that Eli had been too preoccupied to have read his expression.

"But ... what about you?" he managed, eventually.

The other shook his head. "I can always get another," he said. "You have far more need of it in the meantime. Please, Sir, take it. Then at least I shall be able to go home and look my wife in the face when she asks me why I did not bring my friend home when he was in such danger." Eli looked him full in the face.

"She will understand when I explain that, if you are at at the hotel to receive your lady or her 'phone messages, she will not know how to contact you. But if I cannot tell her that, in spite of

85

this, I had done everything in my power, I would be without honour in her eyes and in the eyes of my children."

For one terrible moment, Dutch was on the point of offering to pay for the gun. It had probably cost Eli at least a month's pay and, the gun laws being what they were, he knew the chances of his friend being able to get another for his own protection were slim; but his guardian angel refused to let him speak until he realised the enormity of the insult he had been about to offer.

Chapter 9

The call came at eight-thirty, after Dutch had spent a miserable three hours pacing the hotel bedroom. Several times during the previous hour he had been on the point of 'phoning Morgan; but something had always made him change his mind, and he had put the 'phone down again—on the last occasion, only a few seconds before it rang. His hand was still resting on the receiver, and he recoiled instinctively before snatching it up again, half expecting that the hotel operator would be asking why he picked up the 'phone and put it down again without saying anything.

"Darling?"

"Angela!"

"Of course. Who were you expecting?"

"Where are you? Are you all right?"

"Yes, of course I'm all right. What's the matter? You sound a bit strange. Didn't you get my note?"

Dutch swallowed. Her voice reassured him. He felt a wave of relief sweep over him. Then he got a grip on himself. For all he knew the line was being tapped. He said carefully: "Is Billie all right?"

"Yes, she's just here. I'll put her on."

There was a moment's pause. Then he heard his daughter's voice.

"Dad?"

"Billie!"

"Are you really all right?"

"Yes. But don't say too much over the 'phone. Things have been happening."

There was another pause. Then he heard her say:

"I'm sorry we've been a long time. I'll tell you all about it when we meet."

"Don't say too much Billie."

"Dad—are you sure you're all right?"

"Yes." He paused, then went on: "It's just that some of your friends have been trying to kill me ever since I got here." After all, this would hardly come as news, even if they were listening.

He heard Billie gasp at the other end. Then she said:

"Look Dad—listen carefully. As soon as you've put down the 'phone, go straight outside—don't delay and give anyone time to arrange anything—and take a cab to the main entrance of the Israeli Museum. Don't take the first cab that draws up. Give him a couple of pounds to go somewhere else, but get into the next. Have you got that?"

This was the little girl he had taught her six-times table. Now she was giving him orders!

"Yes, dear."

"We'll see you outside. Don't worry if you get there first. There'll be plenty of people about. If you like, you could talk to one of the guards."

"Thank you."

"All right then. We'll see you in about twenty minutes."

"All right . . . er, Billie!"

"Yes?"

"Put Angela back on, will you?"

"Don't let's waste time. There'll be plenty of time to talk."

"This'll only take a few seconds."

"OK. OK."

There was a pause; then Angela said:

"Hello, I really think . . ."

"Just shut up a minute, will you, and listen; but don't say anything except what I tell you."

"Go on."

"If someone's standing there with a gun at your head, just smile sweetly and say: 'We'll see you in about twenty minutes, then.' But if everything's as it should be, say something else."

"What sort of thing?"

"I don't know. Anything that occurs to you."

"You said just now you were going to tell me what to say,

88

and that I wasn't to say anything else."

Dutch swore under his breath. Then he said grimly: "You've just given the game away."

Angela answered sweetly: "Not really, darling. You asked me to say something else, and I did!"

Dutch contemplated 'phoning Eli instead of going through what seemed to be an over-elaborate charade, as suggested by his daughter. But he decided it was too far to ask his friend to come for such a short journey; and so, feeling faintly embarrassed, he walked out of the main entrance, took a ten-pound note out of his pocket, and bent down to give it to the driver of the vehicle which loomed out of the semi-darkness and glided to a halt next to him.

"Will you please go down to the main Post Office? A friend has just 'phoned and asked me to send a cab."

The driver looked as if he was about to protest; but it was little more than a three-pound fare, and he stuck his hand out instead and took the note.

"What does your friend look like?" he growled.

"About the same height as me. And wearing a light blue rain-coat," Dutch added as a last minute inspiration. It had just started to rain.

The other nodded, and set off.

Dutch glanced up at the sky wondering whether to go back and get his own raincoat; but he thought better of it, and walked towards the front cab of the line which, now his eyes had grown accustomed to the half light, he could see drawn up under the trees further down the drive.

The driver was sitting in the cab talking to one of his mates. As with other conversations between Arabs, they sounded to Dutch as if they were about to come to blows; but they were probably only discussing the price of petrol, and both jumped when he bent down beside him.

"Are you free?"

The driver recovered instantly.

"Oh, yes, Sir." He practically pushed his friend out of the

89

other door, then jumped out himself. But Dutch had already opened the rear door to get inside.

"Take me down into the centre of town," he said for the benefit of the friend, who still stood beside the cab listening interestedly.

"Yes, Sir." The driver resumed his seat. "Any place in particular?"

Was it Dutch's imagination, or did he glance momentarily to his left to make sure the other was still listening?

"No. I'll think of something."

"Yes, Sir. Very good, Sir."

The one beside the cab stood back as they drew away, but just before they reached the main road, Dutch glanced back, and saw the other driver hurrying into the hotel. There might not be any particular significance in it. On the other hand, there might.

When they had been going for a little while, Dutch said:

"What time do the cinemas start their last show here?"

The driver glanced back at him.

"About ten o'clock, Sir."

"And what's showing?"

The driver rattled off a list of titles, and Dutch chose one at random.

They stopped eventually outside a fairly large cinema just round the corner from Zion Square, with a queue outside which would have brought tears of joy to the President of the beleaguered American distributor; but it didn't suit Dutch's purpose at all, and he asked the driver to go on to the next, which turned out to be only a few yards further on. This had the more familiar, abandoned air of a late night chemist's, the reason being that it was showing a picture which the critics had unanimously praised as being the first really worthwhile contribution to the art of the cinema in ten years, and the public should not be put off by the fact that it was in black and white and contained no sex. The driver turned, and made a face which summed up the public's response; but Dutch said: "This'll do fine", and got out.

He paid the fare, and started to walk towards the box office. He became conscious that the driver had not driven away, but under the cover of writing up his log was watching him closely.

He bought a ticket and walked inside. He sat down for about three minutes, and then got up and left by one of the emergency exits at the side. He then walked up the narrow alley which emerged into Hillel Avenue, stopped a passing cab and asked to be taken to the Israeli Museum.

It was a one-way street and, in order to turn back in the right direction, the cab swung left at the end into Salmon Street, and carried on back to Zion Square, where it again turned left.

When Dutch realised where they were going, he shrank down into the back seat. A moment later they passed the cab he had recently left parked outside a public call-box, where he caught a glimpse of the driver talking with evident urgency over the telephone.

Dutch looked back and smiled grimly.

As soon as the second cab had driven away, leaving him standing outside the main entrance to the Museum (which was on top of a hill overlooking a valley, on the other side of which was the easily recognised Parliament Building), a dark blue Renault drew up, and Dutch saw the two girls inside.

"Jump in the back," Billie called urgently. A moment afterwards, they were driving away at speed.

"Darling, where have you been?" Angela said anxiously, turning round to face him. Billie also turned round and gave him a quick grin.

"Hello, Dad!"

"Hello, Billie!"

"Let's get where we're going. Then we'll talk."

"You're the boss!"

"We thought you'd been kidnapped or something," Angela persisted. "And what's all this about someone trying to kill you?"

Billie drove with determination and skill. Her style, perhaps, lacked Eli's flair, but they were travelling almost as fast, and she didn't take any risks. Nor did she do anything to draw particular attention to them. Their route was tortuous in the extreme, but despite this her father's sense of direction told him they were aiming in a generally north-easterly direction.

They passed many new building developments of the kind he had missed seeing before, and then the journey ended as abruptly as it had begun when Billie drove into an underground car park beneath a block of high-rise apartments and parked at the rear, as far away from the entrance as possible.

By mutual agreement, they remained silent going up in the elevator, although there appeared to be no-one else about; but, once the door of the fifth floor apartment had closed behind them, Billie turned into his arms; after they had held each other for a while, he heard her whisper: "Dad—you shouldn't have come. But it's so lovely to see you!"

He looked up and saw Angela watching them ... and she was smiling! Perhaps it was as well the two girls had met first. Men often got in the way, and made a mess of such things!

There was so much to say; but first of all Dutch wanted to know where they were, and why his daughter was in hiding.

"As to the first," Billie answered, "we're in a funk-hole which nobody else knows about. It was rented under a false name a long time ago by the man I used to work with—just in case one or other of us needed to go to ground in a hurry."

"But why? Besides, aren't the people you used to work for among those who are looking for you?"

His daughter nodded.

"So I believe."

She took a packet of cigarettes from the mantelpiece, and offered it to each of them in turn.

"But I meant—the man I *really* worked for."

Dutch shook his head briefly, but Angela chose one, and he picked up the lighter alongside the cigarettes.

"Doing what, precisely?" he asked quietly.

Billie didn't answer until he had finished lighting Angela's cigarette, but when he turned to her she said: "Nothing to be ashamed of, I promise."

They looked at each other for a moment; then Billie lit her

own cigarette from the flame he was offering.

Dutch asked: "Then why are you in hiding?"

His daughter drew the smoke deep into her lungs before answering carefully: "Because they found out about him—and, through him, me. And I didn't want to end up the same way."

"You mean, dead?"

"Yes."

Dutch paused for a moment, then he said: "Look Billie, I wasn't kidding when I told you over the 'phone someone had tried to kill me. Once outside your house, and once in the old City this afternoon."

Angela said: "My God, that must have been all the commotion. But we heard someone had been killed!"

Dutch nodded grimly: "They were. The one who took a shot at me."

"You?" Billie looked at him, white-faced. But her father shook his head.

"No. Someone else got him first. I never saw who." After a pause, he continued: "The guy I was with said he thought the dead man was one of those who had tried to kill me the first time. He must have been lying in wait."

"But how could he have known where you were going?" Angela said quickly.

Dutch looked at her. Then he said mildly: "They must have read your note!"

The girl drew in her breath, then let it out in a sigh.

"I'd forgotten!"

She then turned to Billie miserably, and explained: "I left a note for your father telling him about your call. I knew how worried he was about you."

"Then I was right," Billie said, ignoring her. "We *were* followed. I thought so!"

Dutch rested his hand momentarily on Angela's shoulder. "It was a perfectly natural and thoughtful thing to do."

Then he turned to Billie. "And, if I may say so, young lady, *your* behaviour recently has been anything but. I don't know what you're mixed up in, but both your mother and I were worried sick—and now all this."

Billie's eyes blazed suddenly.

"Who asked you to worry about me?" she flung back at him savagely. "Why couldn't you have both gone on minding your own business?"

All the forgotten hurt as well as the pent-up worry of the past few days welled up inside Dutch's head. He let go of the other girl and, before he could stop himself, slapped Billie so hard in the face that she fell to the floor as if stunned.

"Dutch! No!" Angela threw herself between them as if he was going to hit her again—which was quite unnecessary as he was already looking down bewildered by what he had done. The next second she fell to her knees and gathered Billie into her arms.

"I ... I'm sorry!" he heard Billie gasp. Then both girls started to weep.

"I didn't mean it to sound like that ... it's just that ... I've been so frightened!"

Dutch knelt beside them and put his arms round both of them while Billie cried and Angela wept in sympathy. Clearly she had been under a terrible strain, and to have a good cry was probably the best thing for her. But when it was over, he made them both sit on the settee while he went into the kitchen and made some coffee, before listening quietly—while trying to repress his emotions—to his daughter's story.

She had intended to join the Women's Royal Air Corps on leaving Oxford. But after she had put in her application, she was approached by one of the officers in her grandfather's old squadron while she was still at the University, and she had been recruited into Military Intelligence instead.

She was taken up to London, and there met a man who, she was to learn later, was the Director of the Middle Eastern Section. He had persuaded her that she would be more valuable working under cover and, after taking several weeks to think about it, she had agreed.

A period of intensive training followed to equip her, amongst other things, with the cover of a good shorthand typist—a skill in almost universal demand and short supply throughout the world. After several months as a "temp" in London in her newly acquired "trade", she was ordered to apply for, and was granted, immigration into Israel.

For more than a year she had been a "sleeper", having no contact at all with any other member of British Intelligence. She had gone through the usual processes required of any new immigrant; these included a crash course in Hebrew so that, at the end of six months, she was able to work in both languages, which made it even easier to get a good job. But it was another eight months before Paul Close entered her life.

Dutch wondered, although he didn't ask, how she had felt about deceiving a country which had accepted her as one of its own; and, as if she guessed what he was thinking, Billie went on to say that theirs had been a mainly passive role—not so much gathering information which, if divulged, might have harmed Israel, as finding out what kind of information the intelligence services of other nations were interested in. That was until about two months ago, when suddenly everything had changed.

Billie paused for a moment, then she looked at her father and drew a deep breath.

"Paul disappeared for a while. Then he 'phoned me one night —something he never did normally—and said he had stumbled on something that was so important he had to get back to London immediately. He refused to tell me what it was over the 'phone, and there wasn't time for us to meet in the usual way; but he told me to pack a few things and come up here for a while. He had a suspicion they knew he had found out and, if so, they might be able to trace our connection." Billie looked away, and Dutch saw her eyes fill with tears.

"The last thing he said to me was I must look after myself. I must leave straightaway because they would stop at nothing."

She gave a great shuddering sigh, then went on. "The next thing I knew, he was dead!"

Dutch paused for a moment, then he said gently:

"Were you fond of him?"

Billie looked at him again, and nodded.

"Yes ... but not in the way you might think. He was the kindest man I ever met. He was always concerned to protect me. The bit about him refusing to tell me what he knew over the 'phone was mainly because he thought I'd be safer not knowing."

"Which was hardly true, in the event."

Billie shook her head.

"No. He obviously thought he was going to get back."

"But he didn't, I gather?"

Billie shook her head again.

"No. I heard from London he had been killed."

"How did you hear—I mean—hiding up here?"

"I can't tell you."

Dutch frowned. "Honey, don't you think you've told us so much already? I can't see what difference it would make."

Billie looked back at him, and he saw a spark of defiance re-kindle. Then it was gone, and there was only love.

"I've told you as much as I have, only because I know you wouldn't leave otherwise," she said. "I had no business to, of course. If they knew, I'd be shot out of the Service so quickly my feet wouldn't touch the ground." Again the tilt of the chin. "But I don't owe them *your* life. You're not even British—and you *must* leave, because I think you've been mistaken for the man I've been told to wait for."

It was Angela who spoke first: "You mean Paul Close's replacement?" she said; and Billie turned to her quickly.

"That's right. Paul never managed to tell what he knew. But, whatever it is, London know it must be desperately impor-tant, and they're determined to find out." She shrugged. "They know it's more than I can handle, but they daren't use their other people because they're being watched." She paused for a moment, then went on: "The ones who are looking for me know I'm still here, but they don't know where. Then, suddenly, a man who says he's my father turns up and starts asking questions."

"So you expect me to run and leave you here alone?" It was Dutch who spoke suddenly, and Billie turned to him quickly.

"You've got to. In the circumstances, every minute you're here, your life is in danger."

"What sort of a father would that make me?"

"Dad, it's got nothing to do with you."

"It's everything to do with me as long as you're here."

Billie stared at him, then she looked at Angela.

"Angela, can't you make him see? I love him—but it's not helping—me worrying about him."

Angela shook her head helplessly, then Dutch said quietly: "I'll leave here and now—if you'll come with us."

Billie shook her head: "You know I can't do that."

"I don't know anything of the kind. Frankly, I don't give a damn what you're supposed to be doing here. And to be honest, I don't much care for it either—but I'm darned sure that if it's important enough for you to stay here and risk your neck, it's important enough for me to stay here until either we all get killed or we all leave together."

"What about Angela?"

Dutch glanced from one to the other. Then he said: "I agree. There *is* no reason for her to stay."

"Now just a minute!" Angela protested fiercely. "While you're all giving reasons why you're going to stay, let me make one thing quite clear."

They both looked at her.

"I'm here because I *want* to be—and I'm damned if I'm going home by myself."

Billie shook her head again helplessly.

"You just don't understand," she muttered.

Dutch stood up suddenly, and took a cigarette from the pack. Angela looked at him in surprise as he lit it thoughtfully. He turned to face Billie and said: "You say we don't understand. But there are a few things about this *you* don't know."

He then went on to tell his own story from the beginning, placing particular emphasis on her mother's conversation with the phoney inspector; the description by her friend in the next flat of the intruders, and their behaviour; and lastly, Morgan's total, and apparently genuine, ignorance of the whole affair until Dutch himself had walked into Police Headquarters that morning. He glanced at his watch. "I should say, yesterday morning."

It was already past one o'clock.

"Everything you have said", he went on, "suggests that you believe that those who killed your friend and seek to silence both of us are connected with Israeli counter-intelligence. And yet, surely, if that were so, Morgan would not have let me walk out of his office. And does the double attempt on my life sound like the work of a Government agency operating on its own territory? What was to stop them just wheeling me in?"

He paused for a moment before continuing. "It seems to me, that all the evidence points to someone else—some powerful, but unofficial, organisation. And, that being so, we can be reasonably certain that whatever Close discovered was not an Israeli State secret, in the ordinary sense of the word, but one concerning, at the very least, the security of Britain. Clearly your people in London must think so. Why else would they be so keen to send someone out here to help you get to the bottom of it?

"Which brings me to my last point. Although, at first sight, the continued presence of an amateur such as myself on the scene may seem an embarrassment—disregarding, for the moment our feelings for each other—it does guarantee one thing, don't forget, and that is the safe arrival of your colleague. For as long as 'they', whoever they are, think I am he, they are unlikely to be looking elsewhere!"

There was a period of silence, then Billie said: "I seem to be the amateur."

Angela smiled sympathetically: "What your father really means is that he's just beginning to enjoy himself!"

"Ignoring that last remark ..." Dutch began severely. Then his frown softened into a smile: "I don't think you've been behaving like an amateur at all. On the contrary, you've been under a terrible strain, and have withstood it like a trooper; but seeing we're here, there's no harm, surely, in accepting a little help. At least, until the cavalry arrives, so to speak."

"I suppose not," Billie smiled.

"Fine!" Dutch paused for a moment, then he went on: "And, as for enjoying myself, I don't think anyone really enjoys being shot at, but it *does* make it a little more tolerable if one has some idea why."

Billie yawned, then apologised.

"I'm sorry. I really am very tired."

Her father nodded understandingly.

"You've had a long day. But just tell me the end of the Paul Close episode. You say he was killed before he could talk?"

"Yes. He hijacked an El-Al airliner—"

"I remember that!" Angela said excitedly. "It was in the papers."

"*That* was him?"

"Yes."

"It *must* have been important."

"Yes."

"And the fact—Wait a minute!" It was Dutch's turn to look excited. "The fact that, despite this, Israeli counter-intelligence don't appear to have been alerted—otherwise Morgan would have put two and two together, and held me for further questioning—proves they are not aware of there having been a serious security leak."

"Perhaps," Billie admitted. "But not necessarily. They might have let you go to see where you would lead."

Dutch paused for a moment, then he said: "OK. I admit the possibility—taken apart from the rest of the evidence. But in the *light* of it—go on."

"He was shot leaving the aircraft."

"By one of the crew?"

"No. There was someone waiting in the dark with a rifle. He was shot in the chest."

There was a long pause, then Dutch sighed. "And so no-one was any the wiser."

Billie hesitated a long time. Then she made a decision. She said: "Except for one thing. There was a piece of paper sewn into the lining of his jacket, on which was written a phrase which must be in code, but no one has been able to crack it—yet."

"What was it?"

"Five Gates to Armageddon."

99

Chapter 10

Billie had told him that Close had used the cover of an exporter of citrus fruit to the United Kingdom, and had, in fact, built up a prosperous business. On orders from London she had gone to his apartment to see if she could find anything that might give them a clue as to what had made him break and run, but she had found nothing; and when she herself had ventured into Tel Aviv, she had found the office being watched and had not dared to go back. She was lucky not to have been caught at the apartment, but it had evidently taken whoever it was (she had assumed at the time that it had been Israeli counter-intelligence) that much longer to find out where he had lived—evidence, as she had to agree later, that someone else was involved, for surely there would have been no such time lag otherwise.

Twenty-four hours had passed without there being any sign of the man from London who was supposed to be coming to take charge. He knew Billie would refuse to leave without the information her old boss had died trying to take back to London. The very fact that he had been killed, he knew, had transformed the recovery of it and its successful transmission into a sacred trust for his daughter; but every day that passed increased the danger that her refuge would be discovered, and unfortunately, as far as his responsibility for Angela was concerned, that involved both of them ever more deeply.

He had decided not to go back to the hotel for the time being. Not only because of the risk of getting shot at once more, but of leading those who were trying to follow him to Billie. But Close had kept some spare shirts and underwear at their new address, just in case, and Angela and Billie were about the same size.

He had telephoned to say that they were taking a three-day excursion, knowing the information would be interpreted correctly by their unknown enemies as having gone into hiding; but it didn't change anything, and whatever the receptionist who took the call may have thought, he had little choice but to accede to his request to hold the room in view of his undertaking to pay their full charges. After all, they had left their luggage and most of their clothes.

There was a spare bedroom in the apartment, and after Billie had agreed that they should stay he and Angela had fallen asleep the minute their heads touched the pillow. But when he had woken up the following morning to find the sun streaming between the blinds, he had stretched and realised he hadn't felt so alive for a long time.

Dutch had put out his hand lazily to where Angela's rump should have been to find that her side of the bed was empty. But before he had time to wonder, he heard the shower start in the bathroom which led directly from the room Billie had given them.

He had lain there for a while thinking about Angela in the shower. He had watched her several times with the water running down that glorious body of hers, making it shine almost as though it were made of rubber. But beneath her skin, whose flawlessness gave it the appearance of artificiality at such moments, Dutch knew there were the sinews, muscle and bones of the most perfect mate he had ever known and, after a few more seconds, he got up quickly and went looking for her.

"Is that you, darling?"

Angela heard the door open, and popped her head out to give him one of her best smiles. Like him, she had woken up feeling good; in fact, despite the danger, she almost wished it could go on for ever.

"Do you want to come in with me?"

The artificial light in the bathroom emphasised the difference between the tan she had acquired during the summer months and the comparative pallor round the tips of her breasts and her loins where she had worn one or other of the minuscule bikinis Dutch made fun of by saying that wearing them only drew attention to the parts she was trying to hide.

Sometimes, when her husband was away and the servants were out, Angela had lain by the pool at home without wearing anything. But on one of those occasions—this was before Dutch came into her life—the sixteen-year-old son of one of their neighbours had turned up with his swimming things. She had forgotten the invitation she had made at one of the few parties she and her husband had been able to attend together during a particularly hot spell about a month before, and it had not been taken up at the time. But now, here he was, looking down at her, obviously torn between curiosity and embarrassment, or so she had thought.

He had probably never seen a naked woman before—at least, not one outside his own family—and for a few seconds she found herself trying to remember, quite incongruously, if he had any sisters. Then she had pulled herself together and smiled; if she had shown any embarrassment or dashed into one of the changing rooms, it would only have made the situation worse.

"Hello! Peter, isn't it?" She shaded her eyes with her hand.

The boy swallowed, and nodded.

Angela sat up. Then he said: "I'm sorry. I wouldn't have barged in like this if I'd known."

He didn't *sound* embarrassed. In fact, he smiled back at her quite charmingly. The more she looked at him, the less like a boy he seemed and the more like a rather attractive young man. He must have been six feet tall. But she was sure he was only sixteen.

"If you'd known what?" she challenged, giving him another smile. Good grief, now she was flirting with him!

He had stopped smiling and suddenly knelt beside her.

"That you were like this," he said huskily.

His eyes seemed to be devouring her, but she still couldn't bring herself to move. It was ridiculous. Despite his size, he was still a child at heart.

"If you'd like to change, use the room over on the far side would you," she had said as lightly as she could. But now she seemed to be having difficulty with her own breathing. He might be a child at heart, but he had a man's body.

Oh God ... how long it was since she had held a boy who looked like that and who had looked at her as he was looking

102

now! Not since she was sixteen herself. Then, suddenly, boys her own age had seemed so callow and uninteresting. Suddenly she was grown up and had revelled in flitting from one man to another: Real men who could take her to all the best places and knew what to do and how to behave. Her father and mother had never had money and they had delighted in seeing their daughter swept up into realms they themselves had never dreamt of entering. Then she met Henry—the man she was to marry.

At first, she had not taken him seriously. He was older than the rest, but she had soon learned to take him very seriously indeed—he saw to that. He had decided he wanted her, and she realised later that he had pursued her as single-mindedly and relentlessly as if he had been after a particularly valuable contract. She never stood a chance.

Henry had come into her life too soon. If she had been just a little more experienced ... or perhaps she was the sort of female —she had asked herself this many times—who was too stupid to learn anything until it was too late? He had been genuinely fond of her. There was no doubt of that, but he only wanted her in particular because she was the most sought after young woman in the set in which he moved. He had needed a wife. And like everything else, only the best, the most enviable would do. But if she hadn't been there, the next in line would have done equally well.

How long it seemed since a young boy had looked at her like that, and she felt her heart reaching out invisibly before her hand to touch his sweetness.

But this was insane! She was at least ten years older than he was. What sort of woman was she to be thinking such thoughts? The next thing, she would be frightening him to death.

She moved as if to get up, but Peter had put out his hand quickly to prevent her.

"No ... don't go. Please."

Angela had obeyed the authority of his voice without question. She then looked back at him to see what he would do next, her heart thumping almost unbearably as if it would burst out of her rib cage.

He had bent down and kissed her on the mound between her legs with its guardian forest of curls, so dark against the paleness of her untanned skin.

She had opened her mouth to protest, but her limbs had known better and opened involuntarily as if he had touched a hidden spring, and the next second she threw back her head and gasped as a sensation of unbearable sweetness ran down her legs and up her spine, blocking all but her responsive reflexes and unleashing all her longing.

He had made love to her with a gentleness and skill she had never experienced before and all the time, at the back of her mind, she wondered that such consideration ... and love ... unselfish love ... there were no other words for it ... should lie at the command of one with a face like a young angel.

Then he had stood up, and unhurriedly peeled off his shirt and jeans, and shaken off his sandals before taking possession of her with an assurance and power that surprised her still at the beginning, and left her weak but totally fulfilled at the end.

The spell had lasted all afternoon. Then Peter went home, and the following morning she rang up and forbade him to come again.

She could not bring herself to regret what had happened for its own sake. In fact, she knew it would always be one of her most cherished and secret memories—so secret, in fact, she would never tell anyone, no matter how much she loved them or felt confident of their understanding, for to even try would change it somehow. But when she thought of it in terms of the future, which had seemed to stretch before her in an unending sea of grey, Angela teetered on the brink of despair.

Was this how it would be? The first of a series of distractions that would lead steadily downwards as she got older and more used to what she was becoming until all the sweetness and gentleness was left far behind in a never-ending search for some new experience—anything—which would give her life some meaning.

She had thrust the vision away with an effort of will. Later she had a brief and unsatisfactory affair with one of her husband's managers; one in which there had been no love, only the mutual gratification of desire, and she had known that the process had already begun. Then, suddenly, out of the blue she had met Dutch ... and everything had changed. She had never loved anyone before, she knew that now. And that gave him the power to save or destroy her at will. She had known it as she gave herself to him for the first time, and she knew it even more as she looked at him now, waiting for her. And she was glad, because either was better than slow decay. She knew he loved her and she hoped that sooner or later they would be able to make their life together. Then she would forget the nightmare for ever. But even if it turned out he didn't love her enough for that in the end, and walked away, she couldn't feel anything but happiness now, for then the end would come swiftly. She loved him more than she had thought possible, and no matter what happened, he had already saved her from that which she had feared most.

She had turned off the water and moved to pick up a towel; but he took it from her, and it fell to the floor as she moved into his arms, her skin warm and slippery from the shower.

"Dutch—I *do* love you!"

His arms went round her, and a moment later he picked her up and carried her back into the bedroom.

"What about the sheets? They'll get wet!"

"The hell with the sheets!"

He laid her down on the stone floor just under the window.

For a moment, the stone had been hard against her back, then she had forgotten everything in the joy of loving him.

His proposal to call Eli and go into Tel Aviv to see if anyone was still watching the office had caused an argument at first, with both women siding against him. But as the day had worn on he had become progressively more restless, and eventually Billie had been forced to agree that, although the office had undoubtedly been searched by the others, to have a look for themselves remained the one positive thing any of them could do, and she had given him the key which Close had given her a long time ago.

Rain beat against the window panes as Dutch let himself into the darkened office. He did not turn on the lights immediately, but walked first across to the windows which looked out from the fifth floor of a new block overlooking the sea. He looked to see if there were any blinds or drapes, so he could do what he had come to do without fear of being seen from below; but there was nothing.

He could see by the light of the street lamps on the road below between the building and the beach that the room had been stripped of furniture. This came as no surprise; Billie had warned him that whoever had been after Close would undoubtedly have searched his office in Tel Aviv; but they had been very thorough. As anyone experienced in such matters knew, by far the most efficient method of searching anywhere and of being absolutely sure of not missing anything was to remove everything in it, if possible, to a place where it could be taken to pieces and examined at leisure, while the remaining space was searched for anything which earlier might have been overlooked or hidden. In this case, whoever was responsible had also removed everything that could be unscrewed.

He turned back to the window for a few seconds, and gazed down at the rain-lashed road and the beach beyond. There was less danger of there being anyone out there wondering what he was doing. He walked back to the door and switched on the lights. At least they had left the bulbs behind. He paused for a moment to wonder if it was worth removing them to see if anything had been hidden behind the bulb caps inside the sockets, but dismissed the idea. Paper is a poor conductor, and even the smallest piece would prevent the light from working.

He glanced round the room. The floor was bare concrete—no possibilities there. Then he walked across and opened the door leading into the Principal's office, pausing in the doorway to turn on the lights. But this room was equally bare.

After spending half an hour going through every nook and cranny in both rooms, Dutch stood again, looking out of the window.

Of course, Billie had been right. She had said they wouldn't have left anything, and that he would be taking a risk for nothing. She had also said that part of her training had taught her when to lie low and do nothing, if necessary, for a long time.

He would never make a spy: he was too impatient. He would rather dart all over the place, giving himself the illusion of doing something, regardless of the danger to others. He had been guilty of thinking Billie lacking in initiative, when all the time she was being professional and doing what she was told, while he was behaving like a rank amateur—which, after all, he was.

Dutch sighed. Well, at least, in the event it didn't seem to have done any harm.

The lower casement window by which he was standing rattled in the wind and he glanced down momentarily.

A small piece of paper which had been compressed into a wedge had fallen on to the floor; it could only have just happened, for he would have sworn that the window had not been rattling a few seconds earlier.

He picked it up, and after unfolding it saw it was a page from a notebook covered with shorthand signs.

A quick inspection showed there were similar wedges in two other windows—both pages from notebooks.

Dutch's pulse began to quicken. Evidently his predecessors had not been as thorough as they had thought!

Chapter 11

On the drive back to Jerusalem, Dutch's mind was a whirl. The chances were they were letters or invoices which Close had dictated to his secretary; but until he got back to Billie he wouldn't know, and for once did not wish his friend to drive more slowly.

Eli dropped him at the end of the street, and Dutch walked the remaining two blocks before entering the building through the underground car park.

He waited for a minute just inside the entrance behind one of the parked cars to see if he was being followed; but he saw nothing and went up in the lift.

The two girls were waiting for him anxiously; but their excitement at his discovery turned to frustration and disappointment when it transpired that neither of them could read the symbols on the pieces of paper.

"What d'you mean you can't read them?" Dutch demanded looking at Billie. "I thought you said you could do shorthand in both languages."

"I can. But that's Pitman's—I think. I learned speedwriting."

"Oh, for crying out loud!"

"*I* learned Pitman's—a long time ago," Angela remarked, "but I can't read that. It doesn't make any sense at all." She stared at the paper in her hand, frowning. "At least ... I don't *think* so," she added doubtfully.

"What d'you mean, you don't *think* so?" Dutch said brutally. "Either it does or it doesn't!"

Angela looked at him, tears starting into her eyes. No-one was more disappointed than she at not being able to help.

"I'm sorry," she began; then suddenly Billie said: "Wait a minute. I've got an idea!"

They watched her go into the main bedroom, Angela wiping away the tears with the back of her hand while Dutch looked at her. He felt a complete heel. It wasn't her fault that she couldn't read what was on the paper. But, before he could say anything, Billie reappeared with a shaving mirror from the bathroom.

"Here," she said, giving it to Angela. "Try this."

"How?"

"Hold the paper up, and try reading it in the mirror."

"How will that help?" Dutch asked; and his daughter turned to him.

"Hebrew reads from right to left," she explained. "It just occurred to me that someone who learned to do shorthand in Hebrew might make the symbols the opposite way round. At least, it's worth a try."

Angela nodded excitedly and held up the paper as Billie had said.

"Well?" Dutch demanded after a few seconds. "Does it help?"

Angela frowned, and bit her lip in concentration.

"It helps," she said after a few seconds. "It's almost there . . . but there's still something wrong."

The other two watched in silence a moment longer. Then Billie said: "Wait a minute, I think I know what it is."

She reached into her bag and fished out a ball-point pen. She then went to the small desk over on the far side of the room, and came back with some blank pieces of paper.

"Now what?" Dutch said impatiently.

Billie gave him a smile. "Just contain yourself a moment, darling."

She put the pen and paper on the table in the dining alcove and turned back to Angela.

"Could you come and sit down here,"

Angela did as she was bidden; then Billie said: "The mirror has corrected the shape of the symbols, but if it's in English, it's reversed the words on the paper."

Dutch looked down at Angela. "But, surely you can see that?" he said.

Angela looked at the paper in the mirror again, then she shook her head and glanced up.

"No, you don't understand," she said. "Pitman's is based on sounds, not letters. It's hard enough to read someone else's anyway—particularly if you're completely rusty, like me—but it's virtually impossible if the words are in the wrong order. You have to take it phrase by phrase."

"Oh!" Dutch looked suitably chastened.

"That's why I thought if you re-copied them in the right order . . ." Billie began; but Angela was already hard at work.

The first proved to be part of a letter to Close's business contact in London. It was to do with the shipment of grapefruit.

The second was in Hebrew, after all; but with the two girls working together, Angela making the sounds she thought the symbols represented and Billie gradually getting the sense of them, they decoded a letter to a farming co-operative in northern Galilee which had about the same interest as the first.

The third was a list of appointments. Angela wrote down the names slowly under the various dates. The last was for the day immediately before Close left. This was more like it! There were three names which meant nothing to Dutch, but he heard Billie draw in her breath as Angela wrote down the last name: "Ari Pearl".

The girl sitting at the table also looked up quickly.

"Ari Pearl!" Billie breathed.

"Who is he?" Dutch demanded.

For a few seconds, Billie didn't answer; she was still staring at the name. Then she looked up.

"Ari Pearl was a junior Minister. Paul got to know him through the business. I think he was something to do with licences—something like that; but then they became close friends."

"They visited each other's houses?"

"Yes."

"You said he *was* a junior Minister," Angela commented. "Did he lose his job because of what happened?"

Billie looked at her. "He lost more than that," she said quietly.

"He killed himself!"

Pearl had been an important though not very well-known member of the Government, having come into the Administration from the Civil Service, and his death had been swept from the front pages by the ordeal of those who had been on the hijacked airliner.

It was not difficult to discover the address of his widow. She was living almost in the centre of Jerusalem, as she had found it unnecessary to move after her husband's death—a fact which Dutch found surprising. After all, the widows of Civil Servants were not generally so well off; but perhaps he had taken bribes? The Israeli Civil Service was probably the least corrupt in the entire Middle East, but black sheep were to be found everywhere, and the ex-Minister's particular functions—the granting of import and export licences—did, perhaps, lend itself to such more than most. Nevertheless, Billie told him, there had been no hint of scandal, not even in those periodicals whose life-blood it was, and it appeared that Mrs. Pearl was in receipt of a sizeable Government pension—a fact which itself attested her husband's innocence.

Nevertheless, it was a remarkable coincidence that both men should have died so soon after their last meeting: The one, they knew, was murdered; the other, apparently, shot himself with a pistol. There *might* be some connection. And it was the only thing they had to go on. So, after sweating it out for another day without the arrival of any reinforcements from London, Dutch decided to follow it up.

Eli had to attend a wedding in Bethlehem that afternoon, but he gladly lent them his car. Leaving Billie looking thoughtfully out over the City from the living-room window—she had been doing this most of the morning, and if he had not been so preoccupied himself, he might have thought to ask her why—Dutch and Angela drove to the house of the late Ari Pearl. After walking across the half moon of pebbled drive in front of the house, they introduced themselves to the maid who opened the door as "R. Deutsch and his assistant Mrs. Romay, representatives of

III

IATA, the International Air Transport Authority"—the governing body of all the world's leading airlines. They were shown into an elegant drawing-room while the maid went upstairs to announce them.

In spite of the evident solidity of the walls of the house, sound seemed to travel remarkably clearly. They heard the two of them moving around upstairs, and their conversation in deliberately subdued voices, the acoustic properties of the house being obviously apparent to its owner.

The room in which they found themselves was expensively furnished; hanging on the wall immediately above the fireplace was a painting by Vermeer which Angela, who had taught herself to know about such things, pronounced genuine. Then they heard footsteps cross to the landing and begin to come down the stairs.

A moment later the door opened and an attractive, impeccably groomed woman in her late forties entered the room. She was wearing a kimono.

"Mr. Deutsch?" She advanced a few steps into the room leaving the door leading into the hall open behind her.

Dutch rose from his chair and smiled gravely, as befitted an official of the august body he was supposed to represent. He approached her and stopped; when she made no effort to extend her hand, he inclined his head slightly and said, "Mrs. Pearl, I must apologise for not having asked for an appointment in advance, but we only left London last night at short notice, and this morning your telephone seemed to be engaged so we couldn't get through."

It was a shot in the dark. He didn't even know she was on the 'phone; but surely, someone in her position would have one, and he had learned from Billie that the system did not always live up to the Israeli reputation for efficiency. He continued: "I am the resident Secretary of the European Zone of IATA stationed in London." He wondered momentarily whether he might flash his US Air Force identity card, but thought better of it; the woman was obviously no fool and might examine it closely, whereas he could always plead he had left his papers back at the hotel if she asked to see them. He turned instead to Angela who had come to his elbow:

"This is my principal assistant, Mrs. Romay."

The woman facing them looked at Angela and smiled. Angela usually had that effect on people. Then she extended her hand to each of them in turn.

"I expect the line was out of order."

"Perhaps that was it."

"I was certainly not on the 'phone for more than a minute or two."

"Is it convenient for you to see us now?"

"If you don't mind my receiving you like this. I have the habit of resting in the early afternoon."

Dutch smiled. "That's a habit we Anglo-Saxons should cultivate!"

"Perhaps. What can I do for you? Personally I have never been in a plane, so I do not see that my opinions can count for very much."

Dutch gave Angela a quick look, and she said quietly: "It's not about you we have called, Mrs. Pearl. It's about your late husband."

There could be no doubt about the genuineness of the shock which greeted this remark.

"My husband," she stammered, looking from one to the other. "I don't understand. All that's over and done with.... They promised."

"We're concerned primarily with the hijacking of the El-Al aircraft which took place some weeks ago," Dutch went on hurriedly. "You may have seen something about it in the papers?"

Mrs. Pearl nodded.

"I do remember something about it," she said weakly. "But it was about the time of ... my husband's death. I'm not very clear ..."

"Perhaps it would be better if we sat down?" Angela said gently, and the other looked at her gratefully.

"Yes, yes. Let's sit down. I really don't know what to say. Please."

She waved her hand in the direction of the chairs in which they had been sitting, then she remembered the door and closed it behind her—an action with more psychological than practical significance, for clearly the maid out in the hall would still be able to hear every word if she had a mind.

As soon as they were seated, Mrs. Pearl facing them across the fireplace, Dutch said: "I'm sorry if talking about your husband upsets you ..."

"No, no." The widow, now obviously recovered, waved her hand. "It's not that. He is dead, and that is the end of it. It is just that I was expecting you to say something entirely different. It came as a shock, that's all."

Dutch glanced at Angela, and nodded. They had rehearsed their lines carefully.

"Mrs. Pearl," she began. "According to our records, the man responsible for the hijacking was a friend of your late husband."

"Paul Close." Mrs. Pearl nodded. "Yes, that is correct. They met in business, and became friends afterwards."

Now it was Dutch's turn. "Mrs. Pearl, even though you do not fly yourself, I'm sure you must be aware of the acute anxiety felt by all those in civil aviation at the continued wave of air piracy."

The woman nodded, watching him intently; he went on:

"The motive for political hijackings is not hard to find, reprehensible though the hazarding of innocent lives remains, and it is to some extent predictable." He paused for a moment, then continued solemnly: "But what is unpredictable—and therefore, to that extent *more* worrying—are the isolated acts of individuals."

"Yes, I see."

"On the face of it, these often seem motiveless, and sometimes are. But so that no opportunity should be lost of establishing a psychological profile, as it were, of the apparently motiveless hijacker, to try and see if they have anything in common, and thus give us *some* indication as to the kind of person liable to commit such acts, IATA has decided to probe each individual case in depth." He paused again, before continuing: "It is for this reason, therefore, that we are here in Israel. To find out as much as we can about Paul Close, and it is why we are here this afternoon—to see if you can help us."

Dutch sat back in his chair. It wasn't a bad story, and though he said it himself, he didn't think he'd put it over badly at all. Their "victim" certainly looked suitably impressed.

The next move was Angela's. But Mrs. Pearl was shaking her head.

"I really don't know what I can tell you that you don't know already," she said. "As you know, he was a friend of Ari's. He came here once or twice, but I never visited his home. I didn't know him that well."

"Did your husband?" Angela asked.

"Visit Mr. Close's apartment?"

"Yes."

"I think they played chess together. But, as you know, he wasn't married, and when he wanted to return our hospitality he took us to a restaurant." She paused for a moment, then turned to Dutch.

"Why did you say at the beginning you had come to see me about Ari when you really wanted to know about his friend?"

Dutch looked at her steadily, and saw the beginnings of fear in her eyes. She turned to Angela.

"Why does he look at me like that?" she demanded. "It's upsetting."

Angela said quietly: "He's wondering if there is any connection between the hijacking and your husband's death."

Mrs. Pearl gaped openly for the first time; then her mouth shut like a trap and she rose to her feet."

"How dare you say such a thing! I've had enough of this!"

"Why *did* your husband kill himself?" Dutch asked, as she swung round on him angrily.

"I refuse to answer any more questions. Please leave before I call the police."

"Very well."

Dutch rose to his feet, thus lowering her mounting hysteria just below danger level—in another few seconds she would have been screaming—but he said: "Was your husband the kind of man you would have expected to have killed himself?"

"Of course not!"

"Paul Close, your husband's friend, was not the kind of man you would have expected to have risked the lives of dozens of innocent people."

"What's that got to do with it?"

"He was killed, Mrs. Pearl, in London. He was shot just after the plane touched down."

"I didn't know that."

"Didn't you?"

"Of course not. Why should I?"

"It was a feature of the story you said you'd read about."

"I didn't know anything about it at the time."

"Because of your husband?"

"No. Yes . . . because of his death."

"Didn't the police mention it?"

"I don't remember."

"How did your husband die?"

"He shot himself. Upstairs."

"Was anyone with him at the time?"

"I don't know."

"What d'you mean, you don't know?"

Angela looked at him in alarm.

"I was down here at the time."

"You can hear every word down here."

"No. There wasn't."

"Is that what you told the police?"

"Yes."

"And you have no idea why your husband should kill himself?"

"No! no!" Suddenly she buried her face in her hands and wept.

"Dutch, that's enough." Angela would have moved to comfort her; but he turned on her, eyes blazing, and she froze.

"I won't answer any more of your questions. I won't!" Mrs. Pearl shook her head, her face still clasped in her hands.

"Dutch . . ."

"Be quiet!" His voice was still now, but the words cut through

116

the air.

He waited for her sobs to die away. Then he said quietly: "Mrs. Pearl. I don't think your husband killed himself. I think he was murdered by the same people who killed his friend. There *has* to be a connection."

Slowly she lowered her hands, and now fear started from every pore of her face.

"You have no right to say that," she gasped. "It was proved. The police . . . everyone."

"Everyone except you, Mrs. Pearl. I think you know differently."

He moved as if to walk past her to the door, but she caught him by the arm in an attempt to hold him back.

"Please . . . what are you going to do?"

Dutch looked down at her, and now his face had lost all expression.

"I'm going, as you asked."

"But you must believe me. *I know*. Don't say anything."

"Who to?"

"Anyone. The police. It would only start them asking questions. I couldn't go through it all again."

"I won't talk to anyone. . ."

"Oh, thank you!" Her relief was pathetic.

"If you'll tell me what really happened."

Her eyes were enormous as she stared back at him.

He glanced to see that Angela was ready to follow, then gently removed her hand from his arm and moved to open the door.

Angela went out first, giving him a look of sheer loathing. Out of the corner of his eye he could see, as he paused in the doorway, the figure of the maid watching them from across the hall. He glanced back into the room. The woman was staring at him now hopelessly, seemingly unable to move or even speak.

He said gently: "Don't worry. I won't say anything to anyone until we've talked again. I'll give you a day to think it over, then I'll 'phone to see if you'd like to tell me any more. Goodbye, Mrs. Pearl."

He went to the front door. Angela had already gone outside

117

leaving the door open, and as he closed it behind him, he was conscious of the maid's eyes burning into the small of his back.

"How could you talk to her like that?" Angela stormed as soon as they were safely in the car, which they had left at the end of the avenue under some trees. "I never thought you could be so cruel. You could see how upset she was."

Dutch turned to her. She looked as if she could cheerfully throttle him, but there was no time for lengthy explanations. For the first time he was beginning to see some pattern emerging—as yet undefined—but it was there; and now his eyes fixed once more on the entrance of the house they had just left. He didn't feel particularly proud of what he had just done, but the next few minutes might tell if it had been justified.

"Can't you answer me?" Angela said furiously.

"She was lying," he said without shifting his gaze.

"Well, so what? Say her husband *was* killed, and she heard it all, but was too frightened to tell the police. How does upsetting her like that help?"

"I don't know, honey." Dutch shook his head. He couldn't blame her for being angry. He had gone far beyond what they had agreed, and it was one of the things he admired most about her—the sympathy she felt for other people—but some instinct had led him on, once the interview had started, to push the woman to breaking point. It was like using dynamite in the middle of a log jam: he hoped he hadn't done too much damage, but at least something might start to move.

He did not have to wait much longer. Angela was just opening her mouth to speak when a car emerged from the entrance to the house, and turned in the opposite direction. The chances were they had not been seen.

Dutch started the Mercedes quickly, and followed at a discreet distance. He was right: there *was* someone she had to tell about their visit right away. Someone whose identity was so secret that using the 'phone was out of the question.

Angela glanced at him, but he seemed to be unaware now of her existence.

118

"Stupid bitch!" she thought to herself. She contemplated saying something, but bit her lip instead.

The two cars crossed the City in a south-westerly direction before joining the main highway to Tel Aviv. Then Mrs. Pearl turned right, and Dutch found himself entering an area of obviously upper-class houses, set well back from the road in their own grounds. The gardens of some were surrounded by high walls of brick and stone.

Dutch fell back a little. Clearly they were nearing their destination, and when they stopped he didn't want to be close enough for her to notice them as she got out of the car. In the meantime, Angela had found a large scale map of the city, and was following their route carefully.

In the event, he need not have worried about being seen. After a few hundred yards, the car in front turned in at the entrance of one of the bigger houses, the top floors of which were visible over the surrounding wall. After pausing for a few seconds to speak to a uniformed figure standing just inside, Mrs. Pearl drove on out of sight. Dutch had drawn into the side of the road and glanced at the girl beside him.

"Have you marked the spot?"

Angela nodded. Then she said: "Dutch—I . . ."

He glanced at her, and gave her a quick smile.

"You what?"

She looked at him for a moment, then shrugged helplessly.

"I guess I love you, that's all. And I'm sorry."

"I love you, too."

He leaned over, kissed her quickly, and went on: "We'll drive past to take a closer look at the place. Then we'll get out of here."

"Aren't we going to try and find out who lives there?"

"Yes, but not here. If you're sure you've marked the right place?"

"You know I'm good at map-reading."

"That's true. OK, then. That should be good enough. Let's go. We don't want to be noticed."

He put the car into gear and moved off slowly—but not slowly enough to draw the attention of the man at the gate, who turned out to be one of three armed guards resembling Israeli soldiers, the second of whom was standing nearby. The third was positioned at the bottom of the steps leading up to the front door and at that moment was talking to Mrs. Pearl, who had left her car.

They had a fleeting impression of a large, almost square building of at least four floors set back about thirty yards from the road, in stark contrast to the bolder arrangement of its immediate neighbours, and there seemed to be a temporary wooden building just inside the main entrance—possibly a guard room.

"Well, what do you think?" Dutch said, once they were past.

Angela shook her head.

"Sort of army post?"

"Or someone the Army thinks worth guarding pretty well!"

Angela paused for a moment, then she said: "Perhaps you were wrong in thinking the people after Billie were private individuals?"

"It depends on who's living there."

Dutch found the road forked as it climbed the hill, so he stopped, turned, and drove back.

By this time Mrs. Pearl had disappeared, and the soldier had resumed a position standing at ease at the top of the steps.

"Thirty-four," Angela said, just after they had gone past.

"The number of the house?"

"Yes."

"Good. That should help."

"How are we going to find out?"

Dutch glanced at her and grinned.

"Eli, of course," he said. "Cab drivers know everything!"

By the time they regained the centre of Jerusalem it was getting dark, and Dutch decided to call at the King David. He parked in a street round the other side of the YMCA and, leaving Angela in the car, walked the rest of the way.

He stopped at the desk to see if there had been any messages. If the clerk was surprised to see him, he covered it well; after checking the pigeon-hole beneath the reserve key for their room he handed him an envelope which contained a wire from Helen.

"Worried not to have heard from you. Please 'phone soonest."

"Is this all?" Dutch looked up, and saw the clerk watching him. He'd bet his boots he already knew what was in it.

"Yes, Sir. Do you want to make a call?"

"Why should I want to do that?" The man coloured immediately. He was evidently more stupid than Dutch had thought.

"Why ... in case you should want to send a reply," he stammered.

Dutch looked at him. He probably went straight home to his wife and children every night, and needed the few extra pounds he could make selling comparatively unimportant bits of information to anyone interested. He decided not to pursue the matter.

"I see." He nodded, appearing to accept the explanation, and at once the clerk's face flushed with relief. "No, I don't think so. Not just yet. But I should like to pay my bill up to date."

"Certainly, Sir." The man was now all smiles.

"Have there been any 'phone calls?"

"No, Sir. A note of any calls received is always put with incoming mail."

"I see. OK. Well ... I'm just going up to my room for a few minutes, but I'll be down shortly to settle up."

"Are you checking out, Sir?"

"No. I'd like you to keep the room. You won't see much of us, but we'll be around." Dutch paused for a moment, then a thought struck him.

"Would you like me to pay a week in advance?"

"No, no, Sir. That won't be necessary."

"OK then."

"I'll have your bill waiting for you."

"Thanks." Dutch gave him a final, reassuring smile, then made for the elevator.

He spent only a few minutes collecting some clothes they both needed. Then, after a last look round, turned off the lights, and went back downstairs.

He contemplated sending Helen a wire despite what he had

said to the clerk, but thought better of it. Wires were too public, and, besides, there wasn't anything he could say at this stage that would not simply add to his ex-wife's anxiety. She would have to wait until he had time to write a letter.

He paid the bill with some traveller's cheques, and left the hotel to return to the car where Angela was waiting for him.

He drove back to the apartment, twisting and doubling back several times to make sure that anyone trying to follow would be thrown off.

That, unknowingly, he was unsuccessful probably saved his life.

Chapter 12

The first thing they discovered on returning was a note from Billie: "Decided to pursue independent line. Don't worry if I'm not back tonight. Got to thinking about Paul's last note."

Dutch frowned and handed the scrap of paper to Angela; he went into the bedroom to phone Eli, taking the map which she had marked with him.

Eli had just returned from the wedding, and was in a jovial mood. He agreed at once to borrow a map from a neighbour who was also a driver and kept an identical one in his cab.

After a wait of several minutes, he came back, a trifle breathless.

"I'm sorry to have kept you waiting, Sir, but I took the opportunity to borrow a street directory at the same time. Now, Sir, I have the map in front of me, and am at your beck and call."

Dutch suppressed a grin, then gave the reference:

"It's that road which runs off the main highway at 3B—right the way up to 2C. Do you see it? I think it's called Derech, or it may be called Gan. I'm not sure. One may run into the other."

"Derech Gan, Sir. Oh yes. I have it. No . . . that's all one name. It means Garden Street in Hebrew. I'll look it up in the directory. Just one moment. I will have to put you down."

"That's all right."

This time Dutch didn't have to wait long. He could hear pages being flicked over the other end, then Eli came back on.

"Yes, Sir. I have it. What number did you say?"

"Number thirty-four. It's something to do with the Army. Maybe it's a hospital. I don't know."

"You did say thirty-four?"

"That's right. Have you got it?"

There was a brief pause, then Eli said: "Number thirty-four is the official residence of the Minister of Defence."

Dutch paused, then whistled softly. No wonder it had been crawling with armed guards. But what on earth was Mrs. Pearl doing there?

"What's his name?" he heard himself asking; but before Eli could say anything, he said: "Wait a minute, isn't he the guy who was supposed to have saved the country in the last war? What's his name ... Harzoy, that's it! I saw him on television. But he must be getting on now. Is it still him?"

"Yes, Sir." Eli sounded less than enthusiastic.

"Yes, of course. You've no reason to love him."

"He's probably the most hated man among our people. But we respect him. At least we know where we are with him."

"How old is he now?"

"I don't know. He must be past seventy."

"He must be close to retirement."

"Anyone else would have stepped down long ago, but he seems to go on for ever."

"No one goes on that long."

"No. Of course not. But they say he will die first. There are many younger men who have also proved themselves. But he is a legend, and few dare to suggest that he step to one side in their favour."

Dutch tried to remember everything he knew about the legendary general. Then he realised he was still holding onto the receiver and the longer the two numbers were connected, the greater the risk of anyone tracing them. He said: "Look—thank you for what you've just told me."

"Can I be of any other service to my friend?"

"Not now. But is it all right if I keep the car tonight?"

"Oh, yes." Eli's voice was light-hearted again. "I shall not be answering any calls tonight, saving only from you, if you should need me."

Dutch smiled.

"Have a good night's sleep then. I may well need you to-morrow."

"Very well. As a matter of fact, the wedding feast is still on.

I only came back to be by the 'phone in case you should call."

"You are a good friend."

"I hope so."

"Go back to the feast. I'll meet you with the car where we agreed."

"Yes, Sir!"

Dutch put the 'phone down smiling, but his smile faded as he walked back into the living-room.

"Well?" Angela looked up when she saw him.

Dutch paused holding on to the back of one of the chairs, then he said: "General Harzoy. Israel's most famous soldier ... currently, Minister of Defence."

"My God!"

"Number thirty-four is his official residence."

"What's he doing mixed up in all this?"

"We don't know that he is."

Dutch gazed into the distance for what seemed a long time to the girl watching him, scarcely daring to breathe for fear of breaking his concentration.

"But I mean to find out."

"How?"

Dutch turned, and walked into Billie's bedroom.

Angela waited. After a couple of minutes she heard the door of the hidden floor safe shut, and he came back into the room carrying a field radio receiver incorporating a small tape-recorder and two metal cylinders about two inches long.

"The bugs!" Billie had demonstrated them the previous day to help pass the time.

"If I can remember how they work."

He put all but one of the bugs down on the coffee table then examined it closely for a few seconds.

"You twist it half a turn ... like this: that's supposed to turn it on. And there's an extendable aerial this end. Wait a minute ... here it is." He pulled a piece of wire out for about three inches.

"Remember, Billie said they would work without doing this, but the pick-up and transmitting range is more than doubled if you do."

Angela looked from the bug in his hands to Dutch's face, her eyes wide.

"What are you going to do with them?"

"I'm going to find out what's going on in that house."

"How?"

"With your help, I'm going to plant these."

Angela gasped.

"But you can't. You saw for yourself, the place is stiff with soldiers. What if you're caught?"

"If I'm caught, I can still plant them. And it will still leave you on the outside with this."

He sat on the settee beside her, and switched on the receiver.

"Now ... just let's go on talking for a few seconds and ... with any degree of luck ... we should ... there, that's it—when the needle's dead between the eight and the seven. See?"

Angela nodded helplessly. She felt as if she were being swept along on a fast-flowing current towards rapids in a boat over which she had no control. The thought of him trying to get into that place, with or without her, made her stomach turn to water; but she couldn't raise a finger to stop him and, when the time came, she knew she was going to do whatever he asked.

"Now, then. Let's see how sensitive it is."

Dutch pointed the bug towards the receiver and at once produced a protesting shriek of feed-back. He pointed it away again quickly, then turned to the girl beside him.

"We're too close in here." He thought for a moment. "Look. Let's see how good it is with the aerial pushed right in. Then we'll know the worst. You take the receiver into the bedroom and close the door, and I'll put the bug under the chair and walk away from it counting a step at a time. You listen and tell me when the words become indistinct. OK?"

After several experiments they discovered that, with the tiny aerial retracted, the pick-up range was about six feet; but it was more than they could measure when fully extended.

They set out two hours later to drive back to Derech Gan. Dutch was wearing a dark lightweight suit of Close's he had found hanging in one of the closets, as well as a pair of blue tennis shoes with crepe rubber soles which he had also found. Angela, on the other hand, was wearing the shortest skirt she could find in Billie's wardrobe, and had paid particular attention to her hair and make-up. The receiver was in her bag, which was now resting on the back seat, and Dutch had the two bugs in his pocket, together with Eli's gun which he hoped he would not have to use.

They drew up noiselessly outside the next house but one, and switched off the lights. Then they waited for five minutes to see if they had attracted attention before Dutch got out and shut the door quietly. Angela shifted across to the driver's seat.

Although the front garden of Number Thirty-four was floodlit, the nearest street lamp was more than a hundred yards away, so Dutch was able to cross to the other side of the street and walk past in semi-darkness without risk of being seen. He then re-crossed and moved back towards the guarded entrance, so that he was just outside the zone of comparative light, and moved close under the wall, which he had already judged would be impossible to scale in a hurry without a ladder. The only practicable way in was through the front entrance, and that was what it was going to have to be.

He glanced down at his watch, then cursed under his breath and held it up against the available light. As he did so he heard the engine of the Mercedes, and watched as Angela drove to within twenty yards of the entrance before pulling into the side of the road and switching off the engine once more.

He saw her get out and look down at the tyres one by one, before stopping by the nearside rear wheel and uttering an un-ladylike oath which successfully attracted the guards' attention.

The two soldiers stood at the entrance, but moved no further while they watched her get out the jack. But when she came round into the light so they could see her better—even more when she bent down, deliberately without bending her knees, to poke feebly at the hub-cap with a screwdriver, to give them full view of her sensational legs, it became more than flesh and blood could stand. After glancing over his shoulder at the house, the more susceptible of the two walked towards her smiling and spoke to her in Hebrew.

Angela straightened up immediately and gave him one of her most devastating smiles right between the eyes. The effect was immediate and shattering.

"I'm terribly sorry," she gushed. "I don't understand Hebrew. Do you speak English?"

The soldier, who was a mere boy, grinned sheepishly.

"A little," he admitted. "Are you in trouble?"

"Well, yes—rather. I was visiting friends just down the road, and I hadn't gone more than a few yards when I felt something was a bit funny, and got out to find I'd got a flat." (She had let it half down while Dutch was moving into position.) "And the trouble is, you see, I've never changed a wheel, but I don't like to go back and bother them because I know they were going straight back to bed as soon as I left."

It is doubtful if the young man understood a tenth of what she was saying, but his course was obvious.

"Would you like some help?"

Angela beamed even more and rested her hand on his arm for a moment.

"Oh ... would you really? That *is* terribly sweet of you." The other shrugged, half embarrassed, half delighted, then he set to work while Angela bent down close to him, hindering his movements, although he wouldn't have asked her to move further away for all the tea in China; all the time she was chattering away, ninety to the dozen.

Unable to bear it any longer, the second guard looked over his shoulder at the one standing at the foot of the steps and grinned, jerking his head in the direction of the road outside. The other came to join him, and after glancing back at the house again, they hurried forward to join the party.

As the two of them bent down to help unscrew the wheel nuts, Dutch slipped out of the darkness and through the entrance, plunging immediately into the cover afforded by some shrubbery bordering the open space in front of the house. He paused for a moment, and almost immediately one of the guards raised his voice.

He froze, expecting them to come running back inside, but a moment later he heard another say:

"My friend wants to know why you are driving a taxi with an Arab number plate."

Dutch's blood ran cold and he heard Angela stalling.

"I'm sorry, I don't know what you mean?"

"This is a taxi," he heard the other say patiently, but several degrees less warmly than hitherto. "It also has a brown coloured number plate, which shows that its owner is not an Israeli citizen."

"Oh that!" Angela gave a peal of laughter and Dutch sweated, hoping she could think of something. His own mind was a complete blank!

"Well, you see, we're staying in this quaint little hotel in what I think you call East Jerusalem, and the brother of the manager drives it during the day, but lends it to me in the evening at a positively ridiculous rate. Look—I've got my passport in the car."

There was nothing he could do for her. But now the guards' attention was focussed in a way he couldn't possibly have foreseen, Dutch moved carefully round to the side of the house and out of the lights, where he found a semi-basement window half open.

As he rolled over the sill inside, he heard the engine of the Mercedes fire and the car drive off. God knew what had happened!

Once his feet were firmly on the ground he turned and stuck his head out of the window, listening to the sound of the engine fading into the distance. He expected to hear either the sound of shots being fired or a crash as the half-loosened wheel came off—or both; but neither occurred, and he eventually pulled his head in again and drew several deep breaths to try and stop his heart thumping.

All was still. Somewhere in the house above his head there was the sound of music, but it was barely audible, and certainly not loud enough to mask anyone moving around—as was borne out a few seconds later when he heard a door open and close; the sound of voices; then another door opened and all was quiet once more.

Dutch looked round: Now his eyes had grown accustomed to the dark he could see he was in a larder or storeroom, which led into a large kitchen; this had a back door and a staircase which led up to the rear of the house. It also had a dumb waiter which probably meant the dining-room was directly above, on either the ground or the first floors.

Dutch stuck his head into it, and looked up the shaft between the runners. All was darkness above. He then went to the back door and unlocked it, leaving it slightly ajar. He might be glad of the few seconds necessary to do so later.

He moved to the bottom of the stairs. There was a bend half-way up, which prevented him seeing to the top; round the corner a light was burning, but there seemed to be no-one around; so he began to make his way slowly to where he could see round the corner.

There was a loose board in the fifth or sixth stair which creaked like a rusty hinge. Dutch froze, convinced everyone as far as Tel Aviv must have heard it; but, again, nothing happened, and he rounded the corner, checked to see no-one was in sight, and then went up the rest of the stairs, to find himself almost opposite another back door and at the end of a passageway which led through to the front of the house and a well-lit marble-floored hallway. He had either to go outside or to pass along the passage-way; and so, after pausing to open this door as well . . .

He shut it again hurriedly when a door somewhere else slammed, giving him another few anxious seconds. Then he moved quickly towards the well-lit hallway, and stopped to find himself at the foot of another and much wider flight of stairs, leading up on his right and facing the front door, on the other side of which he realised that by now the guard would un-doubtedly have taken up his position once more.

He wondered again, momentarily, what had caused Angela to drive off like that, and what she was doing now. Trying to change the wheel, in all probability, before coming back for him—if she hadn't lost her nerve; but his rating of Angela's nerve was considerably higher than it had been a short time ago. Even so, the chances were she wouldn't be back for at least another ten minutes.

If the kitchen lift was anything to go by, the door to the left led towards the dining-room; but the house was too big for that to be the only room on that side, unless it was of truly ballroom dimensions. This meant that the door probably opened into a corridor which led to other rooms as well.

He decided against it, and opened the right-hand door instead. It was a large office, in darkness, containing as many as six or seven desks. At the far end was another door, through which he could see yet another desk.

On the wall was an electric clock with luminous hands which read eleven-fifty.

Dutch picked his way between the desks, deducing that this was where the General's personal staff worked during the day, and poked his head around the further door.

The office thus revealed was even bigger. It was laid out more like an operations room, with a huge relief map of Israel and her immediate neighbours on a table in the centre. There were few seats apart from some high stools round the table itself next to hooks where radio head-sets and boom microphones hung ready for those who operated the markers; but there were some chairs on a low balcony overlooking the table and at the desk immediately inside the door.

The only other thing peculiar about the room was its location. That a general should be interested in such a place was unremarkable, but that he should have a fully-equipped operations room covering the whole country at his official residence *was* unusual, surely—even though he happened to be Minister of Defence? But Dutch had little time for speculation. Here was the obvious place for one of the bugs, and it was only a matter of seconds before he had slid under the table and strapped it with some tape to the underside with the tiny aerial fully extended.

Dutch got to his feet quickly and dusted his knees. Then he noticed a small office leading towards the rear of the building. But although this was probably used by Harzoy himself for his own business—whatever that might be—the drawers were locked and the probable result of breaking them open was scarcely worth the risk the noise would entail; particularly as whatever papers were inside were probably in Hebrew.

He moved quickly back across the two rooms, and stood once more in the hallway listening before slowly mounting the stairs. The layout of the first floor was entirely different. A corridor ran the length of the house with numerous doors on both sides; and it was from beyond one of these that the music was coming.

Dutch guessed that the more important rooms would be at the front of the house, and he stood outside the door nearest the top of the staircase for a long time before venturing to turn the handle—at about the same speed as the second hand of a clock—before pushing the door open a fraction of an inch to see if the lights were on—which they were not—then opening it fully and slipping inside.

This was a drawing-room. There was a television set, a number of easy chairs, and a writing-desk by the window on the far side. The air held the stale smell of pipe tobacco, and there was a crack of light under the door to the right of the fireplace.

This must be the old man's private sitting-room. Dutch was sure he'd seen him in the newsreels covering the last war bending over maps set out on trestle tables in the desert, or climbing up on tanks to talk to the crews—*always* sucking a pipe. It was an ideal place to hide the other transmitter.

He looked round, then decided on the chimney. There was an electric fire standing in the hearth, but the fireplace itself did not seem to have been used for a long time.

He took the reel of tape from his pocket and was about to tear off a length, when suddenly the door not a few feet away opened, and an old woman wearing a dressing-gown stood in the doorway, light streaming past her.

Dutch froze. He had forgotten that Harzoy was married, and his wife still very much alive. He remembered reading about her too; she had been a pretty tough nut in her own right.

She said something looking out into the darkened room. It

sounded like a question. Then she noticed the half opened door leading into the corridor and went across to close it. The minute she turned she was bound to see him against the white walls!

At the last second he flung himself behind the nearest chair, and crouched down. She still couldn't help seeing him if she looked directly at him. But perhaps she wouldn't.

He heard a key turn. What was she doing that for? Then it sounded as if she had removed the key altogether, but he dared not look to be sure.

She was coming back. Dutch held his breath. But there was no sudden challenge or cry for help. She walked back within a few feet of him; through the doorway—probably into her bedroom—and closed the door behind her.

Dutch started to take a deep breath when he held it again. She was locking this door as well. How was he going to get out? All other thoughts vanished.

He went to the bedroom door and listened. His heart was thumping so much he had to hold his breath to hear anything. He heard her pick up a telephone and dial. She spoke in low urgent tones.

A few seconds later an alarm bell began to ring downstairs. The old bat had seen him all the time. She'd just made sure he couldn't get away first! He heard the sound of feet running up the stairs. He was trapped!

Dutch looked round desperately. He contemplated breaking down the bedroom door and trying to hold the old woman hostage; but the chances were she'd already got a gun trained on the doorway just waiting for him to try. There was only one other door, the one she'd locked first. There was a tattoo of blows on the outside.

This was it. Already guns would be pointing up at every window. What a fool to think that, just because he had managed to frighten a defenceless widow into doing something stupid, he could come walking into a place like this and get away with it. The best thing he could do was give himself up—if they'd let him!

There was a burst from a sub-machine-gun, and the door blew

133

open. He turned his head instinctively from the noise and saw, for the first time—immediately behind him and to the left of the fireplace—the shattered half-doors of the dumb waiter.

Dutch tore them open with his left hand, at the same time seizing a round stone paperweight from the mantelpiece with his right.

A young soldier jumped into the room followed by another as Dutch rolled the heavy paper-weight across the stone floor towards them shouting: "Look out—grenade!", hoping the word was the same in both languages.

It bounced and spun convincingly, and the two young men, whose eyes had not yet grown accustomed to the dark, suddenly encountered an object of about the appropriate size immediately beneath their feet, and fell over themselves as they dived out into the corridor again.

Dutch had already turned. Beyond the doors of the hatchway was empty space—and two thin ropes.

He had already slid half-way down and was just passing the dining-room when he heard another burst of gun-fire; whether hit by a stray bullet or unable to withstand the unaccustomed strain, the ropes parted suddenly, and he fell the remaining fifteen feet down to the kitchen.

Dutch realised afterwards it had been a blessing in disguise, for in doing so he shattered the bottom of the lift and was able to scramble out into the kitchen. He might otherwise have been trapped.

A hail of bullets fired down the shaft from above blasted the already shattered contraption behind him.

Then he saw the fuse box above the kitchen door.

In a moment he was on a chair flinging the fuses over his shoulder like salt; this took longer than simply throwing the main switch, but that could have been reversed equally quickly.

Section by section the lights went out upstairs and around him until the kitchen itself was in total darkness. Whereupon he flung the main switch, and felt for the remaining fuses by hand.

Upstairs he could hear shouting and cursing and the sound of people colliding. Then he saw a light from the stairway, and he realised several of the guards were coming down with a torch, cautiously—after all, they didn't know if he was armed.

He had just enough light to avoid the tables as he ran for the door. He removed the key as he closed it behind him as quietly as he could. Then he locked it.

There was a flight of stone steps leading up from the back door. He reached the top at approximately the same time as one of the guards; fortunately his eyes were more accustomed to the dark, and he saw the man a fraction of a second before the other saw him. From two steps down he gave him a punch in the groin that made him scream with pain and drop his revolver.

As he doubled up, Dutch stepped to one side and reached out with his other hand to pull the man past him and down the steps. Then he bent down and felt for the gun before setting off for the wall which ran along the front of the house, realising that his opponent had made no further sound since reaching the bottom.

Half-way across the lawn he ran into another soldier and both of them fell to the ground; in the struggle Dutch lost the revolver. He picked himself up, and, although quite badly winded, started off again; but before he had limped more than a couple of steps his right ankle was seized, and he fell over again while his assailant started to shout for help.

Dutch lashed out with his other foot; despite the comparatively soft shoe, he connected with something that gave slightly and turned the shouts into a shuddering gasp. But the damage had been done; already there were others running in the same direction.

He felt for Eli's gun, and pulled it out just as he was caught in the beam of a torch. He ducked and fired at the light, causing it to be dropped on the ground; a moment later a burst of machine-gun fire missed him by inches but hit the man beside him on the ground.

Dutch started to run. Some lights came on just as he reached the shrubbery; but they were evidently expecting him to make a dash for the entrance, and the few seconds grace, aided by the lights, enabled him to disappear from view and begin the frantic search for a tree close enough to the wall to enable him to climb over.

There was none. He reached the right-angle of the wall with the adjoining property. He was about to follow this in desperation, when he noticed that it was two feet lower and was without the usual protective spikes. The bushes also were closer together; this was an advantage in one sense, but they got in the way.

Pocketing Eli's gun, Dutch flung himself at the top of the wall. His elbows, face, and then the whole of his body hit painfully against the rough brickwork as his fingers felt for the edge; but his leap was too low, and he fell back again.

There were more lights behind him now, and he could hear a car being started. Any moment they would realise where he was, and the bushes around him would be raked with a hail of bullets.

He flung himself up again with all his might. He felt the edge of the brickwork cutting into his fingers—but they held. He consolidated his grip, and then pulled himself up; a second later his foot was over the edge, and he was lying on top of the wall panting like a stranded fish.

He heard a command followed by a prolonged burst of fire, which sent bullets smashing into the wall beneath him and showered him with brick chippings. When it ceased, he scrambled up past the spikes on the front wall to the frontage of the adjoining property, which was without such adornment.

Dutch dropped to the footpath, and immediately ran across to the comparative darkness of the other side of the road.

The guards at the gate had been waiting for him; but no sooner had they begun to fire when a car, whose driver was evidently blissfully unaware of what was going on, crossed the line of fire, and they had to stop.

The car slowed down just past the main entrance, and came to a halt, engine revving, close to where Dutch was crouched in preparation for a dash for freedom as soon as it drew level. He looked in amazement as the rear door was flung open and the driver, a man he had never seen before in his life, shouted in English: "Get in ... quick!"

Dutch flung himself in, and the car accelerated away with the door swinging wildly on its hinges behind him before it slammed shut of its own accord.

"Keep down!"

The words were scarcely out when the guards realised they had been thwarted, and opened up with everything they had; but by then the car had already passed the distant street lamp to disappear into the darkness beyond.

When he thought they were out of range, Dutch scrambled up to look out of the rear window; just before a bend cut off his view, he saw a car like the one he had encountered that first morning fling itself out of the entrance, and execute a tyre-torturing left-hand turn before starting after them.

"We're being followed," he shouted at the man in front.

"I should be surprised if we weren't."

The other flung the wheel round almost immediately, as they reached a road junction. When Dutch had picked himself off the floor, he realised they had almost doubled back on themselves, and were accelerating back down the hill towards the main road. There was no sign of the other car following them—yet.

He glanced at his rescuer for the first time, curiosity mingled with relief:

"Thanks."

"That's all right."

"You saved my life."

"Think nothing of it."

"Why did you do it?"

"Just happened to be passing."

"You might have been killed."

"Never really thought about it."

The exchange left Dutch completely baffled; either the man was a complete fool or he was incredibly brave. He glanced out of the window once more, but they had gone round another bend, and he couldn't see for more than a hundred yards. He turned round—and suddenly a shaft of light penetrated the gloom.

"Are you English?"

"Yes."

"My God—we've been waiting for you!"

It was the other's turn to look baffled.

"I don't think so."

"You mean you're not Close's replacement?"

"Who's Close?"

"Then what are you doing here?"

"I told you. I just happened to be passing."

They were nearing the main road, and the street lights enabled Dutch to take a closer look. There was something vaguely familiar . . .

"Do we know each other?"

"Don't think so."

"I'd swear I've seen you before somewhere."

"That's always possible."

He was going to say something else, but suddenly Dutch saw the Mercedes at the kerbside just in front, signalling it was about to pull out.

"Pull up in front of that car?"

"What?"

"That car in front. Don't let it drive off!"

The car slid to a halt at an angle in front of the Mercedes, and Dutch jumped out and ran round to the other side.

He saw Angela's face as she turned, then the Mercedes leapt back, engine revving, as the frightened girl tried to escape.

"Angela—it's me!"

The car jumped forward a few steps, and stalled. Then he snatched open the door.

"Move over quick. We're being followed!"

"I'm sorry, I thought . . ."

"Never mind."

He restarted the engine, then drove forward onto the pavement until he was level with the car in front, and wound down the window which Angela had hurriedly raised.

"Thanks again. I hope to do you a favour one day."

The other smiled briefly, and raised his hand in salute before driving away to join the main highway about forty yards further on.

Dutch brought the car back onto the road carefully. This was

138

no time to break an axle.

"What happened. Did you get in?"

"Sure."

In the driving mirror he saw the lights of a car sweeping towards them, but without undue haste he drove forward, and turned right towards Tel Aviv.

"Where are we going?"

"Back home."

"It's the other way."

"I know. We'll turn later. I didn't want to have to wait to cross over."

As they slipped into a gap in the traffic, Dutch saw the car behind them pull up at the "halt" sign where they had been not a few seconds earlier. It was a small Simca; even so, he drove some way down the road before doubling back; they weren't the only ones capable of changing vehicles. Meanwhile he gave as coherent a picture of what had happened as he was able.

"What happened to the other bug?" Angela asked when he had finished. "The one you were going to put in the fireplace?"

"I don't know." He had forgotten all about it. "I guess I must have dropped it. I really don't remember."

"I don't blame you!" Angela impulsively lifted his right hand to her lips, and kissed his fingers. "Don't ever take such a terrible risk again."

"But you've got a point. What *did* happen to the other bug?"

The girl shook her head.

"I don't care. Having you in one piece is all I care about."

"But if it's found, they'll realise what it is and search the place from top to bottom."

"You're not going back?"

Dutch gave a grin.

"Don't worry. I'm not that crazy! But if they find the one under the operations-room table, it's all been for nothing."

Angela was silent for a while, then she said: "Haven't you any idea where you dropped it?"

"The last time I remember having it was when the old girl came into the room."

139

"And after that?"

"After that, she locked me in, then 'phoned the guards."

"She must have nerves like steel. To see a man hiding in your living-room and not react!"

"She had the reputation of being as tough as her husband."

"Perhaps you dropped it under the chair."

Dutch nodded.

"Somewhere round there, or in the fireplace."

"Perhaps no-one will see it."

Dutch thought for a moment; then he suddenly turned half right into a slip-road which led off the main highway.

"What now?"

"Just a minute."

The road ran up to another which passed over the motorway by means of a bridge before swinging down to the left to join the Tel Aviv-bound stream. After pausing at the "halt" sign, Dutch followed this until they were back on the main road once more.

"Where are we going?"

"Back to the house."

"But you said you wouldn't . . ." Angela wailed.

"I don't mean to try and get inside. Half a mile should be near enough."

"For what?"

He jerked his head in the direction of the back seat.

"To see if we can pick anything up with that. We've woken them all up. They might be having some quite useful conversations.

"But they'll be on the look out!"

"I don't think so. They don't know yet, as far as we know, what I was up to. They'll hardly be expecting a man who escaped by the skin of his teeth to return so soon."

"No-one else would be barmy enough!"

"In any event, like I said, we needn't go too close. I pulled the aerials out of both of them, so about half-way up the avenue where you were parked should be close enough."

"I wasn't parked. I'd just managed to change the wheel!"

"What took you so long?" Dutch suppressed a grin at

Angela's answering snort of disgust. He knew that, contrary to the impression she had deliberately given the guards, she prided herself on her independence and never needed the kind of help women traditionally seek! She probably knew as much about car and aero-engines as he did himself, and could certainly change a wheel faster than most men under normal circumstances.

"For your information, driving on wheel-studs half-loosened jams them almost solid."

"Why did you drive off?"

"I had to. They were getting too inquisitive."

"So you just got in and drove away?"

"That's right. And they stood there and watched me. I made it look as if I thought they were getting too fresh. They were obviously in two minds, but they didn't stop me. They probably expected the wheel to fall off anyway!"

"It's as well they hadn't got any further!"

"That's what I thought. In another few seconds they'd have had the spare wheel out, and I'd let more air out of the other than I'd intended. It wouldn't have lasted two miles."

"Where is it now? The other, I mean."

"In the boot-'trunk', in your language!"

Dutch smiled again.

"Thanks. But I have lived in London long enough to have learned some of your weirder expressions!"

He slowed down. They were coming up to the bottom of Derich Gan. In another few yards they would need to make a right turn into the avenue which ran almost parallel and where, he guessed, they ought to be able to get within a few hundred yards of the General's house while still being at least half a mile away by road.

Chapter 13

"Yes, I'm all right."

Eli read the translation he had made in the pages of an old notebook of the receiver's tape. Then he paused for a moment.

"This is the old woman speaking."

Dutch nodded without saying anything and, after frowning again in concentration, the other continued:

"'I came back as soon as I heard what happened'—this is her husband; we heard him in the operations room earlier."

"Go on."

"'Have they any idea who it was?' she asked.

"'No, but it cannot have been an ordinary burglar,' he answered.

"'Is anything missing?'

"'They're still checking—but don't worry about it. Try and get some rest.'

"'Do you think someone has found out?'

"'I don't know. It's not impossible. But unlikely.'

"'Perhaps . . . you should put it off?'

"'If we do that, it might be too late. Besides, Anderson arrives the day before from Washington. I shall have a perfect reason for not being there.'

"'I don't like it.'

"'We've been into all that. None of us like it, but when the whole future depends on the outcome, what is the death of five or six?'

"'Innocent lives matter.'

"'They are heroes, every one. None will mourn more sincerely . . . but if they had not been so blind, none of this . . .'"

Eli looked up again.

"Then the tape ran out."

For a while the three of them looked at each other, then Dutch glanced at his watch. It was half-past eleven in the morning.

Angela said: "Well, that's the only part with any significance." She looked at Dutch.

"What are we going to do now?"

"What do you make of it?"

Angela shrugged. "If we knew who Anderson was."

"I think I do. He's Under-Secretary of Defense in the US."

"I see."

"He's probably coming over here to discuss arms shipments. The top man usually tries to stay out of it these days. It attracts too much publicity."

Eli snorted with disgust at this; but after a moment, Angela went on: "And so . . . he has a perfect alibi *not* to be somewhere he would normally have been the following day . . . where several people are going to get killed."

"And they're all heroes—but it's their fault; really, things are like this."

"What things?"

"In general, I guess."

"Then he must mean the Government."

"Yes."

Dutch turned away to look out of the window. "You'd never get the whole Government together in one place." He swung round to face them. "But you might get the Cabinet. All of whom have risked their lives for the survival of their country at one time or another."

"And who must now die for the same end."

"Right."

"But why should he do such a thing? It would be an act of treason."

Dutch came back from the window, and stood in front of them.

"Unless he believed them guilty of a greater crime, which only their deaths can purge."

"But what?"

The room was very quiet.

143

Dutch perched on the end of the table, looking down at them, and put his feet on a chair. Then he said: "Because he knew the answer to that is probably one of the reasons why Paul Close died trying to reach London."

"But, Sir, why London?" Eli began. "If he knew such a thing, why did he not go to the Prime Minister or someone else in the Government whose life was threatened?"

Dutch shook his head.

"I've no idea," he admitted. After a pause he continued: "But, on second thoughts, we could make a couple of guesses. In the first place, he may not have been sure who was in on it, and consequently, to whom he could go. After all, a private citizen can't just walk up to the Prime Minister and tell her he has reason to believe she is about to be assassinated. She's surrounded by a security screen that's no less impenetrable for being unobtrusive. Watch the newsreels—it's the same with all of them. They walk up to crowds, and shake people by the hand. It all seems so friendly and spontaneous, but it's always *they* who choose whom they want to meet not the other way round—as you see as soon as anyone else tries to push their way through. The only way would be to try and make an appointment through the Prime Minister's secretary; and unless you could think of some other reason sufficiently convincing, you'd have to spill the beans. And from then on it would be anyone's guess who got to hear about it."

"What's your other guess?"

Dutch paused again; then he gave a brief shake of his head, and shrugged.

"That it's something which involves far more than the security of the State of Israel."

"But how could an attempted coup be so serious?"

"I don't know. We don't even know if that is on the agenda. But if so, I guess it depends on what is meant to happen next."

Angela shook her head frowning, as if a fly were buzzing around inside.

"But this isn't South America! Israel has often been threatened from the outside, but not internally."

144

"I agree. No matter who started it, I don't think any 'coup', as such, would stand a chance."

"Perhaps he's gone off his rocker in his old age!"

Dutch smiled.

"What's funny?" Angela challenged.

"Just the way you put it."

"Oh, well—you know what I mean!"

Eli did not smile; instead, he shook his head and said slowly: "If you are right, it could be bad for my people."

Dutch nodded, and his smile faded.

"I agree," he said. "But I don't believe Harzoy *has* ... gone off his rocker." He paused for a moment, then went on deliberately: "In fact, I think he's very firmly *on* it, and knows far better than we do the likely reaction of his fellow-countrymen to any step he might take. And that could be bad for all of us."

Eli left, promising to return at four o'clock in the afternoon.

Meanwhile Angela slept to try and make up for the previous night, and Dutch lay beside her, intending to do likewise, but unable to do so while all the possibilities coursed through his mind.

Eventually he decided that as soon as Billie returned he would try again to persuade her to return with them to London. The information already in their possession should more than justify her in disobeying orders to remain, and it would achieve the double objective of putting the whole thing in someone else's hands—after all, if one Israeli wanted to knock off another, it was really none of his business—and remove both girls from danger. He also promised himself to take a far greater interest in Billie's career from now on. The British would owe him a thing or two by the time he had told them everything, and he would insist on her being given a safe job somewhere—like counting the yachts in Monte Carlo harbour until she married one of the owners.

It would take some doing—getting Billie to come back with them, not marry a millionaire. She'd probably try and get him to go without her, but he'd refuse point blank. Eli would be able to smuggle them across the border to Amman, and from there it would be plain sailing—unless the Britisher who saved his life last night turned up and started complicating things ...

Dutch woke up with a start and realised there was someone at the front door. Perhaps it was Billie. He got up without disturbing Angela and made his way in stockinged feet to the front door to find Eli standing there grinning.

"My God! Is it four o'clock already?"

He stepped back to let the other in, then shut the door and padded after him yawning.

"What time *is* it?"

"Four o'clock, Sir." Even as he spoke, Dutch heard the call to prayer coming from the Old City.

"Just a minute. I'll get my shoes."

"Yes, Sir. Have you decided what to do?"

"Could you get us to Amman without anyone knowing? That's including my daughter."

Eli grinned broadly.

"Nothing would be easier." Then he looked sad. "That means my friends are leaving so soon?"

Dutch nodded.

"As soon as Billie returns. Hang on a minute."

He went back into the bedroom and fetched his shoes, tie and jacket, then tiptoed out again, closing the door behind him. Women needed their sleep more than men, and there was no point in waking Angela.

When he had finished dressing, he wrote a note telling Angela of his decision, and that he was going with Eli back to the hotel to get their things. Then they went down in the elevator to the underground park, and within a few minutes they were driving back into the centre of the city.

The desk clerk of the King David turned before Dutch had a chance to speak, and pulled two pieces of paper from the pigeon-hole. Both were calls from Inspector Morgan asking him to 'phone back, one timed at nine-thirty that morning and the other about an hour ago.

146

When he had read them, Dutch took his key. Perhaps it would be better to return the Inspector's call from upstairs before checking out—since his arrival he had learned that local events had a habit of altering his plans with little notice. The number of Police Headquarters was given in the first message, and for once he had little difficulty getting through.

As soon as Morgan came on the line Dutch knew something was badly wrong. The Inspector had been pleasant if not affable the last time they had met; but now his voice sounded grim in contrast. Dutch's first thought was that something had happened to Billie.

"You'll be relieved to hear your daughter is unharmed and in perfect health," Morgan answered coolly in reply to his question. "In view of your anxiety, I was anxious to contact you. By the way, where did you spend the last couple of nights?"

"With friends."

"Where?"

"In Tel Aviv."

"Please give me their names and addresses."

"Why?"

"Because I would like to satisfy myself that you are—how shall I put it—on the level, Mr. Deutsch. You see, your daughter was arrested early this morning in a top secret military establishment in the north of the country."

"What!"

"And I should be glad to be assured that you had nothing to do with it."

"There must be some mistake."

"Oh, there was! We're not very fond of foreigners who accept our hospitality and then try to spy on us."

"You've got it all wrong."

"Have I? How should I have it then?"

Deutsch hesitated. Then he made a decision.

"Look, could I come and see you now?"

"I was hoping you'd say that."

"Give me half an hour."

"It only takes ten minutes from the King David."

"I want to fetch something to show you. I also want to tell my wife what's happened."

There was a pause, then he heard Morgan say: "No, I don't think that's a good idea, Mr. Deutsch. I don't want you disappearing again. Besides, according to our records you have no wife. The lady accompanying you is the wife of a well-known British businessman."

Dutch paused for a moment. Then he said: "I'd still like to tell her what's happened."

"Can't you reach her on the 'phone?"

"Maybe."

"Then I suggest you stay where you are and ask her to bring whatever it is you want to show me."

Dutch hesitated again, then he capitulated. There was nothing he could do.

"Splendid," he heard Morgan say.

"I'll still be about half an hour."

"Don't try and disappear, will you?"

"Trust me."

"I'm sure I should. But unfortunately policemen have such cynical natures—it must be the work. Even while we've been talking two of my cars have moved into position outside your hotel. But don't worry. They will not embarrass you in any way, just so long as you do what you say you are going to."

"Don't worry."

"Very well, Mr. Deutsch. Half an hour then."

"Thank you."

Dutch rang off and, before the switchboard could intercept, dialled the apartment where Angela was waiting, having since woken up.

"Get down to the hotel as fast as you can," he ordered. "And bring the recorder with you."

"Is anything wrong?"

"I don't want to talk now in case the number's being traced. Just do what I ask. But make sure you walk several blocks before stopping a cab. And don't come all the way to the hotel. I don't want whoever brings you being questioned."

"Dutch . . ."

"Angela—please!"

"All right. I'm on my way."

He put the 'phone down quickly. It takes at least three minutes to trace a call, even when trained engineers are already waiting at the exchange, and he hadn't been on the 'phone for more than thirty seconds. Then he remembered Eli waiting outside. There was no point in involving him, but how to tell him what had happened without being seen by the men Morgan said he had stationed outside?

He thought for a moment, then picked up the 'phone and asked for an outside line. This was given with some reluctance; it was the policy of the hotel that only local calls could be dialled. But the promise of a substantial tip finally persuaded the operator to put him through.

He dialled Eli's number in Bethlehem where he knew there was a radio controlling all the locally-owned cabs, and spoke briefly to his friend's wife. Then he put down the 'phone and went over to the window.

At first, nothing happened, then suddenly the entire line of cabs, including Eli's, drove away; but when they returned a few minutes later, taking up their positions again in strict order, his friend's was not among them.

Dutch smiled grimly, but he continued to look out of the window until he saw Angela walking up the drive towards the front entrance. Then he turned and went out quickly, closing the door behind him.

"Am I to understand that you expect me to do some kind of a deal with you, Mr. Deutsch?" The Inspector looked at him sternly across the desk.

"That's right. My daughter's freedom to leave Israel immediately in return for information. The kind which, if known, could save this country from civil war."

The Inspector's eyes widened still further. Then he snorted with disgust.

"Mr. Deutsch, I know you have the reputation of being an

imaginative writer, but you mustn't take me for such a fool!"

"I've got proof. Right here." Dutch pointed at the recorder on the desk between them.

"A recording?" The Inspector allowed himself a thin smile. "Anyone knows they can be faked."

"In half an hour? To produce this would have taken the co-operation of dozens of people—all of whom spoke perfect Hebrew—which neither myself nor Mrs. Romay understand."

"So you say."

"Oh, come on!" Now it was Dutch's turn to snort. Morgan paused for a moment, then he said:

"I'll certainly listen. But you could have had it ready against such a contingency."

"I'm telling you, I had no idea where Billie was. Why do you think I came out here looking for her?"

The Inspector dismissed this with a gesture. Then he said: "In any event, I can't promise anything. If your daughter is found guilty of espionage, there is nothing I or anyone else can do to save her from just punishment."

"But she's not guilty. And this will help to prove it. On the contrary, she was seeking information concerning others in high places who are planning to overthrow the Government by force, beginning with the assassination of most of the Cabinet at their next meeting, which is due to be held the day after Marshall Anderson, the United States Under-Secretary of Defense, arrives from America."

"Mr. Deutsch, if you want me to listen any further, I suggest you stop there. I've never heard anything so preposterous in all my life. We still have many enemies, but no Israeli would raise his hand against the duly elected Government. This is a democracy."

"Yes it is—just as long as you keep it that way, and not a moment longer. Do you think you're immune from the forces that always seek to destroy such a seemingly unworkable idea? There are always those who think they know better than anyone else ... and heaven help any nation where one such is already so highly thought of as to be almost above the law!"

The Inspector now looked at him in genuine amazement. Either the American believed what he was saying, or he was putting on the best acting performance he had ever seen, on or off the stage. He swallowed, then said quietly: "And are you suggesting there is such a person here in Israel?"

"Yes, I am."

"Who?"

"General Harzoy!"

After a moment, Morgan opened his mouth to protest; but, before he could say anything, Dutch reached forward and turned on the recorder.

"I take it you would recognise his voice?"

"Of course. He's often spoken over the radio and on television in the past—particularly during our darkest hours."

He turned from the set to look Dutch full in the face.

"Sometimes it seemed only his words and his courage stood between us and disaster. So I'm warning you—if this is a trick, your attempt to besmirch the character of such a man will weigh heavily against you."

Dutch paused; then he nodded.

"This is no trick, I promise you," he said softly. "Listen!"

In the cab on the way to Police Headquarters he had wound the tape back to the beginning of the conversation between the General and his wife. Even as he pressed the button marked "play", he realised how much depended on their assumption that that was who they were. But after only a few seconds, the expression on Morgan's face told him he had no further worries on that score.

When the tape ran out Morgan sat hunched in his chair for a long time. Then he said huskily: "How did you get this?"

"I broke into his house, and left a small transmitter."

"You had no right to do such a thing."

"In the circumstances I hardly think a little matter of breaking and entering makes much difference."

"Who are you working for?"

"I'm working to get my daughter out of this place in one piece. Believe me, until I came here looking I knew none of this. But, as you know, within hours of our arrival I was shot at; and later on that day another attempt was made on my life."

"I didn't know that."

"In this case, the would-be assassin was shot himself."

"Where was this?"

"In the Old City."

"Of course. He fell from the minaret."

"That's right."

"And it was you he was shooting at?"

"Undoubtedly."

Morgan rose from his chair, and came round to face Dutch, who had remained standing after switching on the recorder.

"But why, Mr. Deutsch? If you are a private citizen simply trying to trace his daughter, why should anyone wish to kill you?"

"That was the beginning—asking that question, I mean." Dutch pointed again at the recorder. "And that is the end—at least, as far as I'm concerned."

"And in between?"

"Is quite a story."

Morgan hesitated for a moment. Then he glanced at his watch. "We have all evening," he said, and walked round to his own side of the desk and touched a button. "Would you like some coffee?"

To all intents and purposes, the waiting-room into which they were shown later was a large cell where they were to spend the night while Morgan decided how to act on their amazing information. In any event, he wanted to keep them under his surveillance—for their own protection as much as for any security risk they might present.

Although the bed was hard, Dutch slept more soundly than at any time since their arrival. Billie was in deep trouble; but at least she was safe, and the entire affair was out of his hands—or so he thought. He only hoped Morgan would heed his final warning to be careful himself from now on.

Before asking for the light to be put out, he had borrowed a pen and some paper, and had written a letter to Helen. Then he had lain down beside Angela, who was already asleep from sheer exhaustion.

A breakfast of cheese, rolls, hard-boiled eggs and coffee was brought to them on a tray; then, quite unexpectedly, a sergeant appeared with a message from the Inspector to say that they could return to the King David, but must remain inside the hotel. The sergeant and a constable accompanied them, but waited outside discreetly while Dutch handed over their passports—another condition of their release.

The remainder of the day was spent in enforced idleness. They swam in the pool, read newspapers, and had lunch. Afterwards they went upstairs and made love before sleeping for an hour. The rest of the afternoon was spent by the pool where Angela sun-bathed in a few pieces of bright orange cloth, causing considerable disquiet among the other female guests, many of whom were quite attractive, but could not begin to rival her as she lay on a mattress, apparently unaware of the effect her presence was having. Some of the younger males frantically tried to show off on the diving-board. There was a chapter of accidents as the young waiters serving beside the pool, not always looking where they were going, collided with chairs and tables and trod on guests. A noisy row developed between a middle-aged American and his wife on the opposite side of the pool, which ended when the lady stalked off, with her husband following sheepishly after one last lingering glance in Angela's direction. It all helped to pass the time and Dutch smiled, knowing she was not only perfectly well aware of the effect she was producing but actually revelling in it. He knew she would never betray him as long as he gave her reason to hope; but the admiration of other men was something he would have to learn to live with if they were to be married. He knew it was an important part of her self-confidence, and to become upset about it would have spoiled everything.

That she was beautiful was obvious. That she was also intelligent and amusing, as well as being loving, had been a discovery that had never ceased to delight him, and that she was brave was no longer in any doubt; but something in her make-up, he knew, made her desperately dependent, despite her attempts not to burden him. He didn't fully understand why, but again if they were married, it was something he would have to live with for the rest of his life . . .

"Darling, do you think we should go in now and get changed."

Dutch woke up to find Angela sitting up beside him shading her eyes from the sun, which was settling over the tops of the buildings immediately in front of them. She was so lovely and so loving. He couldn't expect a cast-iron guarantee before he decided—and he couldn't put off a decision for ever. If he didn't know at the end of these days that they were spending together, perhaps he never would; and perhaps that meant he didn't deserve the happiness he knew she could give him.

"I'd like to take a bath to wash off this oil; and then, if we have time, perhaps we could go down to the bar and have a drink before dinner?"

Dutch looked at her and smiled. "I couldn't think of anything I'd like better," he said.

"Great!"

Angela held out her hand, but he stood up before helping her to her feet.

As he followed her inside he was conscious of the eyes of the whole place following them—and he couldn't have felt happier about it!

Dutch heard his name paged, and a boy in uniform came over to their table.

"Mr. Deutsch, Sir?"

"Yes."

"You're wanted on the telephone, Sir."

"By whom?"

"I don't know, Sir."

"Can't I take it here?"

"Sir?"

"All right." Dutch smiled and rose from the table. "Excuse me." He caught the look of apprehension on Angela's face. "I won't be a minute."

He followed the boy out into the lobby, and went into one of the 'phone booths where the receiver was already off the hook.

"Hello?" He closed the door behind him—and at once smelt almonds. He dropped the receiver and tried to pull the door open; but it was awkward, and rapidly he felt his senses slipping away; his limbs seemed like lead, and his legs could no longer support the weight of his body. He fell heavily against the hinge of the door; this promptly gave way, so that the whole door fell out into the lobby with a crash of glass, Dutch on top of it.

He took two gulps of air, and then managed to raise himself on one elbow to wave away the gathering crowd.

"Cyanide!" he croaked. "Get out of here!" The crowd rapidly dispersed. Fortunately the Bishop whom he had pushed to one side some days earlier grabbed someone by the arm, and together the two of them helped him out of danger.

The police were called. They appeared as if by magic in less than two minutes and cleared the lobby, while firemen with breathing apparatus were called to deal with the remains of a small glass capsule which Dutch had unwittingly crushed as he stepped inside the booth. It transpired that no call had been put through by the switchboard and the bell-boy who had called him from the dining-room had never been seen before.

After making a statement, he rejoined Angela in the dining-room who was waiting almost beside herself with anxiety.

"What's been happening?" she hissed as soon as he sat down. "I heard all the commotion, but they wouldn't let us out."

"Eat your ice cream."

"I don't want any ice cream. Not till you tell me what's been going on. And what's happened to your clothes? You look as if you've been rolling on the floor!"

"I have."

"If you don't stop treating me like a child, I'm going to scream!"

"Someone tried to kill me. Again."

Angela's jaw dropped. Then she swallowed.

"How?"

When he had finished telling her, she still didn't want any ice cream. And as he was feeling distinctly detached himself, despite his outward composure, they left the remains of the dinner and went upstairs.

The 'phone rang at eleven o'clock. Dutch looked at it as if he expected it to start belching poison gas, and Angela froze as she turned from the window from which she had been trying to discover the positions of the police who were allegedly watching the building. Then he pulled himself together and picked up the 'phone.

"Mr. Deutsch?"

"Inspector Morgan!" The accent was unmistakable, even if his voice sounded more than a little strange.

"Listen carefully. You were right. Trust nobody. Get to the Prime Minister and warn her. It's the only way."

There was a sound very much like a shot at the other end, and he heard Morgan gasp.

"Warn her . . ." he whispered. Then the 'phone went dead.

Dutch put down the 'phone. Then he turned to the girl who was watching him wide-eyed.

"Come on! We've got to get out of here."

"Was that a shot?"

"I think so. Morgan says trust no-one."

"What about Eli?"

"He doesn't know about him."

Getting out of the hotel without being seen was easier said than done; it was comparatively early, and there were plenty of people about, in addition to the police stationed outside. But Dutch decided they dare not wait, for fear that Morgan's call would have set in motion a train of events which might erupt at any moment.

What was needed was a diversion. He moved back to the 'phone.

Fifteen minutes later two cab drivers drew up outside the main entrance almost simultaneously. One got out and began to accuse

156

the other of jumping the line. A furious argument ensued, and when one of the waiting guests tried to intervene, both men turned on him and the police were hastily summoned. They appeared again with miraculous speed—the same pair, as it happened, who by chance had been passing earlier . . .

They seemed relieved that there was nothing more serious to contend with this time. While they were trying to pacify both drivers and the guests who had joined in meanwhile, Dutch and Angela slipped out the back way, and walked a couple of blocks to where Eli was waiting.

Chapter 14

"The chances are she's not there anyway."

Dutch put down the 'phone, and turned to the other two, who had been listening in silence. He had tried the Prime Minister's office as soon as they were safely back in the apartment; but the call had been side-tracked, and eventually he had become convinced that someone was trying to trace it.

"We'll try again in the morning," he told them; "and if we still don't have any luck, we'll have to think again."

"Good." Eli nodded and rose to his feet. "Then I will come back around eight o'clock; and I'll bring some food. There still seems to be plenty in the freezer, but you need some bread, and some milk—and maybe some eggs?"

"Bless you, Eli. What would we do without you?" Angela got up, and hugged him. The big man grinned from ear to ear as they walked towards the door.

"Then we will make a plan," he said with a confident wink, just before he let himself out. "I have one or two ideas."

They never heard Eli's ideas for reaching the Prime Minister.

The following morning all radio and TV channels were dominated by reports that during the night she had been kidnapped, together with three of her Cabinet colleagues. Nobody yet knew who was responsible or why; doubtless this would emerge when ransom demands were made. During the course of the raid a police inspector had been shot dead, and it had been reliably learned that an American and an Englishwoman who had disappeared from their hotel in Jerusalem a few hours earlier had been seen in the vicinity just before the crime had been committed.

There followed a pretty accurate description of both of them, and people were asked to remain close to their sets so as not to miss developments. The Security Council of the United Nations had been informed, as political motivation seemed almost certain, and early arrests were expected.

Dutch turned the radio down. So that was it! News of the leak had reached Harzoy and, ever a man to turn a set-back to his advantage, he had struck while they were literally asleep!

There was a knock on the door, and he glanced at Angela who was staring at him, waiting for him to say something.

"Eli must have come early." He looked at his watch, then nodded. She went to the door but, instead of their friend, she was confronted by an old man wearing pebble glasses. He smiled.

"Shalom!"

"Shalom!" Angela managed to return his smile. He made a remark in Hebrew, and she looked round for moral support.

Dutch came to join her. "Do you speak English," he asked politely.

The other paused for a moment frowning; then he smiled again.

"Yes. English. You are English?"

Dutch was about to qualify his answer, but he nodded instead.

"We are teachers studying your educational system."

"I am sorry. I do not understand when you speak so fast."

Dutch forced a smile. "Never mind," he said more slowly. "What can we do for you?"

"Ah!" The other nodded. "I live in the apartment just above, and last night it was very cold. My wife and I were wondering if your heat was—working?"

"Yes."

"That's right—working, too; or if the—how do you say it?—the people who own the building?"

"Landlords."

"Yes." The old man beamed again. "If the landlords had not turned it on." He made a gesture and pulled a face. "They always put it off as long as possible!"

"Just a minute, I hadn't noticed." Dutch turned and went to feel one of the radiators, while Angela and their visitor nodded and smiled at one another. Then he came back shaking his head.

"No. Ours is off too."

"Then I will telephone the—landlord—and tell him."

"Fine."

There was a moment's pause.

"We wondered if perhaps there was a fault in our section."

"Doesn't seem like it!" Angela gave him a smile, and Dutch nodded as she made to close the door.

"How do you like Israel, Mr. . . . ?"

"Smith."

"Mr. Smith."

"We like it fine."

"My name is Mindel."

"Pleased to meet you."

"We lived in Moscow. But always our children are saying to us: 'Papa, we should go to Israel'—so one day, we came."

"And are you happy?"

"Oh yes—it is very nice. But we did not expect it to get so cold at night."

"It's the altitude."

"The what?"

"The height. Jerusalem is quite high up."

"Oh, yes. The altitude!" For some reason this amused the old man enormously, and he cackled merrily while Dutch and Angela exchanged glances.

"Look, Mr. Mindel," Angela said sweetly, when he had subsided. "It's lovely talking to you like this, but both Mr. . . ." She looked wildly at Dutch.

"Smith."

". . . Mr. Smith and I have to be at College soon; so if you'll excuse us?"

"Yes, of course." Mindel nodded and smiled pleasantly. "You must go to work." Then he shrugged: "Me, I'm just an old man, I don't have to go anywhere. Except my wife sends me on errands."

"Yes, well—if you *will* excuse us."

The other stood back and raised his hand. "Of course—I talk

too much." Angela smiled, and nodded again as she started to close the door.

"Um ... Now that we've met," Mindel said suddenly stepping forward again and Angela heard Dutch groan behind her.

"Yes?" She managed another smile.

"Perhaps you and Mr. Smith would like to come upstairs and meet my wife."

Angela opened her mouth, but before she could say anything he continued: "I don't mean now, of course. Perhaps one evening?"

"Yes. That would be lovely!"

"Good. When?"

"Well, we're pretty busy at the moment. We often have to stay late at the University."

"I thought you said you went to College?"

"It's another word for the same thing."

"Oh!"

"We'll come up and introduce ourselves our first free evening."

"Fine. When do you expect this to be?"

Unable to contain himself any longer, Dutch turned and walked through into the bedroom and closed the door.

"I'd just like to be sure we're in," the old man continued.

"Well ..." Angela bit her lip. "Do you go out much?"

"No. Hardly ever!" He cackled with mirth again. Before either of them could say any more, the elevator doors opened behind him, and Eli stepped out.

Angela saw him hesitating for a second trying to step back before the old man saw him; but, no matter how bad his eyes, there was nothing wrong with his ears. He turned round at once to see who it was.

Seizing the opportunity, Angela said briskly: "Ah, there you are. Come in a minute will you, we're almost ready."

Eli stepped forward reluctantly, and Angela made way for him before turning back to face the other.

"Now Mr. Mindel, we really must go. It's been very nice meeting you, and as soon as we have a moment, I promise we'll come up and say hello to your wife. 'Bye for now." She then shut the door firmly in his face, and took a deep breath. The bedroom door opened and Dutch came out looking tense.

"Well," he said, "that's that. Hello, Eli!" Then he turned back to Angela. "Now we can't stay here."

"Why not?"

"Why not! Do you have to be quite so stupid?"

"I'm sorry."

Angela hung her head, while Eli looked at him in amazement. Dutch looked from one to the other. Then he took a deep breath, and put his arms round her.

"I'm sorry. It's not your fault."

She put her arms around him, and neither of them said anything for a while; then Dutch glanced at Eli.

"You heard the news?"

The other nodded. "Yes. It's being repeated every fifteen minutes on all channels. That's why I came straight away."

"Thanks!" Dutch then released the girl and held her so he could speak to her. "So you see, it's only a matter of time before old what's-his-name upstairs hears about it and begins to wonder —unless he's deaf as well as blind!" He let go, and moved restlessly to the window to look outside.

"No," Angela said, looking after him. "He's certainly not deaf."

Dutch paused; then he turned to face them. "Then we can't stay here."

"Where will we go?"

"I can answer that." Eli spoke first. Then he turned to Dutch. "You said once you could not come to my home for fear of involving my family."

Dutch nodded.

"And I respected you for it. But now you must see there is no alternative. Already there are road blocks between here and Bethlehem. Every policeman in the country is out—but I know a way we can get through."

Dutch stood in front of him, but there was nothing he could say. After a moment Eli smiled and embraced him warmly.

There were several suitcases in a cupboard, and it was only a matter of minutes before they had packed everything they needed. Dutch insisted on putting in a second receiver/recorder and the remaining bugs—not that he imagined they had any further use, but in case the old man called the police and the apartment was searched, the less evidence left lying around the better.

For the same reason, he decided against leaving a note for the British agent, if and when he ever turned up. It served him right. It was his fault they were all in such a mess, and the way Dutch felt as he finally closed the door behind him and joined Angela in the lift—Eli having taken the suitcases down earlier—the whole of British Intelligence could sink without trace as far as he was concerned.

The route followed by Eli was devious beyond description, relying, as it did, on mainly unmade roads once they were clear of the city. On one occasion they had to pull up and double back when they spotted an unexpected patrol a few hundred yards ahead, and they were lucky not to have been seen. Eventually they arrived unnoticed and unharmed to be received by Eli's wife, Rebecca, and his excited children who included a good-looking dark-eyed girl of about sixteen and eight or nine younger children and a baby.

A room was rapidly prepared. Dutch realised that, by local standards, Eli and his family were well off: The house was quite a substantial one on the outskirts of the little town on a hill with a view of Jerusalem in the distance; even so he felt guilty at the disturbance they were causing until he saw how much genuine pleasure their visit seemed to be giving. But for the knowledge that Billie was trapped, it would have been an experience both of them would have long remembered, chiefly for the way they were accepted by those who offered everything they had with a generosity and affection neither of them had ever met before. Quite apart from their missing passports, flight was impossible. The news broadcast in the early afternoon informed the nation that those responsible for the kidnapping of the Prime Minister and her colleagues had now identified themselves as agents working for Egypt and Syria—this despite reported denials from both Cairo and Damascus—and that the condition for their safe return was a doubling of the compensation to be paid for resettlement of the Palestinian people, together with territorial concessions to both countries in addition to those agreed at the peace conference—which, it was alleged, had been forced upon the Arabs by outside pressure. Their own departure from the original hiding-place in Jerusalem was also reported, and Dutch deduced that the old man upstairs had eventually put two and two together and had reacted as expected.

"But why?" Eli exclaimed when the news bulletin had ended. "They must know the Jews would never agree."

Angela looked at Dutch, who had remained silent throughout the broadcast. "But it isn't Egypt and Syria, is it?" she said.

Dutch shook his head, and again there was silence before he said: "There can only be one explanation. Harzoy wants war!" He paused, then looked at each of them in turn. "It may be an insane ambition, but it makes sense of everything that's happened."

He moved into the centre of the room before continuing: "Don't ask me to figure out why he should want such a thing. Maybe there's logic behind it—maybe there isn't. But one thing's certain, as far as he's concerned the nation's in danger, and that's the only thing that could drive a man like that to do what he's done already."

Eli shook his head in bewilderment, but Dutch went on with growing confidence: "It didn't add up before, that a man who had done so much—given so much of himself to preserve his country—would risk tearing her apart in a civil war; but if he saw some external threat—one perhaps that no-one else would face up to—then he might risk anything."

Angela stared at him. Then she said: "Do you mean he's done all this to bring something to a head?"

Dutch shrugged. "Maybe there are things going on behind the scenes none of us know about," he answered. "Perhaps he feared some kind of deal between the super-powers over Israel's head that would, in his opinion, have diminished her security still further. And maybe no-one else would agree with him. So what could he do? Although the Army's behind him, most of it's out of uniform during peace-time, and the reservists would never have gone along with a forceful overthrow of the Government. So, he comes up with an idea that will not only remove the opposition, but give him an apparent reason for striking at his country's enemies before anyone can do anything about it."

"By having the entire Cabinet assassinated."

"Except for him," Dutch nodded. "But, at least, our involvement has prevented that. In all probability, the four who have been kidnapped are still alive somewhere."

"Where?"

"At his house, I would imagine. Who would dream of looking there?"

"But he can't keep them there for ever?"

"Perhaps not." Dutch turned away. Then he turned back sharply. "On the other hand, once he's done whatever he thinks necessary, it would be in character for him to release them, then throw himself on the country's mercy. And if it could be shown he was right all along, who would condemn him?"

"The super-powers you mentioned just now."

"Possibly." Dutch paused for a moment to think. "Then maybe he'll have to kill them after all."

Eli said suddenly: "It seems to me there are four people in all this we can trust, besides ourselves."

The other two turned to look at him.

"The Prime Minister and her three colleagues."

"That's true." Dutch nodded.

"And I was thinking. If they could be released, so they could tell the people what had really happened, the General's plan, whatever it is, would collapse."

They looked at each other for a long time, then Dutch said quietly: "You're right. There is no other single step we could take more certain to kill it stone dead. The sixty-four thousand dollar question remains—How?"

The discussion went on long into the night. It was a relief in one sense to be able to concentrate on a positive objective; but although there was no shortage of ideas, at least to begin with, each was rejected in turn as being impractical for one reason or another.

Undoubtedly, by that time the guards would have been re-inforced and would be on full alert, particularly if the prisoners were being kept there, although it was extremely unlikely that the lower ranks would have any precise idea of whom they were guarding. But much had been made in the reports of the involvement of the American and the English woman still at large, and the lower ranks would probably have been warned that the break-in the other night was a reconnaissance for an attempt to kidnap the General, if not the attempt itself. Harzoy's appointment as acting head of Government had been unanimously confirmed earlier in the evening by the remaining Cabinet members, and no effort would be spared in protecting him. Even if, by some miracle one or other of them managed to enter his house again, to escape with the four kidnapped politicians, perhaps still drugged or injured, would be virtually impossible.

As the evening wore on, the flow of ideas lessened until eventually the conversation petered out and they were left looking at each other in depressed silence.

Dutch glanced at Angela. She had not said anything for a long time, and seemed completely exhausted. He was feeling pretty tired himself, and Eli looked as if a good night's sleep wouldn't do him any harm either. Perhaps, in reality, the whole thing *had* grown too big for them, and in spite of his impatient rejection earlier of Angela's suggestion that they should try to get back to England without Billie—a suggestion which he knew had placed her in a false position, for she was as concerned for Billie's safety as it was possible for anyone to be who was not her own flesh and blood—he realised, as she had obviously done, that if they were up against a dead end, the only course open which might help would be to tell what they knew to the outside world.

They thanked Eli for everything he had done; but then he asked if they would mind waiting a moment before actually retiring. After a pause, his wife and all their children trooped into the room in their night attire to say goodnight. Dutch realised with a pang of guilt that they had all been waiting patiently outside until they were ready, so that not even the youngest, should fail to wish their guests a good night's sleep under their roof.

When they had gone and Eli had shut the door with a final smile and a bow, Dutch saw Angela's eyes were full of tears, and he realised that she had been equally moved by the little ceremony. He thought then how lucky he was not to have been alone through all this, and how patiently she had borne the rough end of his tongue when things had turned out badly.

He took her into his arms and asked her forgiveness, whereupon she kissed him with surprising strength and then made love with a fierce passion which he realised only later was tinged with despair.

It was long after dawn when Dutch was awoken by a knock on the door. Eli reported that during the night his car had apparently been stolen. He turned to glance at where Angela should have been lying still asleep, and saw that she too had gone. The explanation was on a piece of paper lying on his clothes, which she had gathered up in the night and folded in a neat pile beside the bed.

"Darling," it read. "While you were talking I suddenly realised it was the easiest thing in the world to get into the General's house, providing you didn't bother about getting out again. You just walk up to the front door and knock! I know this only solves half the problem, but I'm taking one of the bugs with me hidden where I hope they won't look, and if I can find out anything which might help you solve the rest, I'll broadcast at hourly intervals on the hour if I can.

I love you. Angela.

PS. By the way, while I was dressing I suddenly remembered. Armageddon is a real place in northern Galilee. A plain, I think, not far from Nazareth. I wonder if Billie got the same idea?

Tell Eli he'll find his car outside the Damascus Gate. I'll take a cab from there.

Chapter 15

With the aid of some boot polish, Dutch darkened his hair and plastered it flat down onto his head. He also borrowed some of Eli's old working clothes, and one of the latter's friends managed to produce some tinted plain-glass spectacles with steel frames. With these, some make-up base, and one or two other touches, he managed to alter his appearance to such an extent that Eli swore his own mother would not have known him. In fact he looked like any number of Arab workmen who, under a recent Agreement, poured into Jerusalem daily from the outlying districts. His bus journey with Eli into the city was delayed for a time while a young Israeli soldier cast his eyes over the passengers; but the man's eyes never paused as they swept over the pair of them, and within a minute they were on their way once more.

The bus station was just behind the Pilgrims Palace Hotel, which almost faced the Damascus Gate, and in a short time they were climbing into the Mercedes, whose keys Angela had left in the ash tray. Dutch rested the bundle of rags he had been carrying, which concealed the other radio receiver, carefully on the seat between them.

There were no control points between the centre of Jerusalem and the bottom of Derich Gan, but as they approached the avenue, Dutch saw that there was a road block across the end of the road, and told Eli to drive on.

"What now?" Eli watched the road block disappearing in his rear-view mirror. The entrance to the parallel avenue was also guarded.

Dutch glanced behind them.

"They certainly don't intend anyone to get near the place."

"Can you blame them?"

"I guess not." Dutch paused for a moment, then he faced the front. "We'd better not go much further. There's bound to be a control point along here. Take the next right if there's nobody guarding it."

The turning enabled them to cross over and head back towards the city. Dutch glanced at his watch; it was just coming up to ten o'clock.

"Slow down a bit, will you?"

Eli nodded. Dutch bent forward and disconnected the lead to the loudspeaker from the car radio, and plugged it instead into the back of the portable receiver.

They reached the point opposite the bottom of Derich Gan just as the last few seconds ticked away. For a moment it seemed there was a signal; then it was lost in a haze of static which no amount of tuning was able to disperse.

Eli took the next turning right again, and climbed out of the valley through which the motorway ran. He pulled off the road and stopped when they were almost at the top of the hill, and they both got out. The road led to the small town of Tsova. Unlike Derich Gan, the top of which they could see running down the valley opposite, the land on that side had few houses, and they were able to wait without attracting attention until eleven o'clock.

For the benefit of any drivers who did happen to pass, they put on a show of changing a wheel; but this did not happen more than half a dozen times and they had plenty of warning, as the road in either direction was visible for half a mile.

Eleven o'clock came, but, although there was less background static on this occasion, there was still no distinguishable signal, and Dutch began to wonder if they were within range.

He made himself concentrate on this possibility. It stopped him thinking too much of any other, and he shaded his eyes as he looked across the intervening distance. "If I had a pair of glasses, I could probably pick out the house from here," he said. "It can't be more than two miles as the crow flies."

Eli followed his gaze in silence for a while; then he said:

"Unless it's lower down the hill." He paused, then looked at Dutch. "How would that affect reception?"

Dutch shook his head. "I've no idea," he admitted. "It wouldn't improve it exactly."

He turned to face Eli, then glanced at his watch.

"Let's try again at noon. And if there's still nothing, we'll try and get closer."

The other nodded, and they settled down to wait. They passed some of the time in desultory conversation, but mainly they were concerned with their own thoughts. Noon passed with nothing to show for it, so they began by jacking up the car and removing one of the wheels, which they locked in the boot so that any police or army patrol who stopped to investigate would think that the owner had taken the wheel to have a puncture repaired— Eli wrote a note to that effect, which he left under one of the wipers. Then, after checking to make sure there were no cars coming, Dutch slung the receiver carrying-strap over his shoulder, and they struck out over the boulder-strewn ground diagonally down the hillside, so that eventually they would reach a point exactly opposite the Derich Gan estate.

The sun was almost directly overhead, and the heat reflected off the rocks so that, before they had walked more than two hundred yards, both of them were sweating profusely. After twenty minutes they had walked back along the side of the valley for about a mile, to reach a point some four hundred feet lower, where they found the top of an escarpment from which the land fell away much more steeply, and they were able to see the whole of the estate quite clearly. The main road below was also plainly visible, as was the house—and even the soldiers guarding the front entrance.

Dutch realised the escarpment had cut off the direct line of sight from the car, and he took heart from the possibility that perhaps this was why they had failed to hear from Angela. But one o'clock passed without them hearing anything, so they waited yet another hour trying to shelter both from the blistering rays of the sun and from anyone on the opposite side of the valley who might wonder what they were doing during the heat of the day; they hid in the shadow of one of the larger boulders which, at least to begin with, fell away from any who might be interested in their activities. But, although the shadow lengthened as the afternoon wore on, it gradually shifted, so they were forced to choose between observation and perspiration, and spent the rest of the time in the sun.

Two o'clock passed; then three. The radio seemed in perfect working order, and now they must be easily within range.

Perhaps the bug had been found despite Angela's confidence that she had hidden it where no-one would think of looking; and, as each hour passed in continuing silence, Dutch found it progressively more difficult not to torture himself by dwelling on all the possibilities—among them, that Angela had simply been taken out into the back garden and shot.

He knew then how much he loved her, and the thought that she had possibly walked to her death to try and help him—because he had led her to believe that he could never be happy if anything happened to Billie, beside whom her own life was less important —almost made him groan aloud with remorse.

He loved Billie, of course. He had risked his own life for her; but, when all was said and done, she was in this because she had wanted to be, and to suggest that he would deliberately sacrifice the girl who loved him more than anything else in the world . . .

"It's almost five o'clock, Sir."

"What?"

Dutch looked up. Then his brow cleared, and he nodded, reaching forward to turn on the set.

". . . have to try now. I may not get another chance—they're waiting outside."

It was Angela. She was alive. A wave of relief and happiness swept through him. If he could ever put his arms round her again, he would never let go.

"She told me there is only one person whose loyalty is beyond question, and that is Brigadier Doud, Commander of the Haifa garrison. Tell him that there are five gates to Armageddon. Then he will know what to do. I must go now. Goodbye, darling.

172

Take great care. I love you."

Dutch and Eli returned to Bethlehem to make preparations for the journey. They decided against attempting it at night, when any patrols would be extra suspicious; early in the morning would be the best time.

During the course of the evening Eli borrowed some papers from a friend living in Nablus who was on a visit to his relations in Bethlehem for a few days. The identifying photograph was over-exposed, and could pass for one taken of Dutch in his new guise; moreover the papers described their owner, Yasim Rokkan, as a fruit and vegetable wholesaler whose business necessitated extensive travel, a good cover if they were stopped and questioned.

They set off, therefore, at five when the commercial traffic was already building up. Although the route down to Tel Aviv and along the coast would be by far the quickest, Eli chose the slower road along the range of mountains which ran like a backbone along the entire length of the country from north to south, dividing the coastal plain on one side from the Jordan valley on the other. The road also passed through Nablus, which gave additional credibility to any explanation they might have to give.

"What happens if they talk to me in Arabic?" Dutch asked as they were getting into the car.

Eli shrugged.

"Tell them you're a Turk. There are quite a few in business there, and they always keep themselves to themselves."

"To the extent of not being able to understand the local language?"

"To the extent of refusing to unless they have to. If anyone tries, just shake your head firmly and answer in English. They'll think you're pretty stupid, but it won't be anything unusual!"

Dutch shook his head as Eli started the engine. Then, with a wave to his children, he drove out of the tiny yard behind the house onto the main road.

"D'you mean to say people behave like that?" Dutch asked when they had finished waving.

"Oh, yes." Eli glanced at him with a grin. "With most it's just snobbery. But it can be useful not to understand *English* on occasion. Particularly when tourists are trying to tell you they want some change!"

They passed the two road blocks on their way into Nablus, and another three between the town and the sea; but in no instance did the soldiers give more than a passing glance to see if they bore a resemblance to the photographs in the top right-hand corner of their papers before waving them on, mainly because of the huge traffic jams that were building up as a result of the checks.

After a while Eli switched on the radio and listened to a news bulletin in Arabic, translating snatches here and there as they drove along. Dutch heard of the world-wide concern being felt at the kidnapping. Harzoy had not said anything yet, but the kidnappers, it was reported, had evidently managed to smuggle their victims successfully out of Jerusalem and probably out of the country; otherwise the almost unprecedented search which had turned Israel inside out would surely have been successful. There were rumours that a helicopter had flown both kidnappers and kidnapped under the radar screens to Alexandria—a story that was hotly denied over Cairo radio—and the Egyptian Government had become so concerned that, in addition to appealing to the Security Council of the U.N. to do what they could to resolve the situation, they had invited the head of Interpol to set up a search organisation in Cairo, promising every assistance in trying to track down the "gang"—if indeed they were hiding inside Egypt's borders.

There were extracts from the world's press and remarks from various heads of Government, all of whom condemned the outrage and forecast dire consequences if the criminals were not soon caught—just when it had seemed that the provisional agreement between the Israelis and their neighbours was showing signs of turning into a permanent settlement, thanks largely to the additional concessions the Jews were reported to have secretly offered. Even the Palestinian guerrilla organisations, which had refused to disband until they were certain that deeds would follow words, condemned the kidnapping as contributing nothing to the just aspirations of the Palestinian people and, more than likely, adding strength to the reactionary forces within the Israeli Government, which was still opposed to a permanent settlement.

Just after they had passed through Nablus, a broadcast of music from Beirut was interrupted with a report from one of the Palestinian organisations that they had just received a 'phone call from the kidnappers—describing themselves as "heroes of the just cause for the liberation of all Palestine"—announcing that, unless there were signs of their demands being met within twenty-four hours, one of their hostages would be shot and his body left in some public place in the middle of Cairo as proof of their intent. Another hostage would be shot every twenty-four hours thereafter.

"They didn't say what they'd do when they'd run out of hostages," Dutch remarked grimly when the news-flash had finished. "But I've a darn good idea."

"War?" Eli glanced at him, and Dutch nodded.

"That's right. They'll kill two birds with one stone—if you'll forgive the analogy! They'll silence those who could have testified that the whole thing was a put-up job, and by the time the fourth body is discovered everyone will be in such a frenzy they'll agree to whatever Harzoy suggests."

"It doesn't give us much time."

"No."

Dutch relapsed into silence. The thought had just occurred to him that, if they carried out their threat to the letter, it was inconceivable they would not also dispose of their fifth prisoner.

Eli had already discovered that the garrison was situated just south of Haifa. This meant that they would not have to drive through the city itself, as the road they were following joined the coast just ten miles short on the same side as the army camp. Soon afterwards they were stopped for the last time, and he was able to get precise directions, explaining that his passenger had an appointment with the Quartermaster to discuss the supply of fresh provisions.

The camp was laid out on the lines of an old British army barracks, with rows of wooden huts on one side and a large parade ground on the other, surrounded by various administrative buildings. The whole area was surrounded by a barbed-wire fence.

In peacetime the barracks were usually more than half empty but now there was great activity, with soldiers everywhere; and the cab had to wait behind a convoy of several trucks bringing in further reservists before they finally drew up outside the guard-room.

Dutch got out and made a display of paying off the driver. There was no point in involving Eli any further; and, if things did not go as planned, it was vital that he remained free to take whatever course remained open. Eli drove away to wait at a pre-determined spot a few miles down the road; if Dutch had not reappeared by sunset, it was arranged that he should return home. He also took the papers Dutch had borrowed; clearly he had no further use for them, and there was no point in putting their real owner to any further risk.

The sentry muttered with impatience while this was going on, but Dutch turned to him as soon as the cab had pulled away and said crisply: "I want to see Brigadier Doud."

"Where are your papers?"

"I haven't got them with me."

"Oh?"

"As a matter of fact, my passport's being held at Police Head-quarters in Jerusalem."

"What?"

"Is he in? The Brigadier, I mean. If not, I'd like to wait."

"Why d'you want to see him?"

"I want to give myself up."

The other looked at him with a faintly dazed expression.

"Why? Who are you?"

"You'd hardly expect me to discuss matters concerning your commanding officer standing here at the gate, would you?" He pointed at the guardroom. "So just run along in there, will you,

176

and find out if the Brigadier's in? Tell him what I've just said. And if he's not around, you'd better arrest me, or he'll put you on a charge!''

As it happened, the Brigadier was not available; but Dutch was told that he had been informed, and was on his way back to the camp. He was put in one of the cells, and given a mug of coffee. This was so awful that he wondered if it was not part of a softening-up process to sap his stamina prior to the forthcoming interrogation; but it had been several hours since he had had anything to drink, and it was getting increasingly warm, so he swallowed a few mouthfuls before pouring the rest through the bars of the window.

The camp was a hive of activity. There was little doubt that the process of mobilisation had started, but how far could it get when, after the last conflict, which had brought the super-powers so close to collision, they had sworn to collaborate instantly to prevent anything similar happening again?

He watched some soldiers cleaning their weapons behind one of the huts, then from behind the locked door came the sound of boots clattering on the floor, as if everyone in the room had suddenly jumped to their feet. A moment later he heard a key being fitted into the lock.

''Stand up!''

A tough-looking sergeant entered the room and stood to one side. Dutch turned from the window to face the next man to enter the room, a swarthy, thick-set man with a luxuriant black moustache whom elsewhere Dutch might have mistaken for one of the brigands who still haunted the Judean hills.

''You want to see me? Who are you?''

''My name is Deutsch,'' Dutch said evenly. ''You may have heard, I am wanted in connection with the kidnapping.''

''You!''

''Yes, Sir. I have come to give myself up. But before you decide what to do, I wish you would allow me to speak with you alone.''

''Anything you have to say would be better kept for the authorities in Jerusalem.''

Dutch took a deep breath. Then he said steadily: "But I have a message for you from the Prime Minister."

"Where is she?"

"I'll tell you, if you will grant my request." He saw the other hesitate, and added beneath his breath: "There are five gates to Armageddon."

Doud looked at him, and his eyebrows almost disappeared beneath his beret. Then he turned to the sergeant and ordered him to wait outside. The man obeyed, casting a look at Dutch over his Commanding Officer's head that was a mixture of curiosity and suspicion.

"Well?"

Dutch took a step forward.

"Perhaps we should sit down?"

Doud glanced at the small table which stood against the wall with two collapsible chairs facing one another; then he nodded, threw his beret on the table, and pulled out one of the chairs. As he did, so Dutch noticed with surprise that, in contrast to his bushy eyebrows and moustache, the top of the Brigadier's head was completely bald.

"Well, start talking," the other said, as soon as they were seated.

Dutch hesitated for a moment, then decided to jump in the deep end:

"The Prime Minister and her colleagues have not been kidnapped by Arabs," he said, "nor by me. The stories reaching the Press are plants designed to mislead the people of Israel and ordinary soldiers such as yourself as to the true state of affairs. The intention is deliberately to create an atmosphere in which another war against the Arabs is inevitable, under conditions that seem justified to World public opinion—in particular, the guaranteeing powers."

"You're mad!" Doud half rose out of his seat.

"Please hear me out before you decide that," Dutch pleaded. The other hesitated, then sat down again. "Very well," he said. "But this had better be good."

Dutch nodded. "Very well. Would you tell me first, please,

why should the Prime Minister say I was to trust you and no-one else?"

Doud hesitated again. Then he allowed himself a brief smile. "Possibly, because I am her half-brother. We have always been a close family!" Then the smile was gone.

"Now you answer me a question. Where did you learn the phrase 'Five Gates to Armageddon'?"

Dutch paused. Then he said: "I think you'd better hear the whole story from the beginning."

It took a long time. So long, in fact, that the sergeant waiting outside the door looked inside once to assure himself that all was well. After Dutch had finished his story with an account of the wait on the hillside and of Angela's last message, Doud remained silent for at least a minute before rising to his feet slowly, almost absentmindedly replacing his beret.

"Well?" Now it was Dutch's turn to ask the question.

The Brigadier looked down at him and his eyes seemed to burn. Whatever the Prime Minister's reasons for trusting him— and Dutch doubted if their blood relationship was the only reason —he really did look a formidable character, and if anyone could do anything about the situation, it might be he.

Doud said quietly: "Leave it to me now."

Dutch stood up.

"You *do* believe me?" he asked.

"You speak like someone who has had a bad dream. But I cannot afford not to believe you. We can at least find out if the process of assembly has begun. And if that is so, the chances are that you are telling the truth."

Dutch looked at him, completely mystified.

"Assembly," he said at last. "What assembly?"

Now it was the Brigadier's turn to look baffled.

"But surely you know," he said. "You yourself gave me the phrase."

There was a period of silence, then Dutch ventured: "Five Gates to Armageddon?"

"Precisely." There was another pause. Then Doud remarked:

179

"It's the code for the assembly of the bomb."

"Bomb! What bomb? An atomic bomb?"

Doud laughed.

"Oh, no, my friend. That's what everyone thinks we've got up our sleeve. But we abandoned that years ago."

"Then what?"

The Brigadier hesitated. Then he made a decision: "Very well," he said solemnly. "If you're telling the truth, you have a right to know."

"And if not?"

"I shall personally see to it that you do not live to repeat what I am about to tell you."

"Fair enough."

"The bomb in question is of a type we do not believe anyone else in the world possesses—not even the great powers. For the want of a better word, it is called a 'neutron bomb'. Its explosive power is beyond even that of the hydrogen bomb; but it is completely clean, so that an army can sweep into a devastated area before the dust has even settled and without any kind of protective clothing whatsoever." He paused for a moment, then continued: "It is so secret no-one below the rank of Battalion Commander even knows it exists, and for security reasons it is dispersed in five separate components at different places throughout the country."

"No-one, other than the commanders of the top secret establishments concerned, knows exactly what it is they are guarding so carefully; no others know where the hiding-places are except the five ministers who must each release the component in his charge for incorporation in the assembly."

Dutch said slowly: "You mean that this thing is so lethal, it takes the five concerned to act together before it can even be assembled?"

"That's right." Doud looked at him with a peculiar expression on his face. "Not even I know where the pieces are—but I *do* know who must give their consent."

Dutch stared into his eyes for several seconds before he realised the significance of the last remark. Then he drew in his breath sharply.

"Harzoy ... and the four who were kidnapped!"

"Which would seem to support your story."

"But what happens if some of the five aren't available?"

The Brigadier shrugged, but Dutch could see beads of perspiration on his forehead; eventually he replied: "I imagine the rest may act without them."

"So, if Harzoy's the only one left—it's up to him alone."

"That would be so. And once the bomb has been assembled, it only requires the Prime Minister and the Minister of Defence in concert to authorise its use."

"But that's him again. He's both, for the moment!"

The Brigadier nodded. Then suddenly Dutch slapped a hand to his forehead.

"My God—of course, that's it. *That's* how he can strike before anyone can do anything to stop him."

"If he uses the bomb, nothing can save them—not even Russia."

"But what happens then?"

"That is anyone's guess ..."

"Does he imagine the kidnapping of four Cabinet Ministers will justify such a thing to the outside world?"

"I suppose it depends on how he intends to use it."

"But millions of people will be killed. Nothing could justify that!"

Doud paused, then visibly pulled himself together:

"I'll do what I can," he said. "But the only one who can be sure of stopping it is the Prime Minister herself."

"Have you got enough men?"

"Not to start a civil war. But that would be unthinkable. I would have to go along if that was the only alternative."

"Even at the risk of starting a world war?"

The Brigadier permitted himself a thin smile. "You Americans and Europeans always get so—how do you say—uptight about that. If you're fighting for your life anyway, it scarcely matters what it's called."

He paused, then went on: "No, I do not think that will be

181

necessary. We have, after all, two advantages: The General does not know how much of his plan is known—and he will certainly not be expecting a raid in strength on his own house at this stage. Of course, if we do this and the Prime Minister is not there—we stand a fair chance of being shot for treason!"

The two men's eyes held each other, then Dutch said quietly: "She's there. And so are the others."

"Well, let us hope so, for all our sakes."

The Brigadier took a breath, then he drew himself up and said briskly: "Now, Mr. Deutsch. While we have been talking I have thought of a plan."

"Can I help?"

"I'm not sure. We'll have to see how it works out."

He suddenly held out his hand.

"If you're right, and I don't see you again, thank you for what you have done already."

Dutch wasn't entirely happy about the way he said this; but he decided against pursuing the matter, and shook Doud's hand briefly before the Brigadier turned and rapped on the door with his cane to be let out. As he was leaving, he looked over his shoulder and said: "Remember the Prime Minister's warning. Speak of this to no-one else. *No matter what happens.*" Dutch barely had time to nod before the door closed—and he was alone.

Around two o'clock someone brought him a chicken sandwich and a glass of beer. After that he was left to his own devices.

Later that afternoon the door swung open and a police Inspector entered the room accompanied by a constable.

"Richard Deutsch?"

"Yes?"

He had been lying on the bed looking up at the ceiling for the past half hour, but at once he stood up eagerly.

"I have a warrant for your arrest on two charges: espionage and kidnapping."

Dutch's jaw dropped as the police officer continued: "You are not obliged to say anything, but it is my duty to warn you that anything you *do* say may be taken down and used in evidence against you. Do you understand?"

"Yes, but . . ."

The Inspector turned and nodded to the man beside him, who produced a pair of handcuffs and, before Dutch could say anything else, stepped forward and fastened them round his wrists.

"If I were you, I should save it."

"Where are we going?"

The Inspector gave him a bitter smile.

"To Jerusalem, of course. They've been expecting you!"

Chapter 16

Dutch sat in the back of the police car, his mind still in a whirl, he barely noticed when it began to get dark. Suddenly he became aware that the car was slowing down, and saw that several cars had drawn across the road in front forming a barrier.

The driver and the Inspector, who was sitting in front, exchanged glances, and the latter made a remark in Hebrew. They were dazzled by the lights of the cars facing them, and both men wound down their windows, to find that they were surrounded by men in civilian clothes, most of whom held guns aimed at them.

Dutch and his companions were made to get out. Those in front were ordered to lean with their hands on the bonnet, but the men to whom he was handcuffed were made to produce their keys and release him.

A short burst of sub-machine-gun fire burst the front tyres of the police car, and another wrecked its radio; then the four policemen were ordered back inside.

Dutch was led away to one of the waiting cars, and a moment later he was being driven away from the scene at high speed down a side road.

Apart from the fact that he was no longer handcuffed, Dutch did not find his situation very different. He was still sitting between two total strangers—both of whom were armed and neither of whom would answer any of his questions. After about ten minutes the convoy drew up at a cross-roads where two other cars were waiting. He was made to get out and to walk over to the leading vehicle, to find the Brigadier grinning at him through the window.

The other got out, and clapped a hand on his shoulder before offering him a cigarette—which for once, Dutch felt he needed.

"I must apologise for the rather theatrical nature of your escape, but in this way, not only is my own loyalty to the Minister confirmed—he must, after all, have his doubts in view of my relationship to the Prime Minister, and news of your arrival in Haifa was bound to reach him one way or another—but also, you can render most valuable assistance."

"How's that?" Dutch drew on the cigarette and felt better.

"By diverting attention, thus giving us more time. News of your escape will soon reach the General. He will then undoubtedly order efforts to be redoubled to bring you in, dead or alive."

"I see."

"You will be the hare, Mr. Deutsch—and while they are hunting you they are not so likely to be wondering what we are doing."

"What *will* you be doing?"

"Moving my best men into key positions. Within twenty-four hours, if we have that long—so maybe sooner—the Prime Minister will be free, and we shall have occupied the television centre in Jerusalem so that she can go straight on the air and tell the people what really happened. Then it will be all over."

"Can't I stay with you?"

"No, no. That would not do at all. You would be instantly recognised. Your new description is everywhere. Besides, I want you to give them a run for their money; you seem very good at it. Why don't you try altering your appearance again?"

"If this goes on, I won't need to. I must have aged ten years in the last couple of hours!"

The Brigadier laughed, and clapped Dutch on the shoulder again. "But it's good you can make jokes. Keep them running, Mr. Deutsch, and leave the rest to us."

Dutch sighed.

"Well, OK. If you think it will help?"

"Help? I'm sure of it." He glanced over Dutch's shoulder. "And now I see my men have changed back into uniform. Where would you like to start? I'm going on to Jerusalem to see the

General. In the circumstances, it would look very odd if I didn't try to find out what was going on." He shrugged. "Of course, I shall accept whatever explanation I'm given, but it will also give me the chance to see how many troops he has surrounding the house. I understand he's moved Headquarters in there officially now."

"When you say 'start', what do you mean exactly?"

"I mean continuing the diversion."

"Well, it might as well be Jerusalem as anywhere."

"Good. We're not likely to be stopped."

In fact, it had already occurred to Dutch there was something far more pressing than merely drawing attention from whatever the other was planning. His mind harked back to what Doud had said about the result of the Prime Minister's broadcast: That it would then be "all over". But would it?

He decided not to discuss what was on his mind. Undoubtedly, bringing the *coup* to a halt must be the Brigadier's first priority; even if Dutch had stopped to argue the point, the chances were that he, as an Israeli, would still have considered this the most important. But it would not be the end of the matter—not if the new weapon was already assembled and under Harzoy's personal control. He would no longer be able to make his purpose seem legitimate, but it wouldn't prevent him from achieving it. He who would so willingly lay down his life for the land he loved would not be stopped from doing what he thought necessary for its preservation, even if the whole world turned against him— providing enough people were sufficiently under his sway to help. And it would not take many in the final analysis—a bomber crew and ground staff; or a rocket crew—whichever method had been chosen.

The Brigadier dropped Dutch outside a 'phone box on the outskirts of Jerusalem. Neither man asked the other what they intended to do next; the two men merely shook hands and hoped they would meet again.

Dutch waited until the two cars had driven away, then he looked round to see if there was anyone about. The box was so well lit he was as conspicuous as if he had been about to step onto a stage—he had already ascertained that the simple expedient of removing the light bulb was prevented by a vandal-proof shield. But, apart from the occasional car, there was no-one. He went inside and dialled Eli's number.

Rebecca answered the 'phone. Eli hadn't returned yet, but she seemed in great excitement, and told him that a friend had been waiting to see him for more than two hours.

"A friend? You mean one of Eli's?" Dutch asked.

"No, Mr. Deutsch. One of yours. Oh, I'm sorry Eli is not here to help you. I know—I will ask one of his cousins."

"Just a minute," Dutch put in hurriedly. "This friend. What does he look like?" By now all the alarms were ringing inside his head. What "friend" could possibly know where to find him? Or anyone else, come to that.

"Well—he's a real gentleman," Rebecca answered. She paused for a moment, then went on: "As a matter of fact, he looks rather like you. Like you usually look, I mean."

Dutch lowered his voice:

"Look Rebecca, if it's the police standing there, just say ... 'I don't know when he'll be back' ... just like that, and I'll know they're waiting for me."

"No, no, Mr. Deutsch. It's nothing like that, really. Would you like to speak to him?"

Dutch thought rapidly. Then he said: "Yes. Maybe that would be a good idea."

There was a moment's pause, then he heard the 'phone being handed over.

"Mr. Deutsch?"

"Yes."

"I hope you don't mind me describing myself as a friend. We've only met once, but I did save your life, if you remember?"

"The Englishman!"

"That's right. Well, we do seem to keep bumping into each other, don't we?"

"Oh, come off it, Mr. . . . ."

"Codron, actually."

187

"Mr. Codron. You're not going to tell me you just *happened* to be passing where I've been hiding from the police!"

"Well, not exactly."

"I mean, I'm very grateful for what you did, but say you stop assing around and admit you're the British Agent we've all been expecting."

"No—really. I hate to disappoint you, but I have no idea what you mean.

"Then, how come you knew how to find me?"

"Well, it so happens I've a very good memory for figures, and I happened to remember the registration number of the vehicle you got into the last time we, er, saw each other."

"So get to the point. What d'you want?"

"Well, I happened to be passing the house where you had, er, a spot of bother the other night. And what should I see but a car draw out—several cars as a matter of fact—and sitting in the back of one of them was the young lady who was waiting for you on that occasion."

"My God, when was this?"

"Um, about three o'clock this afternoon. I—um—thought you'd like to know."

"Did she look all right? I mean, she *looked* all right?"

"I only caught a glimpse. She was very pale—and beautiful, if I may say so. I don't think she'd been injured, if that's what you mean."

Dutch breathed a sigh of relief.

"Thank God for that, anyway."

"Yes. Amen to that."

"What did you say?"

"I said: 'That's a good thing.'"

There was a moment's pause. Then Dutch said: "Did you see which way they were going?" It was a vain hope, but after everything that had happened, anything was possible.

"Well, yes—as a matter of fact I did. I *was* a little curious, and followed for a while. At a discreet distance, of course."

Dutch felt his heart pounding. It could still be an elaborate trap; but if so, why *should* the other have saved his life?

"I lost them in Nablus," he heard Codron continuing; "but, in any event, I was pretty sure by then they were heading north."

North! There were Five Gates to Armageddon—five checks before the bomb could be assembled—signalling, perhaps, the final battle before the end of the world as foreshadowed in the Bible. But Armageddon was a real place, as Angela had pointed out. And there was a top secret establishment there now—where Billie had been caught!

It meant both—the means and the end! And Armageddon was the place where the bomb was to be assembled. Suddenly it was all so clear. That's where Billie was already, and now Angela was being taken there too!

"Mr. Deutsch! Are you still there?"

Dutch pulled himself together. From five points the five parts of the bomb were converging on Armageddon. Perhaps they were there already. Perhaps the assembly had already taken place and it was already too late. But more likely the reason they had taken the mountain road through Nablus, instead of the one along the coast, was so they could pick up one of the parts on the way.

Probably Harzoy himself was among them; it would be typical of the man to want to see for himself the final assembly completed. In any event, it meant there were hours, not days, if anything was to be done.

"Mr. Deutsch! Are you all right?"

"Yes. I'm thinking."

"Oh."

He contemplated trying to get hold of the Brigadier. But if he was wrong? Or was it a trap after all?

He paused for a moment, then said tensely: "Look ... Mr. Codron ... you saved my life once. Would you allow me to return the compliment?"

"I don't quite understand?"

"Apparently my friend is not back yet. But if I don't get to where I think the people you followed have gone, we may be in the middle of a world war by breakfast. I'm sorry if that sounds melodramatic, but I expect you've been following the news."

"Say no more, Mr. Deutsch. I was hoping I might be of service. Where are you?"

In spite of himself, Deutsch still hesitated, then he looked at the instructions printed in English and German as well as Hebrew above the coin box, and read the address: "I'm in a box on the corner of Prophet Samuel Street and Yecheskel."

"How do you spell it? The last bit I mean."

"Y-E-C-H-E-S-K-E-L. Yecheskel."

"OK. I'll find it."

"Hurry. That's all."

"I'll come as quick as I can. But I'd better fill up on the way."

"All right."

"Stay out of sight."

Dutch was about to put the 'phone down when he suddenly remembered.

"Are you there?"

"Yes."

"I don't look quite the same as the last time you saw me."

"So I hear. There's just been a news flash about your escape."

Dutch heard the other chuckling as he put down the 'phone.

Chapter 17

There could be no mistaking the place. On the wide plain at the foot of Mount Tabor was a military complex surrounding an airfield.

For some reason all the road blocks had disappeared as if all troops and police had suddenly been withdrawn, but Dutch had his mind focused on what lay in front of him. He accepted their removal gratefully without reflecting on the significance, and his companion—who still maintained that he was an ordinary British citizen—drove in silence except where it was necessary to seek further directions. Nevertheless, when they reached the point where the road leading down to the airfield turned off the main highway they saw that the entrance, some hundred yards ahead, was heavily guarded as well as brilliantly lit.

Codron slowed down, but did not dare stop for fear of attracting attention; so they had only a fleeting glimpse as they went past; but in that moment Dutch sensed there was much activity beyond the gates themselves.

They carried on for a few hundred yards, still able to see the lights from the airfield through the trees. Then Dutch glanced back to ensure there was no-one behind them, and said: "Pull into the side." He then glanced at the clock on the dashboard. It was one-thirty. It would stay dark for several more hours yet.

When they had stopped, Dutch opened the door. Then he turned to the man beside him.

"Thanks—again!"

"What now?"

Dutch got out, but paused with his hand on the door, and bent forward so they could still see each other.

"Now, you go back and get some sleep."

"How will you get back?"

"Don't worry about it."

"But I *do* worry, Mr. Deutsch. I worry about both of you."

Dutch frowned for a moment, but the other continued: "Are you sure I can't do anything?"

"Do you ever say your prayers?"

"Sometimes."

"Then say one for all of us!"

"But ..."

Any further words were stifled as Dutch closed the door quietly. He waved at Codron through the glass, and after a few more seconds the car drew away, leaving him alone.

He immediately crossed the road towards the airfield, and stepped into the cover of the pines; anyone standing by the roadside at this time of night was bound to attract attention. Then he waited for several minutes to accustom his eyes to the dark; if he was to get inside the camp he would have to step out into the light sooner or later—and judging from the glow, the whole perimeter of the field was floodlit—but he wanted to be able to move around in the surrounding wood first while spying out the land, and to do this he would have to be very quiet for, now the sound of the car had died away, he could hear the voices of two of the sentries talking to each other, and undoubtedly they, as well as others, would have heard the car pull up then draw away again, and might be wondering why. Perhaps, even now, a patrol had gone out to investigate, and was moving up the road silently towards him, ears straining for the slightest sound, such as the snap of a dead twig.

With these thoughts in mind, Dutch moved still further into the wood—but slowly, scarcely picking his feet up at all. Every now and then he stopped, and in the stillness, even the air entering and leaving his lungs sounded like a steam engine, and he had to hold his breath to listen properly.

After a time he became convinced there *was* no-one else close by, unless they were floating through the trees without their feet touching the ground. Besides, he would have seen the light from their torches.

Slowly he drew closer to the lights; then the trees were at an end, and he looked out across an open strip of land, approximately twenty yards wide, to a high double wire fence, the outer layer of which was of taut close-mesh barbed wire, and the inner, two yards further in, was obviously electrified. And judging by the size of the insulators where the wires were supported by the uprights, the charge was at least a thousand volts.

An hour later he had made his way half-way round the field. There were no overhanging trees or buildings close enough to the fence to offer any help in getting inside, but there was a water tower at the edge of the wood close to where he was now standing. Possibly Tarzan might have been able to swing over both fences using a long rope attached to the iron cat-walk running around the top; but, even if a rope had been available, the chances of landing afterwards without breaking a leg were just about nil. However, a series of ladders led up to the cat-walk on the side away from the lights and, although he would still be clearly visible to anyone close by who happened to look up, the chances were they would not be able to see him against the dark background of trees from the other side of the field where all the action seemed to be taking place; and, once up there, he would have an unparalleled view out over the whole base.

As he began to climb, Dutch wondered why the thing had been allowed to be built there in the first place. But experience had taught him never to look a gift horse in the mouth; on at least a dozen occasions in combat he might have been shot down, if the enemy had done the obvious thing; but instead of wondering why they hadn't, he'd shot them down instead.

After pausing at the top for a few seconds to regain his breath, he edged round the circumference of the tower until he could see the main entrance; then the group of buildings a hundred yards or so inside, which he had been able to see before, and which contained a tower not dissimilar from the one he was on—except that this was built solid, and not on legs. Then he saw two things he had not been able to see at all from ground level with the perimeter lights in his face: a line of Golda interceptor aircraft—an Israeli designed machine based on the old American

Phantom, which Dutch himself used to fly, over which they were considered a marked improvement—evidently on stand-by; and just under the tower a Dayan strike aircraft, round which much activity was taking place.

Dutch glanced at his watch. It was almost two-thirty. The chances were it was being prepared for a mission to begin at first light—roughly in four hours, unless it didn't matter about hitting the target accurately.

He felt the hairs on the back of his neck tingle, and started to climb down so fast he missed his grip when he had only just begun the second ladder. He hung for a few seconds by one hand, feet threshing wildly in the air to swing his body back so his other hand could help take the strain. After that, he was more careful, but he still reached the ground in record time.

Dutch stood for a few moments his heart pounding. He had to get in somehow, then he remembered Angela's note. Was it less than forty-eight hours ago?

She had said it was easy enough to get in somewhere if you didn't mind not being able to get out. He thought a few moments longer, and then set off through the woods in the direction of the main road. And this time he didn't bother about the noise.

The sentry challenged him when he was still fifty yards away. He had no idea what the man said, but he stopped at once. A second time he was challenged, and this time Dutch raised his hands above his head to be on the safe side and answered: "I only speak English."

The other looked at him suspiciously, and called over his shoulder. A moment later another guard stepped out of the small building just inside the main gate and, after exchanging a few words with the first, both of them looking in his direction, he barked an order without turning his head, and a few seconds later, soldiers poured out of the building, some to take up defensive positions round the gate, others to surround him and lead him back to where a young officer, who must have appeared while his attention was distracted by the process of being searched for concealed weapons, was now waiting.

194

"Name?"

"Richard Deutsch."

"So! You're the interfering American, are you? We've been expecting you. What took you so long?"

"The buses don't run too frequently at this time of night."

The other slapped him so hard it was like an explosion on the left side of his face. A split second later Dutch reacted instinctively and, while the soldiers on either side and behind him stood rooted to the spot with surprise, both at their commander's sudden action and at the speed of the prisoner's response, it seemed he had all the time in the world to lower his hands, shift his weight to the ball of his left foot, and bring his right hand up in a perfectly executed upper-cut that caught the young officer on the point of his chin and sent his jaw crashing into the roof of his mouth. He reeled backwards and hit the ground.

At that moment the others recovered, and Dutch felt hands seizing him from every direction. His arms were twisted out of harm's way behind his back; then someone grabbed him by the hair, only to let go a moment later with a grunt of disgust as he found his hand covered in boot polish.

Dutch saw the young officer pick himself up, rubbing his jaw painfully; but when he stood once more in front of him, swaying only slightly, he was smiling.

"I'm glad you did that," he said, "because it gives me an excuse, before we hand you over, to show you what we think of people like you."

He glanced up, and nodded at those who were holding him. Dutch felt the hands tighten still further; then the officer hit him as hard as he could in the stomach.

What followed was a confusion of pain, sound, and the sight of whirling fists as his assailant hit him again and again until his eyes became blurred with a combination of concussion, blood and perspiration; but, just as his senses began to slip away, he heard a command shouted from a distance, and a moment later the blows stopped and he fell to the ground, as those who were now supporting, rather than restraining him, relaxed their hold. Then he was lifted up and carried, not into the Guard Room—

that would only have been a few steps—but through the gates—
through the cool night air—until eventually there was a row of
electric lights above his head instead of stars, and he realised he
was being carried down a corridor, and through another doorway before being lowered gently down at last.

"Dutch!" It was Angela's voice.

"Dad!" No, he must have been mistaken. It was Billie's.

"I'm sorry, he's been in a slight accident." Now it was a
man's voice.

"Accident!"

Dutch tried to turn his head but it made him giddy.

"I understand he struck the captain of the guard who, unfortunately, has a very quick temper. But don't worry; I don't
think his injuries are serious. I've already sent someone for the
doctor. He'll be along soon."

Dutch's head was clearing rapidly, but he remained staring
at the ceiling until he heard the door close. Then he turned his
head, and saw both women bending over him.

"Help me up." At least, that's what he had intended to say,
but it sounded more like: "Hell—mm—ur." His lips were so
swollen that he couldn't close his mouth properly, and his
tongue told him he had lost at least two teeth.

"The bastards!" Billie took hold of his hand and raised it to
her lips impulsively, but Dutch looked at Angela and she said:
"I think he wants to sit up."

"But he can't. He's got to stay there till the doctor comes.
God knows what they've done to him."

Dutch was in no mood to argue. It was agony to move; but
strength was flowing back into his limbs and he slid his legs off
the couch so that, if Angela hadn't moved quickly, his whole
body would have followed. As it was, she helped him to sit up,
and a moment later Billie gave him her arm.

"Darling, Billie's right. You really ought to stay where you
are. You can't do anything now."

"No." Dutch started to shake his head, but stopped as it
seemed to make the room fly like the snowstorm in a paper-
weight, and he had to take several deep breaths to stop himself

vomiting. Then he felt better.

"The guard told us," Angela went on, "the General's going to give himself up."

"It'll be too late."

"What will? What are you talking about?"

Dutch pointed at the wall.

"There's an aircraft out there loaded with a bomb big enough to kill tens of millions of people. By the time anyone arrives it will have taken off."

"Oh, my God!" Angela went as white as a sheet.

"Paul," he heard Billie whisper. "He must have known!"

"Help me to my feet."

The last thing the doctor and his orderly were expecting was to be attacked by the two women as they entered the room. The guard, who had waited out in the corridor, came rushing in to help, and the last thing *he* was expecting was a karate chop to the back of his neck from Dutch, who had been waiting behind the door. As the young soldier collapsed, Dutch bent down—an action which sent a shaft of pain up his spine into his head—and picked up his weapon.

"All right. That's enough."

Angela and Billie relaxed their holds, and their two victims turned to find themselves covered by a sub-machine-gun held by a grotesque figure resembling a cross between a badly made-up minstrel and the losing contender in a light-heavyweight boxing championship.

"I'm sorry, Doctor. Surgery will have to wait. Put your hands up, please." Dutch glanced at the two girls. "You other two stand perfectly still."

Apart from the two who raised their hands, nobody moved as Dutch backed to the door until he could glance out into the corridor to see if anyone had heard the commotion. But it seemed deserted, and he stepped back into the room and glanced down at the young guard who was just starting to come round.

"Your call hasn't been entirely wasted. He looks as if he could do with some attention. In any case, I want you all to stay here."

He put his hand on the door.

"Just a minute, what about us?" Billie took a step forward.

"I said stand still," Dutch barked, and his daughter froze.

"You're not going to leave us here?" This from Angela, whose eyes had widened to their fullest extent.

"That's just what I'm going to do"; and, before anyone could reply, he slammed the door shut and locked it. Dutch hurried to the end of the passage and opened the door leading outside, but only an inch—which was as well, for everywhere men were hurrying to complete the final check on the bomber and its cargo only a few yards away. He was right in the middle of the hornets' nest, and whether it was true what Angela had said about Harzoy giving himself up, it was clear he still intended to carry through the main part of his plan, and commanded enough support to enable him to do so. Then he heard a sound behind him and turned, but not soon enough. A gun was jammed into his ribs, and a voice whispered:

"Drop your gun, Mr. Deutsch. Then open the door in front of you and step outside. There is someone waiting to see you."

Dutch was propelled across the space separating the building from the control tower, and their path passed close to the Dayan. A few glanced at them curiously as they walked by, but most were too intent on what they were doing.

When they approached closest to it, Dutch contemplated making a dash for the plane in an attempt to disable it in some way; but he realised it would be a futile gesture. The man behind him had been joined by another as soon as they had stepped outside, and he couldn't have taken more than a couple of strides before one or other riddled him with bullets.

Just another few seconds—that was all it would have needed; from the top of the steps outside the door he could scarcely have missed the fuel tanks, even in his present condition.

There was still one chance after all, the one that had occurred to him when he was still on the water tower on the far side of the field, but that depended on a lot of things—the main one being that, when they thought it was all over, his captors would relax.

"Through the door."

As Dutch approached the main entrance to the tower, the door opened automatically and then closed silently behind them.

"Wait a minute."

They halted in front of a small lift while the two guards conferred in Hebrew. Clearly they were discussing the advisability of being with one who had already shown himself to be a vicious fighter in a confined space where they might not be able to use their weapons effectively; but it was a long walk up to the top—the equivalent of seven or eight floors—and eventually they decided to risk it. They ordered him to the back of the lift, and then first one got in with his gun pressed hard into Dutch's stomach, followed by the other, who turned his back only for a second to operate the mechanism. But they need not have bothered; he had no intention of moving—yet.

When they reached the top, the doors opened, and the second guard stepped outside; then the one who had been covering him backed out and ordered him to follow.

Dutch found himself in a carpeted central lobby. Through one door, which was half open, he could see a room lit only by several radar screens, with an operator sitting in front of each. Behind them stood several men talking in low voices. Then one saw him and pointed, whereupon they all fell silent.

"This way."

Following the guard's direction, Dutch walked in a half-circle round the lift to the entrance of a much larger room, the far end of which was an almost continuous semi-circle of glass overlooking the main runway. There was a group of Army and Air Force officers standing in the middle of the room under lighting, subdued so as not to affect the view outside; just past the shoulder of one of them on the edge of the group Dutch caught sight briefly of the end of the line of Golda interceptors. Then his escort came to attention, and the senior saluted.

"The prisoner, Sir."

At once those in front of them separated, and Dutch found himself face to face for the first time with a man instantly recognisable as General Harzoy.

The General looked at him carefully. Unlike most of the

others, he wore no cap, and Dutch could see his face deeply tanned under a shock of iron grey hair. In spite of his age, his back was straight, and when he stepped forward it was with the suppleness of a man half as old, although he seemed to have aged considerably since he posed for the picture all the morning papers had carried. Despite his smile, Dutch could see that he was desperately tired.

"Mr. Deutsch." Harzoy held out his hand. "Allow me to congratulate you. There is no disgrace in two adversaries shaking hands after the battle; and you almost won!"

Dutch only hesitated for a second before he returned the other's smile and shook his hand. It was not difficult to see why so many had followed him, even to the brink of disaster and beyond. His personality was strong enough to fill the room like a source of light which dazzles all those near it. He said: "I'm honoured to meet you, Sir"—and meant it.

The General's smile broadened into one of genuine pleasure.

"And I'm going to believe you," he answered. "It is a relief to know you are a gentleman. To have had so much of my plan destroyed by a lout would have been intolerable!"

He let go of Dutch's hand.

"And speaking of gentlemen, I must apologise for the treatment you received when you arrived here. The young officer has already been severely reprimanded and ..."—he glanced over Dutch's shoulder—"if you will now give me your word not to try and interfere, you may watch the last act in the drama in which you and I have been participating, while those who accompanied you wait outside."

Dutch shrugged.

"Very well. What can I do?"

"You have done quite a lot, Mr. Deutsch. It may interest you to know that we are already isolated. The Prime Minister and her colleagues have been released unharmed, and Brigadier Doud —now acting Commander-in-Chief, by the way—is already on his way here with an escort to take me into custody."

"You didn't kill them, then."

The General shook his head.

"No. It was one thing that they should die to ensure the success of the operation. But to murder them in cold blood when the truth was already known was unthinkable, and could have served no purpose except to plunge the country into civil war."

Dutch bowed his head for a moment to signify his appreciation of the point. Then he raised it again, and asked: "But what happens when Doud gets here?"

Harzoy glanced round briefly at the men standing behind him, many of whom murmured something; then he turned back:

"Doud has my assurance that there will be no resistance, providing he comes by road and that no attempt is made to attack the airfield in the meantime."

He glanced at the two guards, and nodded briefly; whereupon they saluted and left the room.

"By which time it will be too late," Dutch said.

"In one sense, yes."

"He probably knows it."

"But he, too, is a gentleman. I am sure he will keep his word. Besides, he is above all an Israeli and, like myself, knows that no matter what the consequences, a civil war is unthinkable." He turned away, and the group moved to the window.

One of the controllers sitting at a desk with a pair of earphones made a remark to the General who nodded gravely, then turned towards Dutch.

"Please come and join us, Mr. Deutsch. The plane is ready to take off. They are about to start the engines."

"But what about the consequences?" Dutch blurted out, coming forward. "What about the rest of the world ... and the people who are going to be under that thing?"

Harzoy looked at him for a few moments. Now there was no trace of a smile, and when he spoke his voice was harsh.

"What about the rest of the world, Mr. Deutsch? Who but the Americans cared last time whether we lived or died? As far as the rest of the world was concerned, we could have been butchered to the last woman and child so long as they didn't have to turn down their central heating or go to work on a bus! And now, even the Americans are deserting us. Oh yes—

very soon we shall be back where we started ..." He pulled back the sleeve of his tunic and pointed to a number tattooed on the inside of his left wrist. "... alone—with no one to turn to but each other."

There was a period of silence while Dutch stared at the reminder of a crime so great that no-one involved could ever forget it. The thought struck him that perhaps, even now after so many years, the rest of the world was going to have to pay for having forgotten too easily. In the background he could hear the roar of jet engines.

Then the General pulled down his sleeve and said more gently: "Even so, we have no wish to make the innocent suffer. It is true some must die to ensure our safety, but not in the way you suppose, nor, I pray with all my heart, in anything like the numbers you fear."

The pitch of the engines rose, and he glanced outside, then nodded with satisfaction.

"See—the plane is moving." He glanced at those beside him. "Make room for our guest, gentlemen. He has won so much. It is only fair he should witness our remaining victory."

He held out his hand, and Dutch moved to stand beside him to look down on the moving plane.

"Where are you sending it?" he asked, trying to keep his voice level.

Harzoy turned to him and smiled.

"Why—to Aswan, of course. Where else?"

Dutch drew in his breath.

"The dam!" he breathed eventually.

"That's right. There are few people living close to it."

"But if you destroy the dam, a wall of water will sweep down the Nile valley carrying everything before it."

"Only for the first fifty or sixty miles. It will spread out long before the main centres of population are reached."

"But the sheer volume of water. It will flood everything."

"I agree. At a stroke, both the industry and agriculture of Egypt will be destroyed. But surely that's better than fighting a war in which millions of innocent lives would be lost?"

"Not for the hundred thousand or so who will be drowned."

"But for the millions who will live—and for my people, who will then be able to look forward for a generation without the fear of having to face another attack—next time, without America to help us."

"And at the end of that time?"

"At the end, and probably long before, the world will have rid itself of oil blackmail, and the Arabs will not dare, when they see how few friends they really have."

The plane had now reached the end of the runway and had turned.

"But this isn't the way," Dutch said desperately. "How do you think the rest of the world is going to react when they learn that a country which used to support fifty million people has been turned into a desert overnight?"

"Oh, come now, Mr. Deutsch." The General looked at him with mock disapproval. "Only industry will suffer permanent damage. You must know that the very richness of Egyptian soil has depended for thousands of years on flooding."

"Over a period. Not all at once. This way, it'll be a miracle if there's any left."

"Oh, I think so. And, as for the rest of the world—no doubt they will adjust to the situation."

The controller interrupted with a brief observation and Dutch saw the General instinctively square his shoulders.

"Well, gentlemen," he said in English. "The pilot reports he is ready for take-off. Once he has done so, he will break radio contact so there will be no possibility of countermanding my orders." He glanced at Dutch for a moment, then to the controller.

"Tell him to proceed ... and that our prayers go with him."

The controller nodded and spoke into the microphone.

"You're crazy!" Dutch shouted. "Russia spent ten years building it. It's the symbol of everything she has achieved in the Middle East."

"So, destroying it will win the Americans once more over to our side!"

"She could never accept such a humiliation. You may destroy Egypt, but Russia will destroy you."

There were some excited exchanges amongst those standing beside them, and Dutch saw that the plane had begun to gather speed; but Harzoy persisted: "*Not* if America is behind us."

"Then you know what you're doing, don't you? The one thing that's guaranteed to start a world war!"

"I don't think so."

The plane's nose wheel lifted, and a moment later it left the ground—ponderously, in spite of great power—as if it were carrying a tremendous weight.

Dutch knew he should be moving even now, but he heard himself shouting: "What gives you the right to take such an appalling risk with the peace of the world?"

Harzoy pulled up his sleeve and, exposing his tattooed wrist once more, waved it in Dutch's face.

"This, my young friend," he retorted. "This—and the blood of my family—and of the six million who helped to buy back our native land with their suffering."

"Then what of your own people? What right have you to risk their lives?"

The plane started to bank at the end of the runway while continuing to climb. Harzoy watched it until it was lost into the night sky; then he said:

"I am their conscience. I awaken them from their slumbers, and make them face the future. They may blame me now. No doubt many will, but if we lose our courage and our will to act, we are nothing."

Dutch turned and made for the door. One or two of those in the room moved to stop him; but Harzoy said sharply:

"No. It's over. Let him go. We are in God's hands now."

One officer younger than the others still stood in Dutch's way. The General rapped: "I said, 'Let him go.' He can do nothing now." As the officer obediently moved aside and Dutch left the room, he turned to the others.

"My friends, thank you for your support. And I believe that one day soon Israel will thank you. We have done, as I have told you so often, the one thing that can arrest the slide to disaster. And if we must fight sooner than we thought, we are only facing up to the inevitable, and by our sacrifice we have at least given our people a chance." He looked round before continuing sadly: "I am sorry that it did not work out quite as we had planned, but perhaps it is as well, for sacrifice in a just cause should be its own reward." He paused again, and then added quietly: "When Brigadier Doud comes, I shall be in my private quarters. God bless Israel. God bless and keep you all."

He walked slowly from the room, head erect, looking neither to right nor left. And when he had gone, some wept openly.

If ever the phrase "running for dear life" had any meaning, it was when Dutch sprinted from cover to cover towards the first in the line of fighters. The only relevant fact Harzoy did not know, and therefore had not taken into account when he released him, was his experience in flying Phantoms, the machine on which the Golda was based.

But whether or not this would be of any avail still depended on a number of factors. Were the aircraft fuelled ready for instant take-off? With the Israeli Air Force, the chances were that the answer would be "yes". Again, would the controls and behaviour of the aircraft be sufficiently familiar to enable him to take off and fly the thing properly? He still flew jets occasionally to retain his licence; but the Phantom was years out of date, and he had no idea if he would even know how to start the Golda's engines.

There still remained two questions: Would he be able to catch up with the plane that had just taken off? Even more immediate was another: Would he be able to creep up behind the guard standing in front of the fourth aircraft in order to knock him out before he turned round and opened fire with his sub-machine gun?

He took a breath and then ran to the shadow of the next plane. There he paused for a few seconds to look round, but there seemed no-one else within four or five hundred yards. He was about to dash for the next when there was a muffled but quite distinct shot from the complex of buildings at the foot of the control tower.

Dutch froze. After a few seconds a commotion broke out, and someone ran out into the open shouting at the top of his voice.

He heard the guard mutter an exclamation, and a few seconds later he passed within a few yards as he walked to the end of the line, close to where Dutch had been standing not a moment or two earlier, and looked in the direction of the din which was increasing.

He contemplated getting into the Golda next to him; but no jet engine starts that fast, and it would be at least a minute after the sound of the starter motor before he would be able to move off—all the time in the world for the guard to stop him, one way or another.

For a moment it seemed the problem would be solved for him. The sentry started to make for the scene of the uproar, but after a few steps he thought better of it and came to a halt, though still gazing uncomprehendingly in the direction of the disturbance.

This was it. In another minute he might turn round and come back; now, while his attention was so keenly focussed elsewhere, was the time to strike.

Dutch came up behind him softly. He walked until he was within fifteen yards—still time to stop and put his hands up! Then he flung himself across the remaining space, and felled the man with a chop to the base of his skull.

He seemed unconscious and, after he had dragged him into the shadow of the first aircraft, Dutch searched him, and found a small automatic pistol in a shoulder holster; while he was slipping it into his own pocket, the young man started to come round, and Dutch was obliged to bang his head rather sharply on the tarmac. He then stood up, removed the magazine from the sub-machine gun lying on the ground beside the unconscious sentry, and flung it into the surrounding darkness. If he had not stopped to search the sentry, he would probably have been shot in the back before he had covered more than a few yards.

Then he walked quickly but without undue haste towards the aircraft at the far end of the line. There seemed to be no-one else in the immediate area, and everyone's attention was probably attracted to the uproar still going on behind him; but nothing attracted attention more than a man running and, although his heart was thumping, he consciously maintained a steady pace until he was quite sure he was out of sight. By then he had almost reached his objective.

He ducked hurriedly under the racks of missiles slung under the wings to reach the far side; then he jumped and pulled himself up onto the wing itself. Less than a minute later he slithered into the cockpit and pulled the cover down on top of him.

He found the switch for the light on the instrument panel; but then his heart sank. There were two seats in tandem squeezed into the confined space. The pilot's seat was on the left and, although the main flying controls were duplicated in front of the right-hand seat, the instruments were entirely different. Dutch guessed that the second man's task was probably that of navigator, radar operator and weapons control—an impression strengthened a few seconds later when he leant over and pulled a black leather cover away from part of the instrument panel to reveal a circular radar screen. But the whole lay-out was so different and so much more complicated than anything he had ever seen before that for a minute or two he thought he would never be able to manage. Then he forced himself to concentrate.

He could, at least, be sure that most of the duplicated controls concerned flying and by noting which those were, the pattern of the lay-out gradually began to emerge: throttles for two engines (the buttons at the side undoubtedly controlled the after burners); the aileron, flap and rudder controls; then the radar controls. The radar was on—that would be important later. Ignoring the remaining instruments on the right-hand side, he gradually identified those he would need to use. He could forget the radio; but there was the oxygen mask and controls regulating the flow of gas. That was the automatic pilot . . . and there two buttons alongside the seats, probably the ejectors.

Better get strapped in. Now he was fairly confident. There was no flying-helmet, but that couldn't be helped, and, as far as he could see, there were no maps. But the compass was working and, having watched it take off, he knew roughly in which direction the bomber had set out. With any degree of luck he would be able to pick it up on the radar screen when he had climbed to thirty or forty thousand feet.

The starter motors must be these two here. But what about fuel?

Dutch's eyes scanned the hundreds of dials. At least a dozen of them could have been the fuel gauge, but he couldn't be sure. He'd just have to trust to luck; but it would be remarkable if fighter aircraft on stand-by had not been left tanked up and fully equipped. He had noted there had been four missile tubes under each wing, and there was a row of eight buttons on a black box-like container just in front of the two throttle levers The chances were these had to be activated in some way before they could be fired, but he resolved to keep his hand as far away from them as possible until he was sure. After a final look round, he reached down and pressed the left-hand starter button.

For an agonising moment it didn't seem as if anything was going to happen. Then a low groan started which rose steadily in pitch until the engine fired. Dutch released the button and pressed the other so that, while the first engine idled at twenty thousand revs, the process started again on the other side. He knew that with an interceptor the chances were the batteries were strong enough to start both engines simultaneously; but he wasn't a hundred-per-cent sure, and didn't take the risk. Already the sound of the first engine would have been heard all over the airfield; no matter what else was going on, it couldn't be more than a matter of minutes before someone came running to investigate. Perhaps they were already on their way.

A glance at the rev. counters showed that the speed of the second engine now matched the first. He reached forward, and eased the throttles back a fraction; then he found and released the brakes, and slowly the Golda started to lumber forward. Out of the corner of his eye Dutch saw the lights of a truck heading towards him.

He hadn't been able to find the landing lights of the plane; but there was enough light from those by the fence for one whose eyes had become accustomed to the dark to see a taxiing path leading to the opposite end of the runway. Turning into it, Dutch edged the throttles forward so the pitch of the engines rose to a shriek, and then accelerated to leave whoever was in the truck well behind. It was an uncomfortable ride. Those who had laid out the airfield in the first place had not taken into account the possibility of a heavy fighter aircraft taxiing round the perimeter at over eighty miles an hour, and by the time he began to brake to turn onto the runway itself, the undercarriage had been severely tested, and the wing tip on the port side was badly grazed.

Dutch straightened the Golda with little loss of speed so that it was heading straight down the runway. He had already decided to play safe with three-quarter flaps; but, even as he reached forward and pushed the throttles wide open, every light on the airfield went out, and he found himself accelerating into pitch black with no idea if he was still straight or if he was about to run off onto the grass and turn over—as the drag of the soft ground would undoubtedly cause him to do.

His every instinct was to cut back and brake for all he was worth, but then the action of the guard commander saved him. Realising they stood no chance of catching him, he had been leading a number of vehicles to the opposite end of the runway, and they were taken every bit as much by surprise when they found themselves travelling at high speed through the darkness. But unlike Dutch, the drivers of these vehicles certainly knew where their light switches were, and the end of the runway was suddenly illuminated by the headlights of at least half a dozen trucks just in time.

Dutch corrected the Golda's path very gently; he was already travelling at over a hundred miles an hour, and any sudden change of direction would risk bursting a tyre. But after a few anxious moments he regained equilibrium, and now it was comparatively easy to keep straight, for the commander, with more courage than sense, had led his convoy onto the runway itself, where they had spread out to create a wall of metal, which then advanced towards him at full speed.

The distance between them rapidly diminished. It was like a spectacular game of chicken. Dutch couldn't believe at first that they wouldn't scatter when it became clear he was going too fast to stop, had he wanted to do so; but then he remembered the probable fate of those who had joined themselves with Harzoy in his attempted *coup*, and wasn't so sure. There was certainly no break in the line yet, and they were now less than half a mile away.

He had no idea what the take-off speed of the Golda would be; the wing loading was certainly higher than the Phantom. He guessed around two hundred miles an hour. He must be doing that, surely; but the stick still felt heavy.

Less than five hundred yards—less than ten seconds.

He remembered the after-burners. He hadn't planned to use them on take-off to conserve fuel, but now his hand moved to the buttons on the side of the throttles. A moment later the additional acceleration hit him in the back and the whole airfield was lit with an angry glow.

Dutch pulled back on the stick. He saw the lights of the trucks flash beneath him, and the plane gave a lurch as one of the wheels caught the canopied top of the tallest vehicle.

He fought to regain control. He thought for a second that he was climbing too steeply and pushed the stick forward to avoid stalling; but then the fantastic power of the two boosted engines began to bite, and he realised that although the altimeter showed the plane was still climbing rapidly, the acceleration was increasing.

He pressed another lever and, as the undercarriage began to retract, glanced at the compass, and swung the aircraft round in a half-circle, which took it back over the field again.

The lights were still out, but it seemed there were two trucks on fire in the middle of the runway. They would effectively prevent anyone coming after him.

Chapter 18

At ten thousand feet Dutch turned off the burners, but continued to climb to forty thousand feet remarkably rapidly.

Then he levelled out, but he did not reduce power. It was just over four hundred miles to the dam—probably about the effective range of the plane he was in, but, succeed or fail, there would be no need to return. As soon as Doud arrived, Angela and Billie would be released, and it was far more important to achieve maximum speed. As it was, the dam could not be more than thirty minutes flying-time for the bomber which had taken off at least ten minutes earlier, and he had no idea how much faster the Golda would travel. The chances were it was at least twice as fast, which meant he ought to be able to catch up with at least ten minutes to spare while they were still over the Red Sea; but first the plane had to be found and so, after setting the automatic pilot a few degrees south of south-south-west and leaving the throttles on full power so the plane was still accelerating, he struggled across to the right-hand seat, being careful not to touch the missile buttons, and started to examine the radar screen.

What he saw gave him something of a shock. The bomber was clearly visible about a hundred miles in front, but on the edge of the screen more than a dozen echoes were seen rising from the west. As the minutes ticked past and the distance between them diminished, there remained little doubt that this was a squadron of Egyptian MIG 35s—possibly alerted by the Prime Minister of Israel herself on the direct link between Tel Aviv and Cairo established after the last conflict (nicknamed rather unkindly by the world press the "dateline"). But instead of moving to intercept the aircraft which carried the bomb and was now rapidly closing on the dam, the screen showed that the MIGs were acting as if it didn't exist, and were making a bee-line for him instead!

Dutch glanced at the air-speed indicator, which showed just over fifteen hundred miles an hour. Assuming the MIGs had a roughly similar capability, he had less than five minutes to decide what to do. He throttled back slightly and noticed with satisfaction there was no loss of speed; having reached maximum speed, he had simply been wasting fuel at full throttle.

Two minutes passed. Dutch watched the MIGs pass the bomber at a distance of less than twenty miles without wavering —perhaps, as far as they were concerned, it did *not* exist. But if it had some electronic device which blinded enemy radar, how could he see it himself? In any event, they could see him clearly enough. He changed direction slightly, and noticed how they reacted immediately.

He thought about trying to contact Tel Aviv and asking them to call off the hounds, but there wasn't time. He was going to have to blast his way through—and that meant someone was going to get killed.

Dutch waited until the leading aircraft was within ten miles, and then pressed one of the missile buttons. They were probably still out of range, but he had already been surprised at the sophistication of Israel's home-grown weaponry; perhaps their air-to-air missiles made the ones he had been used to seem like old-fashioned cannon. But nothing happened.

He had seen the missile tubes under the plane. There had been eight of them, but of course he had no idea if they were armed or empty; he had merely presumed that they had been loaded.

The MIGs were less than eight miles away now. Dutch pressed down the second key, then the third, then, with mounting desperation, each of the others in turn. They were all empty. He was defenceless!

He prepared to put the plane into a sharp turn, when suddenly he remembered the activating switch. With his left hand he felt all round the control mechanism. He found it tucked away underneath where, unlike the buttons themselves, no-one could touch it by mistake. He gave a sigh of relief. While his hand was examining it, he glanced once more at the radar screen to see the enemy squadron less than four miles away and starting to spread out.

He never knew how he had managed it, but suddenly there was an explosion as all eight missiles fired simultaneously.

His jaw sagged; but even while his mind was trying to grasp what and how it had happened, his instinct took control. Grasping the control column firmly in his right hand, he reached forward and disengaged the automatic pilot before putting the plane into a steep dive.

Again his hands seemed to work by themselves, opening the throttles once more to maximum power, igniting the afterburners, and coaxing the dive into the trajectory necessary to achieve maximum speed. Then, and only then, did he permit himself to glance back at the radar screen, and was flabbergasted to see that each missile had singled out a separate plane in the formation which had begun to scatter.

The altimeter was spinning backwards like a clock with a broken spring. Knowing that he was still over Sinai, which had peaks of almost nine thousand feet, Dutch pulled out just below ten thousand, and saw his speed had risen to more than two thousand miles an hour. He glanced at the radar screen. It showed the outline of the mountains below, and a minute or two afterwards the coast as he left land behind. But of the aircraft in front and behind there was no sign.

Over the sea there were no clouds, and Dutch could see the water glinting in the moonlight. He knew that if he went right down to a few hundred feet, he would be invisible to the Egyptian aircraft; but by the same token, he would be unable to see the leading plane. Besides, he would burn up far more fuel.

With all the missiles gone, he didn't see how he was going to stop the bomber now, even if he caught up with it. Then the thought occurred to him that if the surviving MIGs saw him on their screens, he might be able to guide them into visual contact with the bomber. It was a vain hope, but there seemed to be no other.

Dutch eased back the control column and glanced at the altimeter. What a rate of climb! What couldn't he have done over Vietnam with such a machine!

At thirty thousand feet the bomber showed up on the screen once more, and he levelled out, cursing when he saw how far off course he had gone in the manoeuvre to avoid the Egyptian aircraft. The Dayan was as far away as when he had last sighted it, which meant it would now be impossible to catch it before it crossed the African coast. But there was no echo from the other planes, and although he stared at the screen until his eyes ached, it was evident they were alone. It was as if a giant hand had wiped the sky clean with the exception of the two Israeli aircraft.

Dutch watched the echo of the plane in front drawing nearer and nearer to the centre of the screen. By now they must know he was on their tail, but they kept on, swerving neither to right nor left—as well they might, for all he could do about it!

But just after they crossed the coast, a hundred and fifty miles from Aswan, he knew the answer. And once the thought had come, he wondered why it had not occurred to him before. It was simple and effective. The only drawback was—he would almost certainly be killed.

The Dayan was losing height, and consequently picking up speed. Was it possible that, by some sixth sense, they had read his mind?

Dutch pushed the control column forward in pursuit, and almost immediately the bomber, now only ten miles ahead, began to bank to the right, and Dutch looked down to see a massive stretch of water beneath them.

For a few seconds he thought they must have recrossed the coast; then he realised that they were further south than he had imagined, and that what he could see was the lake stretching up the valley behind the dam—the waters of the Nile, one of the world's great rivers, accumulated to a depth of hundreds of feet and extending over thousands of square miles.

The bomber was already beginning its run. Even a bomb like the one it carried would have to be aimed with reasonable accuracy if it was to shatter at a single blow one of the greatest structures ever devised by man, a compound of steel, earth and concrete that had taken hundreds of thousands of men and machines more than ten years to complete. It would probably have to be dropped into the water not more than half a mile away—unless, of course, the plane carried more than one. Why had that idea never occurred before?

In any event, he had no means of telling how close they were. The waters seemed to stretch away to the north in the moonlight as far as the eye could see, but at the speed they were travelling they might only be a minute or two away in time.

Dutch put the Golda into a steeper dive to gain speed, until he could see the bomber less than a mile in front and a few hundred feet below. They *must* have seen him by now, and this meant they couldn't be carrying any defensive missiles. But perhaps they wouldn't dare to use them? After all, they didn't know he was unarmed, and as long as he didn't fire at them, they would think they had a chance of completing the mission.

Dutch dropped lower still until he was almost immediately above the Dayan, which itself had throttled right back, and matched his speed to theirs. Since the original idea had crossed his mind, he had been taxing his brain trying to think of a way he could still do it and live; and the solution that had occurred to him depended on the most delicate bit of flying he had ever done in his life.

He noted with satisfaction that their speed had dropped to three hundred knots. That would make it easier to do what was necessary, and he would have a better chance of getting out afterwards. It also meant that the time was approaching when the bomb doors would be opened.

He reached forward, pulled a lever, and listened with satisfaction at the grinding of the undercarriage as it lowered and locked into position. At the same time, with eyes glued to the air-speed indicator, he edged the throttles forward a fraction to compensate for the increased drag. Then gently, like a leaf alighting on water, he lowered the Golda across the back of the bomber.

A split second before the two aircraft ground together, he saw a white face looking up at him from the cockpit. There was the sound of shrieking and grinding metal, then the tail-plane of the Dayan, which was in the direct line of the Golda's engines, caught fire.

Dutch cut the engines completely, and at once they began to lose height. He checked his harness to see it was tight, then put his hand ready on the ejector-seat trigger; but, to his amazement, the pilot of the plane beneath managed to keep on a more or less even keel; there would be no ejection for him. He hoped there was some other way out, but they would have to act fast, for now they were losing height rapidly, and it could only be a matter of moments before the fire destroyed the remaining control surfaces.

Then—suddenly—both planes leapt into the air as if granted a new lease of life. Dutch realised that he had failed; for the sudden movement could mean only that the bomb had been released.

His first instinct was to press the ejector button, but he stopped himself just in time; had he done so, he would have found himself drifting almost alongside the bomb. The longer he could hold on, the further away he would be when it went off.

The altimeter showed five thousand feet. Assuming it was on a parachute, dropping at—say—thirty feet a second, it would take about three minutes to reach the water. They'd probably timed the fuse to allow it to sink to the bottom before it went off to get the maximum effect, and that might take another minute. In four minutes, even at this speed, they'd be well over ten miles away—if they could stay up that long.

Dutch glanced down, and suddenly his heart jumped into his mouth. He could see the dam and generating station. They were only just going over it, and the bomb had been released more than half a minute ago; that was a mile and a half back.

Allow, say, half a mile before the parachute arrested the forward momentum. That still meant it would fall into the water a mile from the dam itself. He might not have failed after all; he had forced them to drop it early. It might hold.

Dutch glanced at his watch; two and a half minutes to go. The bomb was now almost four miles behind them, and every second it was getting further away. Even if it went off while he was still hanging in mid-air, the depth of water might cushion the explosion.

Suddenly he smelt burning. He looked round and saw that the whole of the back of the bomber was on fire and the rear of the Golda was also in flames. They gave a lurch, and started to spiral down. There wasn't going to be any four minutes!

The last thing he did before punching the button was to glance at the altimeter. It showed three thousand feet above sea level. Christ, how far above sea level was the valley round here?

Dutch had ejected twice before, but it was only as the air pressure snapped his head back against the seat, knocking him half unconscious, that he remembered a helmet was more than just an optional extra on such occasions. But everything worked as it was supposed to and, although by the time the parachute opened, he was less than a thousand feet from the ground, he landed safely in an irrigation ditch. Then he stood up to his waist in water, shaking his head and for several seconds quite unable to work out how he came to be there. He saw that the whole countryside to the north was lit up by a huge fire—he could see the reflected glow in the sky—but then he pulled himself together and started to climb out onto the bank.

A minute later he was surrounded by *fellahin*, local farmers, who were in a high state of excitement; many of them were brandishing sickles and other implements. His head was splitting, but he could see his future was still balanced on a knife edge.

"Does anyone here speak English?"

"Yes, Sir. I speak." An elderly man stepped forward, and the others fell back a little. "For many years I work in a hotel for tourists."

"Good."

But he never had the chance to explain what was so good about it, for suddenly the ground began to shake and everyone looked in awe in the direction of the dam about five miles away. To the accompaniment of the most dreadful sound Dutch had ever heard in his life, which was reminiscent of the roar of Niagara and the crack of thunder directly overhead, a column of water arose from just beyond the dam, and reached for the sky with outstretched hands as if to drag the heavens down with it. A moment later the dam disappeared.

Dutch turned and ran—not from the oncoming water; for if the dam had collapsed, nothing could avoid the aftermath. But he would rather drown than be hacked to pieces, and it would not be more than a few seconds before the locals, who had been on the point of becoming friendly, associated him with the destruction and turned on him.

In the event, he had about thirty yards start. Dutch ran through the darkness as he had never run in his life; but within the past hour he had been knocked unconscious twice, beaten up, and subjected to the strain of flying a supersonic jet. He began to tire after only a few minutes, and eventually made the mistake of turning into a small stone quarry, to find himself trapped by high rock faces on three sides.

They came running. Some were carrying torches, and they gave shouts of triumph when they saw he was trapped, and began to advance, brandishing their weapons. It was then he remembered the small pistol. After dragging it out of his pocket, he fired one shot into the air to show what it was.

The farmers came to an abrupt halt. But then, after talking rapidly amongst themselves, they began to advance again, only more spread out this time, deducing—correctly of course—that he could not hope to shoot more than one of them before they closed in completely.

They edged to within fifteen yards. Dutch's mind raced. There was really no point in killing anyone; it couldn't make any difference. But at the same time he couldn't bring himself to submit meekly. Then, quite suddenly, it started to rain. It rapidly became heavier and heavier until it was like Niagara and all the torches were extinguished.

Dutch found he could still stand, in spite of the downpour, and in the darkness and confusion he managed to push past those who had been about to dismember him and who were now wailing in terror. They were brave men when it was something they could understand, but a torrential downpour out of a cloudless sky was beyond their comprehension—and beyond his comprehension too, for a different reason. But, after he had put a good mile between him and his pursuers, by which time the rain had stopped, he stood on high ground, and looked back—and saw the dam still standing serene in the moonlight, as if nothing had ever threatened it.

By dawn he had found his way down to the main road where he hitched a ride in a truck back into the town of Aswan, and there gave himself up to an incredulous sergeant at the local police station.

Chapter 19

It took Angela and Billie almost the whole of the drive to the Airport from Jerusalem, where they had all been handed back their passports, to explain the complicated procedure that had been gone through before he was finally exchanged for the five Egyptian pilots who had parachuted to safety. It was thought that the repercussions of the Harzoy rebellion would be felt inside Israel and beyond for a considerable time, and intense diplomatic activity continued; but when the whole story emerged, and until the moment of his release, Dutch had been treated like a king—which had made it seem all the more ironic when he had noticed, on being given his passport, that the Israeli authorities had stamped across it "Persona non grata".

"It's for your own good," the official from the Foreign Ministry had explained mildly, when he had protested. "There were quite a few people who weren't too happy at the outcome. Perhaps in another ten years or so you could re-apply?"

"But what I don't understand," Dutch said, when the girls had brought him up to date, "is what happened to that English guy who was supposed to come out here. Is it that hard to get help these days?"

He saw Angela and Billie exchange glances, then his daughter turned to him flushing slightly.

"Well," she began. "I wasn't going to tell you unless you asked."

"Tell me what?"

"And I *didn't* know—truly I didn't. Not until I got the message from London when it was all over."

"What? I suppose you're going to say he was here all the time?"

"Why yes. Don't tell me you knew?"

"Well ... there *was* this guy. He always seemed to pop up whenever I needed him."

"What guy?"

Dutch turned to Angela. "You remember? The one who picked me up outside the General's house that time."

"Oh—him!"

"What about him?" Billie demanded, and Dutch turned back to her.

"Well. There are a few things I haven't told you yet, myself."

"Like what?"

"Like he drove me to the airfield where you were being held."

"But it wasn't him."

"It must have been. There wasn't anyone else."

"Oh, yes, there was."

"Who?"

Billie swallowed, then she said huskily: "You, darling."

"*Me!* Dutch looked at her blankly. "What d'you mean—*me?*"

"Well, you see, it's like this. They had to get someone in they didn't think would be suspected of being a British agent."

"That's a laugh!"

"Yes, I admit that bit didn't work. But the rest did."

"Billie, stop playing games."

"I'm not, honestly. But ... well ... you see, they knew all about you. They had to investigate you before I was accepted."

"What?"

"It's done all the time," she went on hurriedly. "And Mummie knew what I was doing. It was because of her I was approached in the first place. Although, of course, I didn't know at the time."

"You mean your mother works for these people?"

"On and off, yes."

"Well, I'll be ..."

"And so, when I went into hiding, they asked her to ring my old apartment to try and find out what was going on—all that was true about the conversations she had by the way. Then they thought of you."

"You mean your mother set me up as a Patsy?"

"No. She was worried about me, and she knew you were very resourceful and so on, and that you'd never leave until you got to the bottom of it."

"Or got myself shot."

"But she didn't think there'd be any real danger. No-one realised they'd catch on so fast."

Dutch took a deep breath while the two girls looked at him anxiously.

"So—everyone knew I was a British agent except me!"

"And me," Angela pointed out.

"And me," Billie put in hurriedly.

"Oh yes?" Dutch looked at her severely, but there was a ghost of a smile at the corners of his mouth. "So that makes three of us. Just you wait till we get back to London and I get the chance to have a few words with your employers!"

Billie swallowed again. "Well," she said, "I was just coming to that. As a matter of fact they asked me if you *would* call and see them. I gather they were rather impressed."

Dutch continued to stare at her for a few seconds; then all three of them collapsed in laughter until he sat up suddenly and said: "But wait a minute. If the mystery man was me, who was Codron?"

There was a pause during which the cab, driven by Eli, who had listened in silence most of the way, nodding and chuckling from time to time, turned in through the main gates of Ben Gurion airport. Then Angela said: "Perhaps we'll never know." But as they drew up outside the terminal building, there stood Codron himself, evidently waiting for them.

"Mr. Deutsch," he beamed as he opened the door for them. "And Mrs. Romay. I trust you are fully recovered from your adventures. Eli, how are you? We never met, but I visited your home once. Charming family, simply charming!" He turned to Billie, smiling. "And this is Miss Smyth, of course. So happy to meet you." He shook her hand while the others stood around looking somewhat dazed. Then he turned back to Dutch.

"Mr. Deutsch, it really has been a very great pleasure. I can't

222

think when I've enjoyed myself more."

"I owe you a great deal."

"No, no really. It is I who should thank you."

"But you saved my life."

"Yes, that's true. Twice actually."

"If there's anything I can ever do for you . . ."

"Well, there is actually. Or rather, something I'd rather you didn't do."

"I don't understand."

"Well, you see, I often find that on these occasions American gentlemen are rather prone to punch me on the nose."

"I'm sorry. I've lost you completely."

Codron smiled.

"But I didn't lose *you*, fortunately. Although I must admit, you did lead me a merry dance." He withdrew two oblong pieces of paper from his pocket and handed one to Angela, the other to Dutch, who looked at it frowning.

"What's this?"

"A writ. Mrs. Romay's husband is suing her for divorce, and you're named in the petition as co-respondent."

"What!"

"Now, Mr. Deutsch. Remember your promise. It'll all be perfectly straightforward. We've more than enough evidence."

"Who the hell *are* you?"

"I've told you. My name's Codron. I'm a private detective."

Angela looked at Dutch with a peculiar expression on her face. She waited for him to get over the initial shock, then said quietly: "Well, what do you say to that?"

Dutch looked at her, then suddenly he grinned.

"What else can I say?" he said, beginning to laugh: "Will you marry me?"

"Oh . . . *darling*!"

Everyone stopped to watch as the American and his two women, together with the cab driver, stood at the kerb-side laughing and hugging each other as if they'd just been rescued from a desert island. Only the fifth member of the party seemed a little out of it, but he was smiling too, and as no-one else was listening remarked to the world at large:

"Well! It *was* just the most unusual case ... right from the beginning!"